Lucy of the Broken States

Also by Cat Stark

Novels

The Elven Prince
The Grey House Book 1
Inside the Grey House Book 2
Protector of the Grey House Book 3
Hell's Junction

Short Story Collections

Contagion: War Stories
Enter the Maze
Revolution: A RAW Anthology

Lucy of the Broken States

CAT STARK

www.catstark.com

For Paul

ACKNOWLEDGMENTS

Thank you to:

Sydney Fox for the hair care lessons.

James Bunnel for the beautiful cover.

Lori Diederich for editing my first sci-fi book.

Jeanette Johnson at PawPrints 3D for graphic design.

Without your help, this book wouldn't be what it is.

ONE

The horse ambled its way into town, past the few wooden buildings that housed a grocery store, a scavenger store, a restaurant, and the sheriff's office. Lucy sat atop Lance and gave him very little direction. Meridune was home and, after riding Lance for three years, the horse seemed to know when they were here. It surprised Lucy that he knew where to go, as many towns in the Broken States looked the same. She wondered if the town smelled different to Lance, but thought it might also be that she relaxed as soon as she saw the town limits sign.

Lucy could move Lance along a little faster, but it was too hot to hurry, and they were both dehydrated. It was a long ride from one town to the other out here, and the sun beat down hard during the summer. From the way the road looked, it had been a while since the last rain. They kicked up a small cloud of dust as they moseyed along. Lance neighed as he went right for the space in front of the saloon. Once he was in front of the post, his nose dipped to the trough, and she dismounted.

"Lucy!"

The voice was followed by the sound of small feet pounding on wooden steps inside the saloon. The young girl's voice carried over the din from the poker tables and music from the standing piano. Someone was pounding away on the keys, their voice almost hitting the right notes. Dean and Meena, twins, loved to play piano and were good at it, but neither could sing. Lucy smirked at the sound as she turned toward the doors of the saloon. She waited until Gracie was outside, then opened her arms wide. The young girl, her blond braids streaming out behind her, ran at full speed, jumped off the boardwalk and into Lucy's arms.

"You're back!"

"Hey sugarplum. Did you miss me?"

"Lots and lots! You've been gone forever!"

"I told you I would be. I had a job to do." She gave the girl an extra squeeze, then set her down. "Where's your momma, sugarplum?"

"In bed. She's not feeling well."

Lucy frowned. "Well, I'm sorry to hear that." She saw Irene and nodded in greeting before turning back to Gracie. "Go say hello for me, would you?"

"Ok!" The six-year-old ran off with as much enthusiasm as when she ran down the stairs.

Lucy looked toward the saloon as five other people came out. She recognized most of the faces, but frowned when she saw what each was wearing. Usually, Irene's Escorts wore shorts or skirts with either half shirts or bras. Sometimes, when the weather was in the 100s, some went with bikini bottoms and were topless. Today, they all wore rather strange clothing.

Irene, the saloon owner and Madam, wore a green dress with a thick, twisted gold rope as a belt. The belt ended in larger than seemed necessary tassels. They looked large enough to grab on to and pull. The dress blossomed out from her waist, fell to the floor, and was embellished with thinner twisted gold rope on most of the hem.

Lucy looked down the line at the other four people who stood at the railing. Next to Irene was a tall man she hadn't met before, in tight white pants, a frilly white shirt, and a purple velvet coat with tails that hung to the back of his knees. His short hair was shaved almost to his scalp, and there was a curious look in his dark eyes. He looked good, but he also looked completely overdressed.

Next was another person she didn't recognize. They had a nice smile, shoulder length hair, thick black eyeliner around their blue eyes, and a five o'clock shadow. They were wearing what could either be a dress or coat that was red and yellow and green and brown, and . . . She tore her eyes away from the technicolor nightmare, and her gaze fell upon Alice's smiling green eyes.

Lucy lifted her light brown leather hat off her head, revealing the red bandana that hid her thick dark hair. Alice wore a gold dress that hugged her body and stopped at her knees. The slim straps showed off her shoulders, which her red hair brushed. Beads hung from the hem of the dress and moved as Alice did. Lucy whistled in appreciation.

"Howdy."

"Howdy yourself." Alice's voice was soft and inviting.

Lucy smiled as she twiddled with the brim of her hat and looked Alice in her clear green eyes again. "It's been a while."

"Need a place to lay your head?"

"I would appreciate that."

The women stared at each other for a moment before Irene broke the silence. "For now, you're needed upstairs, Alice. Moris wants the pleasure."

"I'm sure he does," Lucy said loudly enough for the Escorts to hear, but not loudly enough for her voice to carry inside.

Irene gave her a look. "You know what you can do with that attitude, Lucy."

She put her hat back on her head and turned to Lance. "Yes, ma'am." She gave Alice one last soft look before the woman turned and went back inside.

"The rest of you, go find a lap to sit on. Lucy'll be around for you to talk to later."

This was met with a chorus of grumbles along with a few voices saying, "Bye, Lucy!"

Lucy's thick, dry lips turned up in a grin even as her attention shifted to Lance. Unbuckling his saddle bag, she let it fall to the ground as the sound of footsteps came closer. Irene appeared to her right, near Lance's backside.

The saloon owner leaned down and picked up the saddle bag. "You don't know what's going on with the train, do you? Stella heard it was going to be late."

Lucy turned toward Irene. "It'll only be late by a couple days. A factory Under caught fire. It caused one of the vents to the Above to blow up. There was enough heat released that the area got hit with a few meteorites. The fire and Bombardment stopped the factory for a few days while the miners rerouted the vent. The Regulators confirmed the heat was dissipating correctly."

"Do you know what the factory was making?"

Lucy paused, looked at the sky as she tried to remember, then shook her head. "Nope. I don't think it's something we use here. It's something they use in the mines out west, so they had to delay the train until it was fixed."

Irene nodded. "That's good to hear. We were getting worried. All the rumors."

"There's always rumors, Irene. You don't usually care about all that."

Irene sighed and looked toward her saloon. "There's been a bit of an upheaval. Grace got the Red Death."

Lucy looked shocked. "You're kidding."

Irene scrutinized Lucy. "You weren't with her last time you were here, were you?"

She shook her head. "No, but Gracie and I spent a lot of time together. Does she have it?"

"She tested negative. As soon as Grace realized she had it, she taught her daughter not to get close. It's been hard for them both."

Lucy nodded. "All right. But why are you so keen on the train? Are there any meds on it?"

"No, but . . ." She hesitated, then after a moment, plunged ahead. "Grace wants to talk to you. She said something about the train but wouldn't tell me more."

Lucy frowned.

"You can be in her room. She knows not to touch anyone."

"Wait, she can't work, can she?"

"No." Irene's expression revealed nothing. "They don't have

anywhere else to go. We've all been pitching in to help with her care and food. She had a little saved up."

"Her momma won't take her?"

Irene shook her head. "Grace hasn't dared tell her. She's afraid her mother will take Gracie once and for all."

Lucy shook her head. "That woman . . ." She shook her head again, then frowned a little. "Grace will need a lot of care before she dies."

"I know."

Lucy's eyes narrowed. "What's she got on you?"

Irene's mouth dropped open in shock. Then her eyes opened wide in surprise. "Oh, you little . . ."

Lucy burst out laughing. "Sorry, Irene. I couldn't help it."

"You're in a tear today."

"I like being here. It's home."

Irene nodded. "I get that. Come on, get the rest of your stuff. I'll prepare a bath for you."

Lucy grinned and turned to take care of Lance.

₧₧₧

Half an hour later, Lucy soaked in a tub of hot water in Irene's room. It was the woman's private room, no clients allowed. The tub was porcelain, with claw feet, and weighed so much it had to be on the ground floor. Irene had gladly given up her room on the top floor to have this installed. It was big enough that with her back against the tub wall, Lucy's feet just touched the other side. It was heaven. A lot of places had running water and bathtubs, but Lucy wasn't as friendly with the people of other towns. She wanted one home, and Meridune was it.

Lucy grew up in an orphanage, in the Under, but when she started traveling at the age of fourteen, Meridune, Irene in particular, took her in. The Hired Hand she was following for her Apprenticeship wasn't treating her well and was barely teaching her anything. Irene noticed, took her away from Darrell, and set her up with Cecil, who showed her the ropes of being a Hired Hand. He taught her many things, from filling out the right paperwork to learning how to shoot a gun.

A small sigh escaped her. She missed Cecil, but all roads led to death, eventually. A knock on the door roused her from her thoughts. "Go away!"

The door opened anyway. "This is my room! My saloon. You don't tell me to go away."

Lucy laughed at Irene's irritation. "I knew you'd come in. No one else would have."

Irene nodded as she came in and closed the door. "I suppose that's true. General store had your hair products last month. I wasn't sure when you'd be home, so I bought a couple bottles for you. Want me to braid your hair?"

Lucy's voice was full of gratitude. "That would be appreciated. Thank you."

Irene moved a wooden chair to behind Lucy's head. The chair creaked as Irene sat down.

"You want the orange scented or non-scented?"

"Orange, please!"

As Irene worked her hair, she and Lucy continued to talk.

"If you want Alice's company tonight, she's ready for you. Middleton ran his monthly tests; all my Escorts are clean."

Lucy's voice sounded intrigued. "You only use 'Escorts' when you have a mix. Otherwise, you just say women. When I was here last, you only had women. I saw the new people out there earlier but wasn't sure if they were Escorts or servers."

"Yep. Women, men, and everything in between. Jeremy is homosexual, and Linus is non-binary, bisexual. They might be interested in you."

Lucy sighed as Irene continued to work on her hair. She could take care of it herself, and usually did, but it was a treat to have someone else braid it. "Were both of them outside when I showed up?"

"Jeremy had the purple coat on, and Linus had the very colorful coat."

Lucy frowned. "Yeah, where did you all get those clothes? That's not usually what you wear. And your dress is nice, but it just looks off for some reason."

Irene stopped working on Lucy's hair as she laughed. "It's supposed to. Scavenger came through, oh about two months ago now. They found a practically untouched theater out in the middle of the old farmlands, near the lakes. No one had found the costume department, and the clothes were in cedar chests. Most of the costumes didn't have identifying tags on them, but we all went nuts. We probably spent more on them than we should have."

"What's yours from?"

"It's from . . . It's from a book that I can't remember the name of. I never really liked the title, but it was set in the slave era, from Way Before. At one point the main character . . . shoot, you know how I am with books. I love 'em but can't remember the characters in them. Anyway, the main character, it's after the war, and she has to impress someone, but all her clothes have been taken or destroyed, so she gets her former enslaved servant to make her a dress out of drapes!"

Lucy burst out laughing. "That's ridiculous!"

"It is pretty silly, but when I realized this was from that scene, I had to wear it!"

Lucy continued to laugh as she shook her head. "Some people think up the oddest things."

"I wish I had enough of an imagination to create a book." She placed her hands on Lucy's hair again. "I'm doing four thick braids, by the way."

"That works. Thank you. And you don't need an imagination with the stuff that happens here!"

This time they both laughed. "I suppose that's true." There was a pause as she worked Lucy's hair. "Did you want me to introduce you to anyone new?"

"Though I do like variety, I want to be with Alice right now."

Irene tsked. "I've never understood your relationship with her. I know she doesn't let you pay."

Lucy shrugged. "I please her, she pleases me. I don't know if it can be more than that. I like to travel; she doesn't."

"I suppose if it works for you both."

"It does. When it doesn't, we'll talk further." Lucy sighed again as Irene tied off a braid. "Now, other than helping me with my hair, why are you really bothering me?"

Irene snorted. "It's my room. You're bothering me."

Lucy snickered. She could almost hear Irene rolling her eyes.

"I came to let you know that Grace is asleep already, but Gracie is waiting for you in the dining room. She has some pictures she drew for you."

"I love that kid."

"She's a sweetie."

They were silent for a while as Irene tied off another braid, then Lucy asked a hard question. "What's going to happen to her?"

"Grace's illness is progressing slowly. That means she'll probably be around for another year. Gracie'll be old enough to Apprentice somewhere by then."

"She'll be seven. That's not old enough." There was disdain in her voice.

"Well, not for here, but she doesn't want to Apprentice for me. There are other professions that take them at seven. We'll make sure she gets a good Teacher."

"And if she wants to Apprentice somewhere that doesn't take her 'til she's ten or thirteen?"

"She can waitress in the saloon. She'll be off limits to the clients."

Lucy shook her head carefully. "She deserves to be in school until she's ready to take an Apprenticeship."

"Grace saved up some, but she doesn't have that kind of money."

When Lucy realized Irene had finished another braid, she pulled away to turn and look Irene in the eyes. "I do. I'll give you money to make sure Gracie can go to school until she's ready to Apprentice somewhere."

"And if she decides to Apprentice when she's seven?"

Lucy continued to hold Irene's gaze. "Then you make sure she gets that money."

Irene nodded. "Of course."

"Thank you." She leaned back against the tub wall again. "You have any idea who gave Grace the Red Death?"

"She has some idea, but I don't know. It wasn't a Townie. We're all clear."

"All right. I guess I can ask her myself tomorrow."

"Yep."

Lucy felt Irene tie off the last braid.

"Your hair's all set. I'm leaving the oils on the floor right here. Don't forget to grab them before you go. You can pay me back later."

Lucy reached up a hand to touch the four thick braids. "Thank you, again. It's nice to have someone else do it."

"You're welcome." She sighed heavily and stood from her chair. "I'm going back out for a bit. Take your time, but don't take too long. Gracie is waiting and your dinner's just about ready."

"What'd you order me?"

"Steak, potatoes, and grilled prickly pear. There's cake for dessert."

Lucy made an appreciative noise. "You know what I like!"

"Yep. Just remember it's out there, all right?"

"Yes ma'am!"

Irene opened the door. "It's nice to have you home."

"It's nice to be home," Lucy said with a smile in her voice.

With that, Irene left and closed the door behind her.

TWO

A soft knock on the door roused Lucy slightly. Her mind drifted between awake and asleep, her thoughts aimless in the laziness of a morning with no agenda. Alice, to her left, grumbled.

"Go away!" Alice's sleep-rough voice was too low for the knocker to hear, but the annoyed sound did wake Lucy the rest of the way.

The soft knock on the door came again. Alice pulled the covers over her head and curled up away from Lucy. The door opened slightly, and Irene's voice came through the crack.

"Lucy? You awake? Grace is ready for you. It's best to talk to her when she's feeling good."

"Yeah. I'll be right there," came the sleepy answer.

"Breakfast?"

"I'll eat after I talk to Grace." Lucy rubbed the sleep out of her eyes, or tried to.

"Grace is in room six."

"Thank you."

"Yep." Irene then shut the door.

Lucy sighed heavily and sat up. She rubbed her face with her hands to try and get her mind working, then stood and went to the wash pitcher and bowl. There were two washcloths on the dresser next to it. She smiled, grabbed one, and cleaned up quickly. She could have a real bath later, but this was fine for now.

Cleaned up, she pulled her jeans, blue shirt, and vest on quickly. She tied a red bandana around her braided hair, then sat in a chair to pull on her socks and brown leather boots. Once dressed, Lucy looked over at the bed. Alice was still asleep. Lucy stood and walked to the bed without trying to be quiet. She went to Alice's side and pulled the covers back carefully to expose Alice's flame-red hair. She pulled the covers back some more and saw that Alice was, in fact, fast asleep. Lucy leaned in and gave her a kiss on her freckled cheek.

"I'll be back," she whispered as she pulled away. "Keep the bed warm."

Alice made a noise in the back of her throat as Lucy laid the covers on top of her lover. Lucy smiled down at the bed, then left the room. The hallway was quiet at this time of day. Most of Irene's Escorts worked the night shift, until the train came in. Then, they usually worked double shifts, but mostly downstairs in the saloon at the gambling tables. Though some of the train passengers used Irene's Escorts, it was never that many. Usually, they couldn't afford them. If they were heading west, the clients wanted to save their money for their new life. Those headed west usually went to work the mines or had just enough money to start businesses that would support the miners.

The people headed back east either had enough money to live in one of the big underground cities or were slinking back to their families empty-handed. Either way, life on the East Coast was a bit easier. For reasons scientists hadn't determined yet, the dirt from California to almost Texas was turning rust red from the meteorites that landed during the first and subsequent Bombardments. The red desert hadn't reached past the Mississippi River yet, which meant the land could be farmed. It was still easier to grow crops above ground. Out west, the land was dry.

A sigh escaped Lucy as she moved down the hall and stopped at the farthest door from the stairs. She knocked softly, and Gracie's voice called out, "Come in!"

Lucy opened the door and stepped inside. Gracie was in the far corner, playing with dolls. The young girl looked up, shot up like a rocket, and ran to Lucy.

"Hi Lucy! Are you going to have breakfast with me?"

Before she could answer, a soft voice came from the bed. "No, sweetie. I need to talk to Lucy, alone. Go have breakfast with Linus, ok?"

Gracie looked at her mom on the bed, nodded, and hugged Lucy. When she let go, she blew a kiss in her mom's direction, then headed out the open door.

As Lucy closed the door, she looked at Grace. "She's being very accommodating."

"We had to have some very serious talks when I suspected I had this."

Lucy looked around the room, found a chair, and brought it a bit closer to the bed. Grace was sitting with her back to the headboard, a quilt over her legs. She was paler than usual, which was a feat. Grace never liked going out in the sun, despite growing up on a farm. Most clients were attracted by her pale skin. Now, her ivory skin looked pallid, her thick dark hair had thinned considerably, and her dark eyes were lackluster.

"How are you?"

"Fine, except for, you know . . ."

Lucy nodded. "Irene told me you caught it. When did it start?"

"About six months now. It started on my feet. It's up to my knees now. Middleton estimates I have a year, but if another illness hits me, it may take me sooner."

Lucy nodded, unable to think of anything to say. Grace caught some kind of virus every winter.

"Did Irene say why I wanted to talk to you?"

"No, she said she didn't know."

Grace laughed. "I told her."

Lucy's eyes went wide. "Well, that's uncharacteristic."

"She's been changing. She is getting up there in years."

"That woman hasn't changed in all the years I've known her. I doubt she'll really change now." Lucy crossed her arms and really thought about Irene's attitude. Normally, she wouldn't allow anyone to use her tub, and normally, if an Escort couldn't work, she wouldn't let them take up a room in the saloon. "Ok, maybe she is changing." Lucy shook her head. "I'll leave that for another day. Tell me what's going on."

Grace smiled weakly. "I want to hire you. I want you to find out who got me sick."

Lucy's eyes opened wide. "What?"

"I want you to find the man who got me sick."

"Do you have any idea who it was?"

"When the train came through in February, three men employed me. It was one of them."

Lucy looked shocked. "Three? That's rare."

"Two were business partners and were with me at the same time. One was a man who won some money downstairs and decided to spend time with a woman."

"Do you know their names?"

"They didn't give me their names, but the businessmen said they were opening a pet shop out west. They were real proud of their idea. They want to sell the mutated animals as pets. I think they said they had both Apprenticed as vets and were branching out."

"Anything else on them?"

She shook her head. "They looked about the same. Taller than me, well fed. One had a purple suit, said it was his favorite color. Both had brown hair and thick beards. One had a real deep voice," she giggled. "and the other had a crooked dick."

Lucy burst out laughing. "Well, I'm not getting close enough to find that detail!"

Grace's smile blossomed largely on her face. She briefly looked like her old self. "Yeah, I know, but if you talk to some Madams out there, you might be able to find them that way."

Lucy nodded. "Good point." She gazed at Grace for a moment, then asked, "What about the third man?"

"I have a feeling he was the one who infected me. He couldn't stop touching my feet. The other two men didn't touch me too much, but I think it's best if you talk to all three."

"Who were you with last?"

"The lone man."

"Ok, so if he did infect you, the other two won't have caught it from you."

Grace shook her head. "No."

"You got any information on him?"

She shook her head. "He was headed out west to work in the mines. He said he didn't have anyone back home and that he planned on working until he had enough money to marry, then he would head back east."

"Got a name or nickname or anything?"

"He said people called him Deter, but that he didn't like it. He said going to the mines would allow him to leave that name behind for a while."

"Shit, Grace, you're not giving me much."

"The only other thing is that he spoke with an accent."

"Underground accent or something else?"

"Something else. Remember when the Orators came through a few years ago and they had that main speaker who had that weird accent no one had heard?"

Before answering, Lucy thought about it. The Orators came through town about twice a year. Usually, Mr. Bradly was the main speaker. He had a clear voice that carried over the crowd. She squinted as she thought about that other man, and his voice came back to her. She nodded. "I remember the accent. It sounded like it was from overseas, but I don't remember where."

"I don't either, but this man sounded like that. He," Grace looked away, "he did try to tell me where he was from. He was really talkative, but he finished before he could say the country. Then he was too tired to talk."

Lucy laughed. "All right. I do remember the accent, and if I have a nickname he didn't like, that might help." She sighed. "He didn't say what city or mine, did he?"

There were many mines out west, all being worked by people who wanted to make money until they had enough to raise a family. Lucy wasn't sure why there were so many mines, but there were always rumors. Some speculated scientists wanted more of the Red Rock used in the meteorites during Bombardments to learn more about it. Some speculated people were looking for metals that could be scavenged, from when the cities were obliterated. Some even speculated that the Under was trying to expand beneath the Pacific Ocean. No one really knew for sure, but the mines employed a lot of people and paid well.

Grace's soft voice cut through Lucy's thoughts. "He said he was fascinated by the Red Rock, but most people are."

"All right. I can try and track these men down, but I gotta ask, why is this important to you? If he's sick, he might die before I find him." Lucy sighed sadly. "You might too."

Grace looked away. "I know, but . . . I don't know; it feels important. I can't really say much more than that."

Since Grace refused to look her way, Lucy knew something was up. "You're lying. What's going on?"

Grace looked briefly at Lucy, then looked away. "Alright, there are two reasons why I want you to track these men down, the lone man in particular." She paused and took a short breath. "I'm pregnant."

Lucy was silent as she digested the news. "You don't know it was one of them."

"I do. The month before the train came, I was at mom's place. She wanted to see Gracie. She doesn't approve of what I'm doing, but she likes to see Gracie. We were there for a month. I got my period. I came back, the train was here, and that night I saw those three men. I found the spot on my foot the next morning. I didn't get my period after that.

"After three months, I had Dr. Middleton run a test. He confirmed I'm pregnant. I'm almost six months now." She placed a hand on her relatively flat stomach. "Because of the Red Death, I can't keep any weight on. We also can't do too many exams, but the baby is fighting. Deter got me pregnant. The other two men were using me as a ruse. They were more interested in pleasing each other than in being pleased by me. They touched me some, but when it came to the end, they weren't anywhere near me."

There was a lot Lucy wanted to say, but she felt it best to let most things go. "Well in this day and age, you'd think they would just ask for a room."

"Some men can't. They think they have to be careful. I don't get it, either, but it's money. I don't question people's desires unless they want to hurt me."

Lucy nodded in agreement. "All right, so you need me to make sure the businessmen aren't sick, and you want me to tell Deter he's a father."

"Yes."

"Then what?"

Grace looked confused. "I don't . . ."

"When I find Deter, do you want me to simply tell him he's probably the father of your child and let him go, or do you want me to bring him back here so you can talk to him?"

Grace's eyes went wide. "Oh! I hadn't even thought of that."

Lucy stood silently as Grace looked away and seemed to think about her options. Finally, she slowly nodded. "I want to talk to him. Can you bring him back here?"

"I can try my best to do so."

"Ok. Thank you."

Lucy nodded, then looked at Grace but didn't say anything. The woman seemed to understand.

"I can pay you. I'll leave everything of mine to you."

She shook her head. "I can't take kids."

"I didn't . . ." Grace seemed to think about what she said, then tried again, "I'll give you everything I have minus Gracie and the new one. She's almost old enough to Apprentice anyway."

"Do you know what she wants to do?"

"She wants to be a doctor."

"Middleton is getting old. Does she want to Apprentice with him?"

Grace shook her head. "She isn't old enough to make that decision, but I talked to him about it. He wants to stop working. His hands shake too much. The town is looking for a replacement, but we're having a hard time. Most want to be on the East Coast or Under, where it's easier."

"It isn't any easier Under. People like to lie to themselves." The women looked at each other for a moment, then Lucy continued. "When she's ready, I'll take Gracie to another town, if needed. I know a doc or two that should be amicable to having an Apprentice. They aren't so far away she won't be able to visit home when she wants. And one's a woman. Doc Caster loves to teach."

Grace relaxed back against the headboard. "I like the idea of that, but I don't know what she'll do until then. I have some money, but not enough to keep her safe until she's old enough and pay you."

"You let me, and Irene worry about Gracie's education. We'll keep her safe."

Grace gave Lucy an odd look. "She has changed."

"Not for this. Leave it alone." She added the second part quickly as Grace looked about to speak.

"All right. Well," she sighed and sounded more tired than she should, "I suppose that's all buttoned up then."

"I still don't understand why you're having me do this."

Grace blinked and opened her mouth. "Middleton told me something interesting after he diagnosed me."

"Lay it on me."

"The Red Death doesn't affect everyone the same way."

"Oh?"

"Some people show symptoms right away, like me. Some show symptoms years later, and some never show symptoms. If the dad doesn't show symptoms, it's possible he won't die from it early. I want my kid to have a chance to know their dad."

"And if he is sick?"

She shrugged. "At least the dad'll know." She looked toward the corner of the room, where all of Gracie's toys were laid out. "I wish I knew who Gracie's dad was."

Lucy leaned back in her chair. "Would make things easier." She frowned a bit. "Is the baby going to have the Red Death?"

"Middleton's never seen a woman who had it who was pregnant. He's trying to find out, though."

"How?"

"He asked on the wire if someone else has seen it. Other towns close to us are asking towns they're closer to. He said he sent out an 'all hands' message, which he said would spread the question until it reached the end of the line or until someone came back with an answer. Doctors in the Under are getting asked too."

"That's a lot of towns."

"He says he's done this before, says it helps other places too. Remember that odd rash Vera got last year?" When Lucy shook her head, Grace corrected herself. "That's right, you weren't here for that. Vera got a rash on her arms after working in the garden. Wasn't like poison oak or ivy or sumac or anything like that. Turns out she's allergic to the toxins in the rhubarb leaves. Middleton found out about it by asking the docs on the wire to put out an 'all hands' bulletin."

"Well, ain't that something."

"He's still helpful."

"Yeah, but he needs to stop before his shaking hands make him slip up." She sighed and looked at Grace. "You sure about this?"

Grace nodded to indicate she knew the conversation had gone back to the hiring job. "I am. I want my baby to have a chance. This is probably it."

Lucy nodded and stood up. "I'll get the paperwork sent off today. And I'll do my best to finish this job."

Grace smiled. "You usually do. Thank you."

Lucy nodded once, then left the room.

THREE

Irene opened her bedroom door and nodded to Lucy. "Get it all figured out?"

"Yes and no. I have some questions about you now."

"Oh?" Irene started to straighten up her room as Lucy came in.

Before she made herself comfortable on Irene's bed, Lucy looked around the room. The room was already clean. Due to Irene moving around and avoiding her eyes, Lucy figured the woman didn't want to talk. She persisted anyway. "Why are you letting them stay here?"

"They have nowhere else to go."

"Last year, you kicked Fawnna out when she got sick. She didn't have anywhere to go, either. The year before that, Ty got sick, and you kicked them out. You don't have a good track record for keeping sick workers, Irene."

Irene sighed audibly, shook her head, and sat in the nearby chair. "Well, first off, Fawnna and Ty both tried to cheat me on numerous occasions. I don't stand for that. Grace has always been truthful." She paused. "I don't know, though. Feels different with her. She was my Apprentice. She's been with me so long; she feels like family. I was Grace's midwife for Gracie. When she confessed she didn't know who the father was, I decided it didn't matter, and Gracie felt like my grandkid."

She looked down at her hands and picked at some lint on her skirt. She still wore the same green dress as yesterday. Lucy didn't say anything. She had never seen Irene look anxious before. Finally, she spoke.

"I don't know if I ever told you. I can't have kids. All the stuff that happened during and after the Bombardment, some people were rendered sterile. I was born on the East Coast. My great-grandparents lived on land that was highly irradiated. They didn't know. They were able to have many kids, as was my dad. He met Mom coming home from the mines. She was from around here. I was born on my dad's land, which was passed down from my great-grandparents. My siblings and I were all born sterile. Radiation was supposed to have gone by the time I was born, but scientists say it's still there. Grace feels like my kid, even though she isn't blood."

Lucy gazed at Irene for a long time before Irene finally looked at her. "I'm sorry you can't have your own. I know how much you love kids."

She gave a weak smile. "I feel like it's best that I couldn't, with what I do for a living, but I still wish . . ."

"I don't understand fully. I don't want my own, but I've heard this story too often."

Irene smiled weakly again. "I love her, and Gracie, and I'll do what I want concerning them. And one or two others."

Lucy nodded. "I get that."

They smiled at each other and let the conversation lie between them for a moment before Lucy started in again.

"I get all that, really I do, but before yesterday, you never let me use your tub."

Irene waved the statement away. "And I would not have allowed it this time either, but a very good client asked to use the one upstairs with one of my Escorts."

"You've made others wait."

Irene gave Lucy a pointed look. "I already said there were one or two others that I feel are my own."

Lucy gave an embarrassed but happy smile and looked away. "Aw, shucks."

Irene sighed again. "Any other questions, little miss?"

"A ton, but none you can answer."

"Did you take the job?"

"Yep. She wants me to find the men she slept with who weren't from here. She said she slept with three men before getting the Red Death. Said she was at her mom's place for a month prior. Is that true?"

"It is. I remember, as one of her regulars was rather angry that he couldn't have her for a month. Then she came back, and the others paid more for her time, so he couldn't have her that night. And the next morning, we found the spot."

"I didn't know it started that quickly."

"It can if the person is prone to illnesses. And you know Grace is always sick. Middleton said something about her immune system being weak. I don't remember too much about human bodies unless it's how to please them."

Lucy laughed. "Yeah, that stuff never stuck in my head either, but I do remember something about an immune system. We all have it. It's what fights diseases." She vaguely remembered more but wasn't confident enough to continue. "So, it can show up that quickly? We sure it wasn't her mom or one of her mom's farmhands who had it?"

"We asked. We also had Middleton run the test on all of them and on everyone in town. He said no one had it except Grace."

She stared at Irene. "We have nearly two hundred people here. That's a lot of tests."

Irene caught Lucy's real meaning. "The test is now free since it's destroying towns. They're starting to worry it'll get to the Under and destroy those too."

"Oh. Wow, that's . . ." She was quiet for a moment. "Maybe I should get tested. You know, just in case."

"He'll run the other tests for you too. The ones my Escorts get."

"He ran those for me the last time I was here, and the only one I've slept with since is Alice."

Irene nodded, then went back to an earlier question. "What's Grace paying you, if you don't mind my asking?"

"All that she has, minus Gracie." She left out that Grace was pregnant, as she didn't know if Irene knew.

"What is she asking you to do?"

"Find out who got her sick."

"Why?"

Lucy paused and gave Irene a level look. "How much did she actually tell you? I know she talked to you, but I don't know how much."

Irene returned the level look, then sighed. "I know she's pregnant."

Lucy nodded. "She wants me to find the dad. She's pretty sure she knows who got her pregnant. If he's the one who got her sick, she wants to make sure he's aware he's sick."

"Why does she want him to know she's pregnant? She didn't tell me that."

"She wants to give the kid a chance to know him. She regrets that Gracie doesn't know her dad."

"But if he's dying . . ."

Lucy held up her hands. "I'm for hire, Irene. I love the woman and Gracie. I'll do what I can to help her, even if it's a fool's errand."

"You're not going to earn enough for your troubles."

"I don't want this getting out, but I've done a few jobs that earned me a lot of money. I can take on jobs that don't pay much if I feel it's for a good cause, or for a friend."

Irene gazed at Lucy for a long, silent moment then, "Only one type of job gets a Hired Hand a lot of money."

Lucy didn't look away. "Yeah, the ones where clients pay lots."

Irene opened her mouth to say more, then thought better of it. She gave a curt nod, looked away, and stayed silent.

"I know what you were thinking." Lucy's voice was soft. "Did you really think I wouldn't take one of those jobs?"

"I've heard it changes people." Her voice was soft too, as if she didn't want the discussion to continue.

"It did, but Cecil told me how he felt the first time he took an assassin's job. He told me that it was my decision to take one or not, and that when I did, I should schedule about two months to myself afterwards to really reflect on it."

"Oh."

"Irene, my first assassin's job was when Cecil was still alive."

She whipped her head back to stare at Lucy, her eyes as large as saucers. "Oh!"

"These last two weren't assassin jobs. They just paid real well." She chuckled. "Rich people will pay anything if they think something is worth it."

"Oh." Irene sighed audibly as she processed the conversation. "I just never thought."

"It's best when people don't suspect we're available for those jobs. It brings all kinds."

"I suppose it would, wouldn't it?"

"There are three women and four men in this community who have approached me about assassinations. It was after I became full-fledged. They came to me and said if I ever decided to take on an assassination job, that I should come see them. They all want their spouse or sibling dead for various reasons. What they don't seem to understand is that a Hired Hand who is willing to approach someone about an assassination job is someone they don't want to hire."

There was a gleam of curiosity in Irene's eyes. "Is there a situation in which both spouses hired you to kill the other?"

Lucy laughed. "No, but I'm waiting for that to happen."

Irene laughed as well and that seemed to ease the tension. She leaned back in her chair and gazed at Lucy. "So she wants to find out who got her sick and who got her pregnant?"

"Pretty much. She's sure it was one of those three from the train that did it."

Irene nodded. "When are you going?"

"On the next train west. It's just my luck that the train heading west will be a couple days later than the one heading east. I want to check if the men are heading home already."

"You going to be able to identify them?"

"I don't know. Everyone gets off the train here. Last stop with a real bed for miles and miles, and a chance to see the sun. I'll borrow you for the night and see if you recognize any of them. Do you remember what they look like?"

"Vaguely. One sounded like he was from Deutschland."

"That's it!" Her eyes opened wide in excitement, and her voice went up an octave. "Grace said he sounded like that Orator who came through a while back. I couldn't remember where he said he was from."

"Oh, that's right! I knew I'd heard that accent before."

Lucy gave Irene a curious look. "Do you remember what Grace's client looked like?"

"Had large ears and nose. Average height and thin."

Lucy nodded. "You didn't get his name, did you?"

Irene shook her head. "No. They rarely give names."

Lucy nodded again. "What about the other two? Grace said they were partners, in more ways than one."

She made a noise in the back of her throat. "Yeah. I asked if they wanted a room of their own, but they looked embarrassed. I don't remember how they looked though, other than too well dressed. I feel like they'll end up selling their wardrobe if they run out of money."

"Grace mentioned one liked purple?"

Recognition lit up Irene's eyes. "Oh, that's right. I remember that now. We guessed he had to. He was dressed head to toe in purple, including a top hat." Irene placed a hand over her heart and raised the other in the air. "Oh, but he was handsome in that suit. So regal!" She lowered her arms. "The other was demure and had a simple black suit. But the suits fit very well, and it was hard to see the stitches. Good craftsmanship. Rare for people going out west."

"Well, that's something."

Irene nodded. "So, you're not going to stick around too long?"

"Since we really don't know how long Grace is going to live, I'm leaving with the train. It's the best thing to do. I'll give you money before

I leave. Maybe stick it in a bank for you."

"You think that's necessary?"

"It's almost the end of summer, Irene. Grace usually gets sick in September, or sooner if anyone else gets a cold. And since the train only runs once a season, I'll be lucky to get back before she dies. I want to make sure there's money for Gracie in case something happens."

Irene nodded. "What are you going to do if you can't find the men?"

"I don't know. I'm pretty good at finding a needle in a haystack. I feel I have a chance."

"You already have a plan."

Lucy laughed. "Yeah."

"All right. I guess I should have known that."

The women looked at each other for a moment, then Lucy stood. "All right, I'll get out of your hair. I have paperwork to file, anyway."

"What are you going to do while you're in town?" Irene stood, as did Lucy.

"Check the job board to see if there's anything I can do quickly. I don't like being idle." She gave a small shudder as she moved to the door.

"All right."

"Can I see Alice after I'm done filing my paperwork?"

"If she's at the tables, you can talk to her. Just don't keep her from her job."

"Yes, ma'am." Lucy nodded her goodbyes and left the room.

FOUR

When the train heading east came a few days later, Lucy sat on the back porch of the hotel, Irene close by. The entrance building to the train station was near a natural hot spring. The warmth of the springs hid any heat caused by the steam engine in the underground tunnels. The building was small, with only a waiting room and a long ramp. The waiting room had double doors and some windows. It wasn't meant as a place to stay. Those disembarking or embarking moved through it to the town beyond.

The small building faced the back of the hotel, which was across the street from Irene's Saloon, Gambling Hall, and Escort service. A lot of the passengers came toward the hotel. A few approached Irene, but she advised them to go to the saloon and talk to Alice. The ladies watched as what seemed like the last person exited the building.

"I didn't see them."

"You think anyone stayed on the train?"

"No idea. It's hard to say how many people take the train east. Sometimes it's full, sometimes it's not. Talk to Stella. She'll let you on the train." Irene rose from her chair.

"You going to come with me?" Lucy stood as well.

"I have to get back to work."

"What are the odds they'll be on the train, do you think?"

"Usually takes a year for people to realize they've made a mistake and head home."

"So, slim?" Lucy placed her hands on the railing in front of her and stared at the building, as if it would reveal anything.

"It's worth knowing."

Lucy gave a noncommittal grunt.

"It leaves in a couple days, and the train west isn't here yet. You have time."

"Yep."

Irene leaned against the railing. "What's got your thoughts?"

"I really don't understand why she asked me to do this, you know?"

"Her baby needs a chance. Life in a saloon around Escorts isn't always good. Gracie's seen too much."

"If the dad's sick, the baby isn't going to have too many options anyway."

"There are orphanages," Irene offered quietly.

Lucy turned her head and gave Irene a look of disdain. "Have you seen those places?"

Irene was quiet for a moment, then shook her head. "No. No, I have not."

"Don't put those kids in one, all right?"

"We'll do what we can."

"If she dies before I get back, you do everything in your power to keep them out of an orphanage, you hear me? Even Grace's mother is better than an orphanage."

Irene looked shocked, but she acquiesced. "All right."

"Good." Lucy looked at the building, then stood tall. "Well, I guess I'm going on a hunt."

Irene had the audacity to laugh. "And for a man at that."

Lucy's face cracked into a grin. "Oh, hush."

Irene laughed and turned to leave. "You sleeping at the saloon tonight?"

"Alice wants time to herself. If you got a room I can use . . .?"

"We'll work something out. Come by later."

Lucy nodded and Irene left. Lucy turned and headed to the building. She opened the door, made sure it closed behind her, then walked quickly across the floor and onto the ramp. When the train west came through, there would be cargo unloaded up this ramp. She walked at a good pace down, then turned right. There were two elevators on this level that went all the way down to the station. One was for humans, and one was for cargo, though even the cargo elevator could be used for humans, if there were enough.

In front of the elevator operator, she nodded. He nodded back. The man was shorter than her by a few inches and wore a blue pinstripe suit. There was a name tag close to the buttons on his suit. Lucy looked pointedly at the tag.

"Hey, Randall. Care to take me down?"

"Sure." He took a good look at her, cleared his throat, looked at her right lapel again, then looked in her eyes. "Pardon me, but . . . are you here on business?"

Lucy smiled. As she was on the job, she wore a pin on her right lapel indicating her profession. It was a copper pin with the letters HH embossed on it. It was standard procedure unless the job was to kill. Not many people realized that last part. "Yes, but I'm looking to talk to someone."

A small frown knitted his eyebrows together. "You have to say if you're here to kill, right?"

She looked surprised. Though she felt like kidding with him, it was probably best to tell him the truth. "You're new, ain't you?"

He cleared his throat. "Um . . ."

She nodded as if to answer her own question. "You're new. Randall, if I was here to kill someone, I wouldn't wear the pin, and I would be in a better disguise than this. I'm trying to find out if someone is on this train, which I'm allowed to do."

"Oh." He cleared his throat again. "Ok."

Randall moved out of the way and pushed the iron gate aside. Lucy rolled her eyes at his inexperience with Hired Hands, then got on the elevator and moved to the back. He moved inside, closed the gate, and started the box down. She could hear the cranks and gears as the rickety sounding elevator was lowered. It took a minute or two, but soon they were on the station platform. As Randall opened the door, she placed a gentle hand on his shoulder. He turned and gave her a nearly fearful look.

She held out her other hand, in which lay a gold coin. "For your trouble. And, really Randall, get familiar with Hired Hands. We have rules to follow, or we lose our license. Most of our rules are documented and accessible by the public. It'll save you trouble in the long run, especially if you keep working on the trains, ok?"

He nodded and took the coin. Lucy tipped her hat to him, then left the elevator. She made her way to the ticket station nearby. Unlike the elevator operator, who worked for the train and rode with the train from station to station, the ticket salesperson usually worked for the town the station was under, or a town nearby. This one was manned by Stella, who lived in Meridune and knew Lucy. The woman also knew the rules of Hired Hands, which made things easier on Lucy.

At the ticket window, Lucy could see Stella behind the counter. She was a petite woman with a stern look on her wrinkle-lined face. She didn't look up from the paperwork in front of her when Lucy knocked on the wood counter to get her attention.

"Destination?"

"Stella, it's me."

The woman looked up, a startled expression on her face. "Oh! Hey Lucy. I was expecting customers. How can I help you?"

"Can I get on the train? I'm looking for someone."

She rolled her eyes as she repeated the usual, in a bored voice. "Railway policy states you have to tell me why. No killing on the train." She looked Lucy in the eyes. "And don't tell me the rules again. You know I know them."

Lucy laughed at Stella's apparent annoyance. "I'm looking to find the man who got Grace sick. Not to kill him but to talk to him. I want to make sure he didn't end up on the train home."

"Oh! Yeah, let me get you the ticket. If anyone on board bothers you, you show them this and they'll leave you alone." Stella grabbed a thick paper ticket from the backboard and handed it to Lucy.

She took it and shook her head. The "ticket" was on thick paper, about a foot long and three inches wide. It could be stuck into a back pocket but not easily forgotten. "This is ridiculous."

"Pay for a real ticket."

"Train's not going the right way."

Stella gave Lucy an inquiring look. "That's not your usual response."

"If the gentlemen aren't on board, I'll be heading west."

"Well, I guess it's your good luck that the train is late this time."

Lucy smiled wide. "Yep!"

Stella smiled and her hands went back to her paperwork. "Need anything else, Lucy?"

"Not yet. Thank you, Stella!"

"Welcome!" She turned back to her paperwork as Lucy turned around, walked the few steps to the train, and boarded.

ᛒᚷᛒᚷᛒᚷ

"Any luck?"

Lucy sank into the chair at the surprisingly empty blackjack table and shook her head in Irene's direction. "No, but the steward remembered the man with the accent. The one Grace said didn't like being called Deter."

Irene frowned as she fiddled with a glass of whiskey. "What's the steward's name?"

"Jamie. Young man of about twenty. Had short, red-tipped hair. Spray of freckles across his cheeks."

"I think I know him. He's got a good memory for people." Her frown deepened. "If he was on the train west in February, he would have returned to the East Coast on the May train."

Lucy shrugged. "I can't speak on that. All I know is that Jamie says he remembers Deter, or rather Dietrich, because the man almost started a fight in the dining car."

Irene looked shocked. "Over what?"

"Over who was in line first."

Irene stared at her for a moment, then shook her head. "Some people."

Lucy shrugged. "At least I have a name."

Irene nodded. The women were silent for a moment until a tall man came over with a plate and placed it in front of Irene. He looked at Lucy. "Need anything, Lucy?"

She looked at the fried chicken on Irene's plate. There was also corn on the cob and mashed potatoes. "That looks good."

"How much chicken?" the man asked.

"Same as hers."

The waiter nodded and walked back to the kitchen.

Irene caught Lucy's attention again. "You leaving soon, then?"

"I already have my ticket for the next train west. It'll be here in a few days."

"Do you know when, exactly?"

"Stella confirmed it's on its way from River Falls. Should be here in two days. Meaning I'll leave in three."

"Make sure you say goodbye to all the right people." Irene gave Lucy a pointed look.

"I will, especially since I need to get some money squared with you, soon."

"For Gracie?"

"And the other, if needed."

Irene nodded. "If you want to take care of it now, we can go to my room?"

Lucy pointed out the plate of food. "Your food is going to get cold."

Irene stood. "Almost always does. Now or later?"

"I have to go to the bank."

"Ah. All right."

Irene sat back down and started on her dinner. The women were quiet as she ate. Before too long the waiter came back with a plate and set it in front of Lucy. As he left, Lucy turned to Irene.

"Why is this table empty?"

"More customers wanted to have sex than gamble."

"Ah." Lucy turned her attention to her food.

ᏸᏣᏸᏣᏸᏣ

Lucy knocked softly on Grace's door. It was late, but she wanted to talk to her if possible. She didn't hear a response but knocked softly again. This time, she heard small feet hurrying to the door. It opened to reveal Gracie. The little girl's eyes opened wide, and she looked about to squeal.

"Shhhhh. Is your momma awake, sugarplum?"

Gracie contained her excitement and looked at the bed. "Mom?"

"Send them away, honey."

"It's Lucy!" Her voice was excited.

There was a mumbled response then, "Ok."

Gracie opened the door wider and let Lucy in. Lucy turned to the girl and looked her in the eye. "Let me talk to your momma alone, hun."

Gracie looked downtrodden. "That's been happening so much lately!"

Despite the protest, she left without another word. Lucy closed the door, then went to Grace's bed. "I'm sorry to bother you."

"It's fine. I might fall asleep while we talk."

"I won't be long. The train heading east came in. The men weren't on it. I'll be heading west in a few days."

A look of resignation came to Grace's face. "All right. Thank you."

Lucy looked at Grace and tried not to worry. The woman looked like death warmed up. She was pale, her hair was stringy, and her skin was shiny with sweat. "You all right?"

She shook her head. "No. Some days the pain is so terrible I want to ask Doc Middleton to chop off my legs."

"That doesn't stop the illness." Once someone had the Red Death, it was too late. If an affected arm or leg was chopped off, the disease came back but started in the stump.

"I know, but still. It hurts so much."

"I'll be out of your hair in a minute. Grace? Why not have your mom take your kids in?"

A more haunted look took over her face. Fear and anger seemed to give her the determination to sound confident and strong. "I don't want them being raised by that woman. I'll go visit and let her see Gracie, but not unsupervised." She shook her head as tears started to form. "I can see what she really thinks about Gracie when we visit. She's said some nasty things while my child has been in earshot. On top of how she treated me as a kid? No way."

"I didn't realize." Lucy's voice was soft. "I'm sorry it's like that."

A tear slid down from Grace's eye, and she wiped her face with shaky hands as she nodded.

"I'll do my best to find the men."

Grace nodded and smiled weakly.

"Do you need anything?"

She laughed. "A cure?"

Lucy patted her pockets. "Sorry, hun. Fresh out."

Grace laughed, smiled again but it quickly faltered and turned into a yawn.

"I won't keep you. I just wanted to give you an update."

"Thank you."

Lucy turned to the door and placed her hand on the knob. She stood for a moment, then looked back and caught Grace's eye. "I left money with Irene for Gracie and the baby. In case I don't come back before you pass."

This time the tears flowed freely as Grace spoke. "Thank you, Lucy. A lot."

Lucy nodded, then left the room.

FIVE

The train rocked gently as it moved through the tunnels. To say it raced would be a misnomer. The spotters had to be on the lookout for cave-ins and other debris on the track. Not all the tunnels were cemented over yet. That was still in the works. Also, the faster the train moved, the more heat it generated and released through the vents. That couldn't be risked, as it would draw the Aimers attention and bring a Bombardment. Though the engineers and miners who built the tunnels were confident a Bombardment wouldn't reach the train tunnels, no one really knew, and no one wanted to find out the hard way.

In about a week, they would be under the mountains, which meant they would be able to go faster. The walls of the mountain tunnels were cemented over and the steam vented at natural springs and geysers. Lucy sighed as she settled back into the stall she shared with Lance. Though most didn't try to bring their horse underground, Lance was an easy horse. To get him onto the train, she put blinders over his eyes while they were still on the surface. She was then able to lead him into the building and onto the ramp. He neighed nervously while on the freight elevator, but once in the stall, with hay on the floor, he was fine. Now, he lay in the hay next to her, asleep.

Lucy preferred to be on the surface; she hated being cooped up, but traveling on horse to either coast from Meridune was too slow. She had gone to the East Coast on Lance for her last job, but that hadn't been on purpose. Her job had taken her out farther than she initially thought she had to go, which meant she was gone way longer than she wanted to be. With Lance, she could ride eight to ten hours a day. At a steady pace, he walked about twenty miles per hour. The train had enough conductors that it moved twenty-four hours a day. Even though most times, the train didn't run higher than eighteen miles per hour, it was still, overall, faster than a horse.

If the train west hadn't been delayed, she would have ridden Lance out, but that was dangerous. There were too many Bandits on the road and too many critters that liked to hunt humans. Also, there wasn't an easy way through the mountains unless she took the train. By horse, she would have had to go over the top. It was cold in the mountains even now. Therefore, she got herself a ticket and did as she had to.

There were plenty of seating arrangements on the train for people, less so for animals. At least they had a car with stalls for horses. Lucy could have paid for a seat, or even a sleeping car. Sleeping in Lance's stall was cheaper, and it kept people from thinking she had any money. Being near Lance on the hay was also comforting. The smell and his soft neighing could help her forget she was underground. It made for a peaceful ride. She smiled, laid her head back on her bag, and was slipping her hat over her face as she heard the car door open.

Lucy listened to the steps approach and opened one eye. To the casual observer, her hat covered her eyes, but she could see under the brim. She watched as a tall, lanky man walked into view, turned toward her, and squatted. He wore black jeans, a button-up black shirt, and black leather boots. His black leather cowboy hat was tilted just a little bit back, showing off more of his forehead. An HH pin was on his right lapel. She addressed him without moving her hat.

"Yes?"

"Looking for a Hired Hand."

"And you think I'm one because?" Her pin was hidden under her coat.

"We really going to play this game again, Lucy?"

She moved the hat out of the way a bit and smiled at him. "How are you, Roger?"

"Fair to middlin'."

She grinned. Cecil used to use the phrase every day. Lucy sat up and leaned her lower back against her saddle bag and moved her hat completely out of the way. "What do you need?"

"Got a job, if you want it."

The smile dropped a bit, and she asked more pointedly. "What do you need?"

He paused and looked at her, seemed to realize something, and nodded. "I'm with my Mistress."

She snickered.

Roger narrowed his eyes. "The woman who hired me, Ms. Bauer, needs another guard."

"Why?"

"When she told me she wanted to go west, I advised her that I would need help so I could sleep. She agreed, but she is . . . rather opinionated. She alienated him, and he's now back in Meridune, waiting for the train back to Boston. I'm sure he'll regret his decision once he realizes how long he has to wait."

She nodded. "How did you know to look for me?"

"It took a while to hear that a Hired Hand was on the train. When I heard someone was back here, sleeping in the horse stall, I knew it had to be you."

"To be clear, you're looking for someone to help you guard so you can sleep?"

"Yep. Need someone all the way to the coast. I'll pay twenty gold."

Her eyes popped wide. "That's a lot for a train ride."

He took a deep slow breath. "She's a lot. Her uncle, her only caretaker, died four months ago. She's been sheltered. She's on her own, young, and doesn't know how to act around people yet. Her uncle hired me for her about two years ago, and she hardly ever came out of her room. She seems to think that just because she pays me, she has the right to every minute of my day and night. It won't be an easy trip."

"Why are you still working for her?"

"I'm making good money." His eyes popped open. "I married Susie! She's expecting. We have the use of a small guest room on Ms. Bauer's property. It's helped me see my family a lot more."

"Congratulations!" Lucy said with a smile. It quickly dropped. "Which one was Susie?"

Roger laughed. "About as tall as you, has a bald head most of the time. Fixes train engines."

Lucy nodded. "I think I liked her."

"You did. You also couldn't stop making fun of me with her the last time we were all together."

Lucy laughed. "I remember her now."

Roger smiled. "You want the job or not?"

"Just until Sacramento?"

"Yep, and if she's too much, you can walk away. All I ask is that you don't talk back to her."

Lucy made a face full of discontent. "It's good money, but you know how I am."

"And I'm still asking for your help."

They stared at one another for a few minutes before Lucy nodded. "When do I get paid?"

"When we reach the end of the line."

"And if I walk away before the end of the line?"

"I'll pay you for the days you stayed."

She held his gaze for a while as she thought about it. Finally, she nodded. "All right."

Roger stood. "Want to go meet her?"

"Sure. She going to care that I smell like a horse?" Lucy asked as she stood and brushed some hay off her backside.

"Probably not." He turned toward the car door and took a few steps. He talked over his shoulder. "She has an area for your horse too. At least Lance will be closer."

"Stop trying to sell me on this venture, Roger. Twenty gold is twenty gold." She followed him toward the door.

"You don't always take jobs for the money." He opened the door to the car, stepped through, and held it open for her.

Lucy stepped through and waited for Roger to lead the way. He looked at her, expecting an explanation or rebuttal, but when none came, he nodded and moved forward. They had a few cars to walk through. The cargo cars were behind the stable. In front of the stable was a dining car, then three passenger cars. In front of those was a sleeping car. The number of passenger or sleeping cars changed based on the number of tickets sold.

In front of that one was another dining car, this one with a few gambling tables. The patrons in this one were better dressed than the other, as were the servers.

Lucy glanced at the clock as they moved out of the dining car and understood why there weren't that many people up and about. It was eight o'clock. People were settling in to get some shut-eye. There were some lights in the train cars, but most of those were being dimmed. It made it easier to see out the windows, which showed the blackness of the tunnel beyond the train. The wall was closer on the right side of the train than the left. Two trains could move in the tunnel at once, but usually only met each other once, at the Meridune station. It wasn't the middle point of the track, but with the speeds the trains had to maintain, it ended up being the meeting point.

Finally, they reached a car marked "Private." Roger led the way through that one, quickly. There was a hallway with a door on one wall and windows on the other. The patrons in this car were well off. The cars up front had a private bedroom, a living area, and some had a small stable. At the other end of the car, Roger opened the door and waited for Lucy on the small platform for the next car. There was a sign on it that read "Private" as well.

Roger opened the door to the car and stepped through. For all other doors, he had opened the door and let her pass first. She took note of it but didn't say anything about it as she looked around. The car had a hallway, with one door on the left in the middle and two doors on the right, one on each end. Instead of moving forward, he looked at Lucy.

"We're in this one. The car after is the tender, then the locomotive."

"For some reason, I always thought the rich people were in the back of the train, away from the coal."

"Turns out, rich people would rather suffer with a little coal smell than be killed by Bandits. They're more likely to strike at the cargo cars than the passenger cars. If they see a rich person back there, they think they can ransom them."

Lucy nodded. When she didn't say anything, he turned and walked to the left. Roger waited for Lucy to move behind him and knocked twice.

"Come in!" a high-pitched feminine voice called from the other side of the door.

Roger opened the door and again stepped through first. "Evening, ma'am. I'd like to introduce you to Lucy. Lucy, this is Ms. Adelia Bauer, my employer."

The woman stared at Lucy from her seat. Her dark hair was tied in a tight bun at the back of her neck. She had the same pale skin as most Undergrounders, with green eyes. Despite the stern look on her face, she looked about ten years younger than Lucy, which made her around the same age as Roger.

Lucy nodded then looked around the car. Ms. Bauer sat at a small round table, situated under one of the two windows. There was a vacant seat across from her. A teacup sat on a saucer in front of her. There was a cart nearby with more tea settings. There was a couch along the far wall across from the windows. Next to the couch was a door. Another door sat across from it on the right. Against the right wall was a record player. Lucy wondered what was powering it before turning back to Ms. Bauer and looking her in the eye.

Ms. Bauer raised an eyebrow and looked her up and down. "Did you get a good enough look?"

Lucy held the woman's gaze. "If I'm going to help guard you, I need to know the space you'll live in for the duration of the trip. Standard procedure."

"Roger didn't do that."

"Roger had the plans memorized before the train left the station." Lucy held the woman's eyes as she spoke. Ms. Bauer seemed to bristle, which made Lucy smirk.

"You dare think you know him?"

Lucy's smile became more pronounced. "I apprenticed with his father. I helped raise the brat."

Roger let out an annoyed, "Hey!"

Lucy's eyes were fixed on Ms. Bauer though, and she saw the woman's lovely reaction. Her eyes grew wide; one hand came up and hid the laugh that bubbled out of her chest. She composed herself quickly, but her eyes still sparkled with mirth. It was a genuine laugh of someone kindly amused. It made Lucy feel that Roger's assessment of Ms. Bauer might be off. She filed that away in her mind and caught the woman's eyes again.

"You need someone else to watch you?"

"Roger believes I do, but we could both sleep at the same time. I'm not sure what can happen on a train."

"Bandits. We're coming up on their territory. They strike at all hours. Best to have two or even three people watching you. Let's them sleep in shifts."

"He said the same thing, but I don't understand. How are there Bandits in these tunnels? They're well secured."

"Though the Rail does a good job of keeping the Bandits out, they do find ways down here. Sometimes they make new tunnels, sometimes they use the vents, sometimes they simply invade the town a station is in."

Ms. Bauer looked a bit shocked. "I didn't realize."

"There's always someone trying to make some gold off of someone else's hard work."

Ms. Bauer looked away. "I suppose." She cleared her throat. "If I hire you, would you sleep during the day or night?"

"Roger's used to being awake during the day. I'm used to sleeping when I need. I'll take the night shift."

"What will you do during the day?"

"There's plenty to keep me occupied after I get some sleep." Lucy didn't feel like filling in the blanks.

"You gamble?"

Lucy shook her head. "Though I've been known to place wagers on shooting contests, I don't play cards much." To stop the questions, Lucy decided to give one possible location. "There's an observation lounge in the furthest dining car, in the upstairs. It's open to all and has plenty to do. But I'll stay close until we're in the mountains, when it's harder for the Bandits to raid."

"You seem to already have a plan in mind."

"If Roger's been in your employment for a while, you should understand that's how we operate. Always plan and always be ready to abandon those plans when necessary."

Ms. Bauer gave a light frown. "I don't believe he's had to 'abandon plans' with me, yet."

Lucy looked Ms. Bauer in the eye. "Perhaps 'change at a moment's notice' fits better."

Ms. Bauer sat taller. "Well, when things change, we must all do our part."

Lucy fought the urge to frown, as the thought seemed too automatic a response. She let her thoughts go, cleared her throat, but didn't say anything else.

Ms. Bauer stared at her for a moment, but Lucy kept her mouth shut. The rest was up to the woman. She could either accept or reject her and at this point, Lucy could take the job or leave it. Twenty gold was a lot of money, but she had more stashed away in the bank at Meridune.

After a moment, it seemed like Ms. Bauer realized it was her turn to speak and cleared her throat. "Do you have any other questions for me?"

"Nope."

"All right. Roger, I accept your choice."

"Good. Thank you. Lucy, let me show you the bedroom we're going to be sharing. And you can't move Lance until the next station."

"Figured." She nodded to Ms. Bauer and followed Roger out.

SIX

ucy followed Roger out of the room and to the door closer to the head of the train. He opened the door there and revealed a small bedroom with two cots, a chair, a dresser, and a wash basin.

"It's not much, but it's enough."

That earned him a snicker from Lucy.

"What?"

"For having been raised by your ma, and not Apprenticing with Cecil, you sure picked up a lot of his sayings."

He gave a small smile. "He might not have been around much, but he had a big influence on my life."

Lucy looked Roger up and down pointedly. Roger was the spitting image of Cecil, down to the black clothing. His hair was cut in a fade and not tied up with a red bandana like Cecil, but everything else mimicked the man to a T. "You think?"

He opened his mouth to speak, thought better of it, and looked at the room. "You can bring your saddle bag up from the stable, then get yourself situated."

"How tired are you?"

"I could sleep."

"My bag is fine with Lance. Why don't you get some shut-eye, and I'll watch her? Do I sit in the living room?"

"Yep. The couch is comfortable, but not too comfortable. Let me show you the books."

Lucy gave a gasp and her eyes lit up. "I didn't see a bookshelf."

"That's why I'm showing it to you." There was laughter in his reply.

She smiled and followed him out of the small room and back to Ms. Bauer's room. He knocked but when he didn't receive a response, opened the door.

"She tends to go to her bedroom early, but she's hardly ever asleep. She likes to read." He led the way to one of the other doors in the room and opened it. It was an all-purpose closet, with clothes on one side and a small bookshelf on the other.

"She's got old world books?" Before the Bombardment, most books were bound in thin paper and had glossy plastic covers. Special ones were hard bound with either thicker paper or leather. Now, if they were paperback, the cover was thicker but still flexible, with no plastic. Lucy reached out and grabbed a paperback off the shelf. It felt odd in her hands.

Lucy opened the book to the last page. It was over 100 pages long. She brought the open book to her nose as her eyes closed and breathed in deep. It had a clean smell, of wood or sawdust. The pages were yellow with age, and the ink was smeared, just a touch, showing it had been read many, many times. She closed the cover and slowly looked it over. She didn't pay attention to the title, cover art, or writer's name, but looked at the flecked paint, the little tears and the hills and valleys of the book's imperfections. Her hand caught on a couple tears as she ran her fingers down the spine. It was lovely.

"You need some time alone?"

She glared at Roger.

He gave a small laugh. "Yeah, I know you like books, but do you ever really read any or do you just fawn over the textures?"

"I like to read, but old books are, I don't know, they tell us a little more of who we were."

"You and Dad, full of emotions over something you don't even seem to have much of."

Lucy gave Roger a steady look. "I own all the books I've ever picked up. I just store them out in the world for other people to pick up too. Hoarding books seems to be a waste of knowledge."

"I've heard that before the Bombardment, people had libraries in their homes."

"I believe it. We just shouldn't have that luxury. Not enough books in the world and it's getting harder and harder to print."

"Boston Under was starting to print more."

"I heard it takes a lot of heat to make books."

"A group of monks found out how to make parchment. It's what we used before paper, long time ago. I think they found an old printing press from the Way Before."

"Whatever gets us more books."

"Alright, well, don't stay in here fondling the books too long. It's getting late, and I need my beauty sleep."

"All right, all right." Lucy held on to the book. "You sure I can read them?"

"She told me I could. You can tell her I let you, if it becomes an issue."

Lucy nodded, turned, and headed out of the closet. She went to sit on the couch. It was comfortable, but there were lumps in a couple bad spots.

It would keep her awake, probably.

"You need anything more?" Roger asked from the doorway.

"Coffee. I was awake today."

"I'll get you some. Oh, and if someone comes for the tea cart, just roll it over to the door."

Lucy looked at the table and realized that the tea cart she'd seen not moments earlier was still in the room. "I dismissed that as part of the furnishings."

"Nope, belongs to the dining car."

"I'll wheel it to them when they show up."

"Great. I'll be back with coffee. Still take it black?"

"Yep!"

"All right." He walked out and closed the door behind him.

Once she was alone, Lucy opened the book to the first page and started to read.

ဆောကြသောကြသောကြ

The rattle of the doorknob woke Lucy the next morning. She was standing with her hand on her gun when she realized she was still clutching a book to her chest. Both her arms lowered as the door opened fully, and Lucy and Ms. Bauer stared at each other. Ms. Bauer looked Lucy up and down and raised an eyebrow.

"Did you get a good night's sleep?"

"No ma'am. I took a nap, but that doorknob woke me."

Ms. Bauer opened her mouth to speak but appeared surprised by Lucy's response. She shut her mouth with a snap and started to walk to the table. As she did, Lucy looked her up and down, admiring the cut of the woman's suit. It was dark blue and hugged her body like a glove.

"I would like breakfast."

"Am I supposed to order it for you?" she asked, sincerely. "I didn't ask Roger the protocol last night."

Ms. Bauer nodded as she sat down, but a knock on the outer door changed her words. "Come in."

The door opened to reveal Roger and a server with a food cart. He nodded to Lucy and allowed the server to wheel the cart in. Roger then nodded to the man and closed the door behind him.

"Morning. I woke up early enough I figured I'd ask for breakfast. I ordered your usual."

"That's fine. Thank you, Roger." She looked at Lucy. "You can go get real rest now. I don't want a repeat tomorrow morning."

Lucy nodded and left the room.

₧₨₧₨₧₨

"Morning." This time, Lucy sat upright on the couch, the book in her hands instead of lying on her chest. She spoke before Ms. Bauer did. This morning, the woman was dressed in a red suit. It hugged her body well, and Lucy had to stop herself from whistling. The woman was beautiful, but it wouldn't do to get distracted and say the wrong thing. Cecil always said, "Never flirt with your Assignment. It only leads to sloppy jobs." She took his rules to heart. They made sense and kept her safe.

"Did you want me to get you breakfast?" Lucy asked as Ms. Bauer took a seat at the table.

"Please. I'll have tea and toast this morning."

Lucy nodded, stood, and placed the book on the couch. She left the room and found Roger in the hallway.

"Morning."

"Morning. I'll go order her breakfast. You sleep ok?"

"Yeah." He nodded. "I'm happy to be able to sleep a full night all at once."

"I'll be happier when I can get Lance moved up here."

"We should be arriving at Station Six in a few hours."

She frowned. She didn't remember there being a station with numbers for a name. "Station Six? Is that new?"

Roger shrugged. "I have no idea. There are a few stations that run north and south from it, all with numbered names."

"Anyone know why?"

He shook his head.

Lucy nodded. "All right then. I'll move Lance later today. You watch her. I'll get breakfast. Can I get us something too?"

"Yes, just don't have them put it on her cart."

Lucy almost laughed but thought better of it and nodded. "All right. I'll be back."

"Yep." Roger moved to the door as Lucy walked away.

⁎⁎⁎

In the dining car, she gave them Ms. Bauer's order, then looked at the menu. "What do you have that's quick that I can eat while I wait for the cart?"

The young woman behind the counter in the gold and black uniform scrunched her face into a thoughtful frown. "The daily surprise is cold, but ready now."

"I'll take one if it's large, two if it's small."

The girl looked surprised. "Oh, sure. It's about the size of two sandwiches."

Lucy smiled. "One then, but I'm also getting breakfast for someone else. Can I try it out before I pay for it? I don't want to pay twice."

"Um . . . as long as you pay."

"I always pay for my food."

The girl gave her an odd look, then glanced behind her. Lucy looked over her shoulder and realized no one else was in the car. When they were looking at each other again, the girl nodded. "Sure."

She turned, grabbed a pastry partially wrapped in butcher paper off the back counter, and handed it to Lucy. There were grease stains on the paper, and it looked as if the grease had started to congeal. It looked overstuffed and the pastry was flaky.

Lucy folded the butcher paper back a little and took a large bite. The pastry made a satisfying crunch. The flavor of the lukewarm contents made her sigh. The texture was that of partially melted cheese, scrambled eggs, and meat. The flavor was not familiar.

"Meat, eggs, cheese. Why call it the Daily Surprise?"

From behind the young girl, a loud, robust voice called, "Because we're not going to tell you what animal the eggs are from or what type of meat it is!"

Lucy looked to the larger man in the kitchen part of the car. "And the cheese?"

"Whatever we have laying around!" Came the booming voice.

Lucy laughed a little. "Well, this is good. I'll take another to go, and two coffees if you have them."

"You don't want any of that on the cart, right?" the girl asked when she rang the items up on the cash register.

"How did you guess?"

"The woman in car one doesn't like anything on her cart except her things."

"How long did it take to remember that?"

The young girl smiled at Lucy but didn't really answer.

Lucy chuckled a little. "All right, keep your secrets."

"I will get her cart and the rest of your order out at the same time. Doesn't take much and we're not busy."

Lucy looked around again. She was still the only one in the car. "I wondered about that."

"To keep congestion down, we have a couple people that take a cart of food to the passengers. The Rail decided to do that in case of Bandits."

"Keeps people out of the way." Lucy offered.

"Yep."

She nodded. "How much do I owe you?"

The woman rattled off the total for her items, which Lucy hurriedly paid. She then found a seat at a booth and continued to eat her pastry. She wanted to finish it before it turned completely cold. Even after a few bites, she couldn't identify the meat, cheese, or eggs, but everything tasted good, so she didn't think about it. She was down to her last few bites when a porter called out.

"Food cart for car one ready."

The uniformed man stood in the doorway of the dining car. In front of him was a cart, and in one hand was a tray. When she stood, he nodded to her and indicated the tray.

"Did you want to carry all this?"

"Isn't that what she wants?"

"We can have someone carry it to the car for you."

Her eyes went wide. "Oh, no that's unnecessary." She took the tray, placed it on the counter and looked at the porter.

"You can start ahead. I'll catch up before you reach the furthest door in the next car."

He nodded and Lucy looked at the tray. As there was still no one else in the dining car, she stayed where she was and looked at the items again. There were two 16 ounce plastic cups of coffee, with lids secure. Like most places, the train used whatever plastic ware they could find from Before. Even after eighty years, it was still around, waiting for the Scavengers to find it. She read once that plastic took a very long time to break down. Since it took too much heat to make more plastic, Lucy figured it was good that it was still around. The world had lost too many things from Before.

She pulled her head back to the task at hand and looked at the cups. On one lid, in black wax pencil, was written "2 S," for two sugars. That was Roger's coffee. She popped the top off the other one, took a sip and smiled. Coffee, black, and it was smooth, just how she liked it.

Lucy grabbed the pastry and Roger's coffee in one hand, her coffee in the other and headed to the door to follow the porter. At the door, she balanced her coffee on top of Roger's and headed out. She hurried into the next car and did, in fact, catch up to the porter before he came upon the furthest door of the next car. They walked together to car one, with Lucy in front. At Ms. Bauer's door, she knocked and waited for Roger to open up.

Lucy moved out of the way and Roger took the cart. The porter left, and Lucy waited for Roger before they both went to their room. He opened the door and waited as she set everything down.

"She wants to know if you're awake enough to talk to her."

Lucy looked at Roger sharply. "Did I do something wrong?"

"No, she wants to talk."

The frown showed her worry. "About what?"

"She didn't tell me."

The frown deepened. "Has she ever 'just talked' to you?"

Roger opened his mouth to speak, then shook his head. "No."

"Should I be worried?"

"I really don't think so, Lucy. She didn't seem mad."

"Ok. Now?"

"Yep."

"Ok." She pointed to his coffee. "That's yours. I'm taking mine. In the bag is the Daily Surprise. Cold, but good. Eggs, meat, cheese."

"I've been avoiding that."

She snickered. "That's because you don't like surprises. I already had one. It's good. Try it out. I'll get you something else if you don't like it."

He eyed it suspiciously. "Fine."

"I'm going to talk to her."

"I'll be here when you're done."

Lucy nodded and left the room with her coffee. She knocked on the other door and waited for Ms. Bauer to say, "Come in."

SEVEN

Lucy stepped inside the car, nodded to Ms. Bauer, then shut the door. She sipped her coffee as she moved forward. "You wanted to see me?"

"I did." Ms. Bauer sat at her breakfast table, her hands moving the silverware around. She wouldn't make eye contact.

"Did I do something wrong?"

Ms. Bauer frowned and finally looked up at Lucy. "No. I . . . no, you didn't. Would you like to sit down?"

Lucy eyed the chair, then slid her gaze back to her employer. The look on the woman's face was odd. It wasn't unreadable, more like she was trying to figure out how to look. Lucy gave up. "Fine."

She sat opposite Ms. Bauer and placed her plastic coffee cup on the small table. She noticed that the rest of the place settings were porcelain but didn't match. The saucer was green, the cup was white with flowers, and the plate was white with gold trim. Some of the gold had flecked off. The utensils were also mismatched, but they looked like metal.

"Nice settings."

"I asked for the best."

Lucy looked the woman in the eyes. Her tone wasn't snobbish but matter of fact, as if fine things were the usual. When she didn't say anything more, Lucy spoke. "Look, I don't know if this is a test or if you're angry with me and nonconfrontational, or what, but I can't do this. Either talk to me or let me leave. I have to get some shut-eye."

Ms. Bauer looked at her in shock. When she didn't say anything, just sat with her mouth hanging open, Lucy shook her head. "Can I leave then?"

"I . . . I don't know how to start this conversation."

"That's a start." She crossed her arms as she waited for more.

Ms. Bauer looked down at her utensils and rearranged them around her plate nervously. "I'm . . . I was raised by my uncle in Boston Under. My parents died when I was rather young, and I was brought here on a sailboat."

"Ok."

She sighed heavily as she looked at Lucy. "When he found out I . . ." She looked down and started picking at something on her pants. "When he found out I didn't want to marry a man, that I wanted to be with women, my uncle shut me in our house and swore I would marry a man."

"Oh." Lucy uncrossed her arms. "That's not a fun time."

Ms. Bauer gave a bitter laugh. "No, it's not." She sighed again. "He died four months ago, and I've been trying to find out how to meet other women. I go to clubs and libraries and other gatherings, but I don't know how to talk to anyone. I only saw him and my cousin growing up. I wasn't even allowed to talk to the help."

Lucy raised her eyebrow at the word but didn't say anything.

"I wasn't even really allowed to talk to Roger until after my uncle died."

Lucy frowned. "That's not what this is about though, is it?"

Ms. Bauer shook her head. "I still don't know how to talk to him. Or the others who work for me. He seems like a nice person, they all do, but I don't know how to talk to people."

"Not calling them 'the help' or thinking of them like that is a good start." She tried to control her voice, to speak in a friendly manner, but the shocked look on Ms. Bauer's face revealed Lucy's harsh tone. They stared at each other for a moment until Lucy forced a deep breath in and out, and asked somewhat pleasantly, "And I'm here now because?"

The shocked look melted into one of battered hope. "I thought perhaps you could help me learn?"

Lucy gave a laugh. "I'm not the best person to ask for help on how to socialize, ma'am. As you witnessed, I tell people how I feel. And I talk to my horse more than I talk to people."

"Do you know how to play cards?"

Lucy stopped herself from sighing heavily. She did not want to be trapped trying to help anyone learn how to socialize. She liked her solitude. "Like I said yesterday, I don't like to gamble."

In what felt to Lucy as a rather empathetic moment, Ms. Bauer nodded as a look of understanding crossed her face. "I understand it may not be fun for you to help me. All I ask is that you come to the dining car with me one night and play a round or two of cards with other women there."

Lucy groaned inwardly but found herself nodding. "Fine."

Happiness exploded onto Ms. Bauer's face as she clasped her hands together. "Thank you!"

"You're welcome."

"Would tonight be alright?"

"We should be hitting a station in a couple hours. Not sure what'll be available there. Also, I want to move Lance, and you'll want to get up top. It's a good idea to move around some while you can. We have this stop, then Bend before we hit the long stretch with no stations. How about we see how things go tonight, but plan on the night after we leave this station?"

A soft look of confusion crossed Ms. Bauer's face.

"This is one of those 'change at a moment's notice' things I told you about when we met."

"All right. Will you go up top too?"

Lucy nodded. "Once Lance is situated, sure, but Roger will take you up and I'll join you after."

"All right. Well, thank you." She looked Lucy up and down. "I imagine you would like to rest now?"

"Yes."

"Can you send Roger in?"

"Sure." Lucy got up and made as quick an exit as she could without running. She went to the room she shared with Roger and sat heavily on her bed before acknowledging him.

"What's up?"

"She wants me to play cards with her to help her talk to other people."

He opened his mouth as if to say something, paused, then continued. "I guess that makes sense. When Heir Bauer was alive, I hardly ever saw her."

"You said she was sheltered. I didn't realize how badly."

"Yeah, he was an odd man. Didn't treat either her or his own son well."

A look came across Lucy's face, and Roger held up his hands.

"I know, not your business." Roger sighed and dropped his hands. "You going to play cards with her and help her out?"

"I'll try."

"You look thrilled."

"I am not opposed to helping people learn things, but this seems daunting. I don't even know how she wants me to act."

"Just be yourself. It's more, well, natural and might put her at ease."

Lucy made a noncommittal noise in the back of her throat, then changed the subject. "I was told to send you in."

"Figured. I'll wake you when we hit the station, if you're not up."

"Fine. Thank you."

"Yep." With that, Roger left the room.

As Lucy settled onto the cot to sleep, she realized with annoyance that her coffee was still sitting on the table in the other room, and she had no desire to go get it.

ნႽნႽნႽ

A soft knock woke her later. Lucy sat up and looked toward the door. "Yeah."

The door opened and revealed Roger. "We've stopped."

"You two heading up?"

"I convinced her dinner in town is a good idea."

Lucy nodded. "I'm moving Lance and then I'll see you."

"Sure. By the way, you left your coffee in the other room. I brought it in for you this morning, but you were already asleep."

She followed his pointing finger and saw it on the nightstand. Her eyes opened wide, and her mouth made a small *o* of happy surprise. "Oooo!

Thank you!"

Roger left as Lucy went for her coffee. She grabbed the cup, removed the lid, and chugged the cold coffee. When it was done, she let out a satisfied "ah" and smacked her lips. She then got up and readied herself for the night.

‟‟‟

Lance was not happy with the move.

"Come on, you silly horse. It's no worse than getting you down here." She spoke in a soft voice, to try and entice him off the ramp and to the left of the train. Since the door to the stable in car one was to the left, it was easier to get off the train and onto the space between the two tracks. The dirt floor between tracks was large enough to accommodate a horse.

"Come on, Lance."

When he gave a protesting neigh, she sighed and closed the gap between them. She rubbed his nose and pulled some carrot bits out of her pocket. She let him take them, then reached into her other pocket and brought out horse blinders. She slipped the blinders on him gently as he ate, then took his reins and pulled carefully. This time, he didn't complain and allowed her to lead him down the ramp and off the train. She breathed a sigh of relief and started to walk next to the train.

As she walked, she looked around. There was a lot of light down here. The concrete walls were being painted white, to reflect the light better. As she walked, she listened to the people in the scaffolding call out to each other. It reminded her of her childhood, of sneaking out of the orphanage and to the Above. Their voices even sounded like the people back then. The camaraderie was obvious in their jovial voices.

"Hey! It's almost quitting time! Let's hustle and get a little more done."

"Oh, come on! We've been doing this long enough. It was quitting time ten minutes ago!"

"All right, all right!" the first voice called from a little farther down the tunnel. "Put the lids on the containers and pack everything up. Remember to take your brushes and wash them out. Keep your equipment clean! Replacements are hard to get!"

She heard the people moving their equipment and smiled again as Lance neighed. She looked to the end of the train and realized she was halfway there. Even with the doors and connecting cars, it was easier and quicker to walk in the train. Of course, she wasn't leading Lance while walking through the train.

As she continued along, the clattering of people descending ladders echoed in the tunnel. She chuckled as the voice of the man who seemed to be the boss called loudly to another person.

"Terry! I swear to Aimer! If you don't clean up your equipment, you're going to lose your job. Enough is enough! I've had to remind you for too long."

There was a little bit of grumbling, but Lucy saw a worker climb back up a ladder. As she approached the person's location, she watched as they closed paint can lids and grabbed a paint roller and brushes. As the person descended the ladder again, she drew up to them. When they were on the ground, they turned and looked right at Lucy, surprise in their eyes.

"Oh, hello. Not often we see a horse down here."

"No quicker way to get to the coast." She stopped abreast of the worker.

The clothing the worker wore made it hard to see too much about them. Their overcoat was thick and made of dark material. It had a high collar, and Terry had turned the collar up.

Terry shook their head. "I mean, it's not often I see one," they gestured to the tunnel in general, "here."

Lucy smiled. "Moving from one car to the other."

Before the worker could say anything else, a voice rang out. "Get a move on, Terry! You're holding up the elevator!"

Terry waved to Lucy as they turned and started away. "Coming."

Lucy smiled and resumed walking. People didn't change much, not really. When she was younger and would escape to the surface, the workers acted the same way. They were nice if they engaged with her, but more often than not, they were too busy with their own lives to pay attention to her. It made her escapades to the surface easier at least. She heard an elevator door close and turned her attention to her goal. She glanced back at Lance, then moved them a little faster down the tunnel. She wanted him in the stall so she could go to the surface. She always preferred open air to canned.

EIGHT

Lucy walked to the saloon slowly and enjoyed the night air. The town around her was as boisterous as Meridune. The people were out and about despite the late hour, and shops were open. When the train stopped, most towns opened their stores in case anyone wanted to make a purchase. Lucy knew it helped Meridune; she assumed it would help all towns.

A slight smile on her face, Lucy entered the saloon and looked around. Though there were patrons, most of the Escorts were at tables, trying to catch people's eyes. When the Madam caught Lucy's eye, she nodded to him but headed to the bar. The bartender was a young man of around sixteen. He nodded and greeted her.

"Howdy! Welcome to Austin. What can I get you?"

"Any town specials?"

"We have a drink and dinner special . . ."

"I'll take both."

There was a rather surprised look on his face. "You don't want to know what they are?"

"Nope. If I don't know what they are, I'll try it out. If I like it, I'll finish it. If I don't, I'll order something else. Either way, I'll pay for it."

The boy nodded but still looked surprised. "All right. One daily special coming right up!"

Lucy nodded, turned, and placed her back to the bar as she surveyed the room again. The Madam made eye contact and came over to lean against the bar as well.

"You come in on the train?" His deep voice was friendly.

"I did. I'm Lucy."

"Bernard. Can I get you anyone?"

"Not sure. You all don't look busy."

"Seems most folks don't want a companion tonight." His voice was open and friendly and invited more conversation.

Lucy looked at Bernard, then around the room again, and back to Bernard. "My employer asked me to help her with something, and I thought I was going to wait a couple days, but since you have people available . . ."

He glared at her. "I don't like cryptic."

"Fair. If I want to hire someone to play cards with me and my employer, would that be doable? Preferably a woman, preferably bi. Flirting is up to the Escort, as is anything else that happens that isn't cards, but I'll be the one paying."

He gave her a funny look. "You serious?"

She rolled her eyes. "Yeah."

He seemed to think for a moment, then shrugged. "Sure. You want Beatrice to dress in any particular way?"

"Nope."

He nodded. "I'll talk to her. If she agrees, she'll come over."

"Thank you."

Bernard nodded and walked away as she heard a heavy glass being placed on the bar behind her. Lucy turned and regarded the drink and the bartender. The drink was served in a thick glass, had the consistency of orange juice but was reddish brown. It wasn't the most appetizing drink she had ever seen. She picked it up and sniffed it. It smelled fruity but she wasn't sure what fruit it was. A sip revealed a sweet but strong taste that didn't trigger any memories. It had the texture of orange juice though.

Lucy caught the bartender's eye. "Ok, I have no idea what this is. It's tasty, but I've never tried anything like it."

"Scavengers found a box of liquor in a town up north. It had some of this in it. The bottle said Cassis and had a picture of berries on it, but none of us are familiar with it. The label is in a foreign language. We think it's French or Spanish, but we're not sure. None of us can read it. We mixed it with some fresh-squeezed orange juice."

"It's good. I like it."

"Good. Food will be here in a minute."

Lucy took another sip and nodded as he walked away. She liked the taste. She turned again and looked at the crowd. There wasn't much of one. Some people gambled, others talked, but it was quiet. She turned around again as she heard a plate being set down behind her. The smell of oranges wafted up from the full plate.

There were noodles to one side, a green vegetable that looked like cactus, and a quarter of a bird. The meat didn't have the same color as chicken, and the skin looked fattier. There was a sauce on the bird. The bartender set a knife, fork, and napkin next to the plate.

"Oranges again?"

"Train heading east had some. We're trying to use what we bought before they all go bad. Most of it's being made into marmalade or sauce."

Lucy nodded, grabbed the knife and fork, stabbed a piece of meat, and cut herself a little bite. She popped it into her mouth and let the flavors mingle as she chewed. The bartender, a curious look on his face, stayed close by, as if waiting to hear what she thought. Lucy took two more bites before nodding to him.

"I have no idea what this is, other than a bird. I see a wing here."

"Do you like it?"

"It's different. I'm not sure if I like it or not yet."

The boy grinned. "It's duck with orange sauce."

"Duck?" She was astonished to hear that.

"Yep."

"The water bird? Quack, quack, quack?"

His grin grew wider. "Yep!"

"In a desert? They need water." Her confusion only grew as did his grin.

"Yeah. We have a lake."

Her face scrunched up in confusion. "In a desert?"

This time he laughed. "Yeah, we have a lake that's practically underground." He nodded to Lucy's right. "Have Beatrice show you. Won't take too long."

Lucy looked at the woman on her right. She was as tall as Lucy with dark eyes and dark, straight hair that fell past her waist. She wore blue eye shadow that matched her crop top. Her jean shorts were snug and barely hid her behind.

Lucy smiled. "Hello."

"Hi. What am I showing her, Ben?"

"The grotto."

Her eyes lit up. "Absolutely!"

Lucy looked at each of them in turn, then shrugged. "Let me finish my meal first."

"Sure. And you can tell me if Bernard was pulling my leg. You want to pay for my time to play cards?"

Lucy took a bite of food as she nodded. She continued to nod as she chewed then swallowed her food. "My employer wants to play cards and learn how to talk to other people. She's been pretty sheltered. I talk to my horse more than other people, so I figured if I had an Escort help me, we might both be able to instruct her. Escorts are usually friendlier than I tend to be."

Beatrice looked relieved. "That's no worse than what I've been asked to do in the past. I'm ok with it. Do you want me to flirt with her?"

"Only if you want to. If you end up sleeping with her, I'll pay."

"Do you want to keep my job a secret?"

"No."

That seemed to surprise her a little. "Ok. Well, I'm game."

"Thank you. I'm going to finish my meal, then we can find a place to play. I'd prefer someplace out of the way."

"That's fine. We have a back room. I'll ask Bernard if we can use it. Finish up your food and I'll take you to the grotto first."

"All right." Lucy dug into her food as Beatrice walked away.

⛧⛧⛧

"This . . ." But words failed her. They were by a lake that was protected from the elements. It wasn't underground, but it was surrounded by rock walls. There was a ceiling as well, high up, but light still streamed through from somewhere. "There's so much light."

"There's a full moon tonight and this place is limestone. If I remember correctly, that reflects light."

"Where are the ducks?" Though there was a shore and some bushes around the edge of the lake on a small ledge, she couldn't see any animals.

"We have a few farms for them. They bring them here during the day but then take them in at night. Coyotes and other critters like to try and eat them."

Lucy looked around again and sighed. It really was beautiful. The lake was clear and almost still. She could hear some trickling water somewhere, and there were tiny waves lapping at the edge of the lake. She wanted to stay here longer, but there was work to be done. She turned back to Beatrice. "I would love to stay longer, but . . ."

Beatrice smiled. "But we have cards to play." She turned and headed out of the grotto. "You can come in the morning and see the ducks."

"I think the train leaves too early for that."

"Yeah, you're probably right." After a few steps they were out of the grotto and headed back to town. It wasn't a long walk, and Beatrice liked to talk. "Do you like her?"

"Who? My employer? I'm still figuring that out."

"Why are you helping her then?"

"To figure her out."

They caught each other's eyes and laughed. They walked for a little in silence, which Lucy thought was odd for the woman. Beatrice had talked all the way to the grotto, but Lucy let her have her silence. Just before they reached town, Beatrice stopped and turned to Lucy.

"So, what if I want to flirt with you?"

Lucy took a deep breath and let it out slowly. She spoke softly. "Though I appreciate the offer, I have to decline. I don't sleep with anyone while I'm on the job."

Beatrice frowned. "Why not?"

"Distractions cause problems."

The young woman nodded. "That makes sense."

A smile lit up Lucy's eyes. "Next time I find myself here though, if you're still interested . . ."

Beatrice returned the smile. "That sounds like a plan!"

Lucy gave a larger smile as she licked her lips. "Let's get back before things get out of hand."

"Ok." Beatrice's voice held joy, and it made Lucy feel warm and happy. She turned and headed back into town before her desires took over.

☙❧☙❧☙❧

"That was an interesting idea." Roger stated as soon as she walked into the bedroom.

"What?"

"Getting an Escort to play cards with us? Weren't you going to wait a couple days or something?"

Lucy shrugged then stopped her words as she felt the train lurch into movement. "I thought we had a few more hours before the train left?"

"They were able to unload fast and don't feel like waiting longer, since they were late to begin with."

"Makes sense. Did everyone get on board?"

He leaned back on his cot and gave her a long look. "You really care?"

"Interesting information to know."

He laughed and shook his head. "You just want to make fun of people."

"Maybe a little, but not much."

Roger shook his head again. "You're also avoiding the subject at hand."

"Look, she wanted to talk to women, and now she has a better idea on that. It's not that hard. Also, the Escorts weren't busy and they know how to engage others and make them comfortable."

"Weren't you complaining about talking to people yesterday?"

She gave him a pointed look as she sat down on her cot. "Don't you need to go watch her?"

He laughed but got off the bed. "Yeah, yeah. I'll see you tonight."

"Yep."

Lucy watched as he left the room, then stripped down to her underwear, climbed under the covers, and breathed a sigh of relief. Playing cards with Beatrice had gone well, but mostly because the woman kept flirting with Roger and Ms. Bauer. It kept the conversation light. At the end of the night, Ms. Bauer was laughing along with Lucy at Beatrice's antics. A smile came to Lucy's face. She felt Roger was wrong about Ms. Bauer and hoped to show him that as the train continued west.

NINE

The next station they came to was Bend, so called as it was the last station before the tracks turned north and headed under the mountains on its way to Sacramento. They would be stopped here up to three days to unload the goods, fuel up, and ensure the track was clear. There were a lot of towns Above and Under, therefore half of the remaining cargo cars were being moved. It was a daunting task. When the train stopped, Ms. Bauer was eager to go up top and almost didn't wait for Roger. He let her go ahead of him and turned to Lucy.

"You really going to let Lance out now?"

"Though the stall is large, he hasn't had much chance to walk around. I want to make sure he's ok."

Roger shook his head as Ms. Bauer looked on semi-patiently from the train platform. "All right. We'll be at the hotel."

"Yep."

Once Roger left to escort Ms. Bauer, Lucy turned and climbed back into Ms. Bauer's car. She went to Lance's stall and opened it up fully. The car had a sliding door in back, and a ramp, that allowed her to move Lance quickly. Once on the ground, she walked him a little bit and tried to stay calm. For some reason, she was on edge and kept looking around as if to find something in the shadows. She had been fine until they reached the station. She thought maybe she was worried about Lance, but now that she was walking him, the uncomfortable shiver up her spine grew instead of quieting.

Lucy looked hard at Lance for a few more minutes and ran her hands along his body to make sure he wasn't hiding an injury. When she realized he was fine, she put him away. Lucy left out the front of the car, but instead of going right to the platform, she turned left and headed back to the tracks. She went and placed her back against the wall, under a scaffolding. Eyes closed, she breathed deep and tried again to calm the uneasiness eating away at her mind. Her eyes popped open as she realized how quiet it was down here.

When they'd arrived at Station Six, it was probably eight o'clock. The workers were still on their scaffolds, yelling at their boss to end the day. It was six o'clock here. There were no workers on the scaffolding. She moved from under the scaffold and looked up at the paints. She couldn't see them from here, so she found a ladder and climbed it until she could see the workers' paints and brushes. There were open canisters sitting on the scaffolding, brushes left haphazardly on the boards.

Bandits! Her mind screamed.

Lucy nearly ran down the ladder, but thought better of it and slowed her movements. If anyone was watching, she didn't want to appear concerned. She lowered herself down the ladder, then went back to Ms. Bauer's train car. She went to the bedroom she shared with Roger and sat on her cot. The drape on the window was closed already, for privacy. Lucy breathed deep and closed her eyes to better concentrate on the sounds around her.

Even this far from the cargo cars, she had been able to hear the workers when they removed one at the last stop. She couldn't hear those noises now. That was a good sign. It might be that there weren't any Bandits down here yet, but she wasn't sure. She needed more information, so she stood and walked calmly out of the car and to the platform. Lucy looked around carefully, as if seeing the station for the first time.

When she didn't see anything out of place, she went to the elevator and took it up, noting that the operator was not the same person as had taken her up at Station Six. It should have been. She had talked to enough elevator operators in her time. Elevator operators stayed with the train. They did odd jobs as the train traveled and tended to the elevators when at the stations. Some years ago, one told her the Rail found it cheaper to do it this way.

As the elevator went up, Lucy looked at the man's back. His hair was ruffled and dirty. Most operators had their hair combed neat and tidy. The Rail wanted to set an image. The man's clothes were nice but faded and looked like they were a little big. She guessed the clothes were stolen from the actual operator on this train. He had been a tall man with wide shoulders. This one was of average build, so closer to her size. Lucy didn't see a gun, but she bet he had one under his jacket, at the back. The coat was bunched up over something just above his belt. She nodded to herself and looked away from the man's back just as the door to the elevator opened.

"Thank you!" she said as she exited. "Have a great day!"

"You, too!" came the voice from the elevator.

Well, at least he was polite, she thought as she headed up the ramp and to the door. Outside, she plastered a smile on her face and looked around as she moseyed along. Like in Meridune, the station opened near the back of the hotel. Not seeing anyone, she wandered around to the main street, climbed onto the boardwalk, and looked in the shop windows. That allowed her to look inside and use the windows as mirrors. She walked along and tried to find the things that were out of place. She didn't immediately see anyone suspicious, but that was to be expected. Bandits were usually smarter than that. It just meant she had to look harder.

At the end of the boardwalk, which was the end of the main road, she turned to go back. A commotion in the street drew her attention and she stopped. In the middle of the street were an older man with dirty clothing and a girl who looked to be fifteen or sixteen. Their sides were to Lucy, which meant she could look at their expressions somewhat. Though there were a few people in the stores, no one came out to find out what was going on. Lucy watched and stopped herself from running to the girl's aid. She needed more information before she could help.

"Shut your mouth!" The man was taller than the girl and loomed over her as she held her cheek. "I'm sick of all these questions! Get out of my sight!"

His voice drew no other watchers. Lucy moved slightly and leaned against a pole holding up an awning on the boardwalk. It wasn't large enough to hide her, but leaning against it made her look more relaxed. The man and girl on the street hadn't noticed her yet. The girl said something, and he slapped her cheek again. He didn't seem to hit her that hard, but she fell. Lucy cocked her head as she realized the girl had made herself fall. Lucy licked her lips to stop herself from saying anything out loud. The man kicked the girl in parting and headed away, down a side street. When the girl didn't move right away, Lucy ambled down the stairs, into the street and to her side.

She held out her hand and looked the girl in the eye. On a hunch, she offered her services but spoke softly. "I'm for hire, if it's needed."

The girl locked eyes with her, took her hand, and spoke just as quietly. "Not here."

Lucy raised an eyebrow as she helped the girl to her feet. She whispered, "Where?"

"Saloon. Ask for Jasper," the girl whispered and ran away.

Lucy made a big show of rolling her eyes. She spoke in her normal voice. "Ungrateful brat."

With that, she turned, headed onto the boardwalk, and moved in the direction of the saloon. No one was on the street, and she didn't feel eyes on her, but she still looked into the shops to see if she could detect anyone watching her. When she did not, she picked up her pace and went to the saloon. Once there, she looked for the Madam but couldn't immediately tell who it was.

Irene constantly watched the door to see if anyone coming into the saloon was a known client, a new client, or known trouble. When someone came in, she immediately nodded to them and walked up to them to start the conversation, if she could. If she could not, she would nod very deliberately to acknowledge the person and ask for a moment. Bernard had done the same thing at the last stop. No one was doing that here.

There were people gambling though, and there were people at the bar and tables eating dinner. There were a couple people who were obviously Escorts, and they didn't look that happy to have the men touching them. And then Lucy realized, all the clients in here were men in outfits that looked just a bit too dirty. She quickly went to the bar and nodded at the bartender as he came over. She was actually impressed that he had seen her as quickly as he had. There were a lot of people lined up at the bar. The man looked exhausted.

"Help you?"

"I'm looking for Jasper?"

"He just went upstairs. You can have him next. Is this your first time in Bend?"

"No, but it's been a long while."

"This your first time with an Escort?"

"No."

He nodded. "I do things a little different here. You go upstairs, do what you want, and when you're done, Jasper will tell me what you owe me."

"That's fine. I'll wait. If you have a menu, I'd like to order some food."

"I'll bring that right to you." He looked beyond her shoulder. "Looks like he's already done, actually."

Lucy turned to see a young man, probably in his early twenties, coming down the stairs with a woman who looked angry. The woman was yelling at Jasper.

"This isn't fair!"

"I'm sorry. I know how to get a woman off! I told you it was going to be quick." As she reached the end of the stairs, he yelled after her as she headed toward the exit. "You still have to pay!"

"I won't pay until you learn how to take your time!" With that, she stormed out of the saloon.

Most saloons have a rule: if you don't pay, you don't get to play. Lucy knew that woman would not be allowed to use any of the Escorts here again. She turned to the bartender. "She was feisty."

"She's a handful." He turned his head to look at Jasper. "Jasper! You have another one!"

"Gerald! Mirabell didn't pay!"

"I saw. Don't worry about it. Take this one instead."

Lucy nodded, then turned and waved to Jasper. He nodded and turned back to go upstairs. She followed, and in moments they were in a room with one window, a bed, a dresser, a wash basin, and a stack of washcloths next to the basin. The room had two doors: the main one they came in through and one Lucy thought might be a closet.

The tall, lanky gentleman leaned against the door and regarded Lucy. "So what can I do for you, or to you?"

Lucy smiled and wished she had the time. He was handsome. "A man on the street hit a woman twice. When I offered my services, she told me to come here and ask for you."

A doorknob rattled, and when Lucy saw it wasn't the one on the main door, she turned toward the closet and pulled her gun. When the young woman came through the door, she put her hands up. Lucy quickly looked at Jasper, then at the young woman. They had the same shaped head and facial features, which made it obvious they were related. As she put her gun away, she heard Jasper's annoyed voice.

"Shit. Rose, what the hell?"

She glared at him but looked back at Lucy. "I want to hire you. There are Bandits in town. They're here to rob the train."

"Shut up!" Jasper whispered harshly.

Lucy moved and was instantly in his face. She placed her hand on his chest and pushed him back against the wall. "I already knew this before coming up to the surface. You will shut your mouth and let us talk."

She stepped back and gave him some space. Rose came into the room and closed the door behind her. Jasper looked at the women with a sorrowful look on his face. "I don't want to die."

"If you do this right, you won't." Lucy caught his eye and watched as he moved to the bed and sat down. She then looked at Rose. "What do you know?"

"It's a big group. Twenty or so."

"Most of them seem to be downstairs, then."

She nodded. "They're insisting on using the Escorts for their pleasure."

"The man who hit you, is that the leader?"

Rose shrugged. "He's either the leader or the second in command. I'm not sure, but he's not downstairs. There are five or so hiding out somewhere in town, waiting."

"Do you know anything about the five men?" Lucy crossed her arms.

"They seem to be the top people. They boss everyone else around."

Lucy nodded. "What was he yelling at you for?"

She seemed to shrink into herself. "He says I'm old enough to be an Escort and kept saying he was going to take me away to his camp. I became as annoying as possible and kept asking him questions about the camp, about the heist and about him and his men. You know," she grinned, "like the most annoying kid on the planet."

"Well done. It looked like you fell on purpose?"

"I've been practicing. I've heard it's a good idea to know how to take a fall."

Lucy narrowed her eyes. "Why?"

Jasper groaned. "Don't you dare say it."

Both looked his way, Lucy with contempt in her eyes, Rose with annoyance. Lucy looked back at Rose and raised an eyebrow.

Rose stood tall, "I want to be a Hired Hand."

Jasper groaned and both ignored him.

"How old are you?"

"Fifteen. I'll be sixteen in three months." Rose said with confidence.

"We'll visit that conversation another time." Lucy turned the conversation back to the Bandits. "When are they robbing the train?"

"Tonight, while everyone's asleep."

"And you have absolutely no idea where the boss is?"

"Frank won't tell me. Neither would his men."

Lucy nodded. "Do you know what time exactly?"

"I think they said midnight or later."

Lucy nodded again. "How many people in town want to stop this?"

"They have all our families." Jasper's voice sounded strained.

Lucy looked sharply at Jasper. "Come again?"

"That's why we haven't overtaken them, even though there are more of us then there are of them. They took our families. Or everyone else's family. Rose is the only family I have left."

Lucy nodded. Taking hostages was a common strategy for Bandits across the Broken States. "All right, is there anyone in town willing to help despite the situation?"

"I am. So are a few others." Rose said with confidence.

"I need numbers, girl." Her voice was hard.

"Sorry. Six, seven if we can find more guns."

"Don't count on us finding guns unless you know where they are. Do you have a gun?"

Rose shook her head. "Frank took it."

Lucy nodded. "Do you know more of their plans?"

"They took over the station early this morning. They put all the workers in the freight elevator, sent it to the Under, and broke it. It'll need to be fixed from up here. They waited for the train and, when it arrived, kidnapped the conductor on duty, his assistant, and the elevator operator.

I don't know if they kidnapped all the conductors or just the ones on duty. And I don't know if they're still alive. I think they were able to use the passenger elevator and get back up here before anyone else from the train saw them."

"How do you know so much?"

"I was with them for part of the time. Told Frank I wanted to be with the Bandits. That's when he said I would be a better Escort than Bandit."

Lucy made a noise and raised her eyebrow in exasperation. She hated most Bandits, and these weren't turning out to be any better.

"Do you have a plan?" Rose's voice was full of hope.

"I may. I need my partner here to plan, though."

"I can go get them."

"You sure?"

Rose nodded. "Frank doesn't want me around. I got him angry enough."

"All right. His name is Roger. He's in the hotel with our employer." She turned to Jasper. "Where is it safer, here or at the hotel?"

He looked at Lucy then at Rose. "Why not ask her?"

"You don't seem to take chances. People who don't take chances know where the safe places are, usually."

Jasper seemed to think about it for a moment, then nodded. "Here is safer. The door that Rose came through is a closet with a secret staircase behind it. That leads to a basement no one ever uses and probably forgot about."

"How do you know about it?" Lucy was intrigued, and it showed in her voice.

"Our mom was an Escort. We grew up in this building. We used to go exploring when we were younger. No one ever mentions the basement.

When we were rearranging some furniture once, I asked Gerald if there was an extra room someplace, like an attic or basement, and he said no. No one seems to know about it."

Lucy nodded and turned back to Rose. "All right. Go get Roger and Ms. Bauer. They're at the hotel waiting for me. Roger is about as tall as I am and is a little older than your brother. He's in a black shirt, jeans, and cowboy hat. If his hat is off, his hair is cut short in a fade. He's got dark hair and eyes, and almost the same complexion as me. She's in a blue suit that hugs her body well and looks like she has money. Talk to Roger. Tell him, 'Lucy said Charleston was for fun, this one's for real.' Once he remembers what that means, bring him and her here."

Rose nodded, thought about it for a moment, nodded again, and left the room via the closet door. Lucy turned to Jasper.

"How much to keep you here for the evening?"

His mouth dropped open in wonder.

TEN

Lucy and Jasper were sitting on the bed, playing cards, when the closet door opened again. Jasper assured her over and over that no one knew about the secret entrance but him and Rose. He even took her down the stairs so she could see it herself. There were old moldering boxes and a lot of dust and not much else. Satisfied, they went back up to the room. Therefore, when Rose came through the door with Roger and Ms. Bauer, Lucy didn't have her gun out.

As soon as Roger was through the door, he gave Lucy a look. "Bandits."

"About twenty to twenty-five." She stood from the bed. "Rose gave me all the information she had. They want the stuff from the train. We're going to put Ms. Bauer and Jasper in the basement with Rose while you find out where all the conductors are, and I find the people we need to talk to."

"I want to help!" Rose said a little loudly.

Lucy put her finger to her mouth to shush the girl. When she quieted, Lucy looked her dead in the eye. "Have you ever killed a man?"

Rose opened her mouth to speak, thought better of it, and shook her head.

Lucy walked to her and placed her hand under the girl's chin. She was about a head shorter. Lucy looked Rose in the eye and spoke carefully. "This isn't the time to be brave. This is the time to do what you're able. If you've never killed a person, that's ok. You stay behind and keep Jasper and Ms. Bauer safe. That's your job. Do you understand me?"

Rose nodded.

"Good." She moved away and saw that Ms. Bauer had a confused look on her face. "Yes?"

"I still don't understand what's going on."

"Bandits took over this town. They plan on robbing the train tonight, when everyone is asleep. The basement downstairs is the safest place we know of, as no one in town knows about it except these two. You and Jasper will be spending the night downstairs. Rose is keeping you safe. Roger and I will be finding others who know what's going on and taking care of the Bandits."

"Why?" Her voice was full of curiosity. "Everything on the train is replaceable. Human lives are not."

"Sure, it's replaceable, but it won't be replaced for three months. In that time, people on the coast don't get their supplies. Some of which is absolutely needed, like medicine. The Bandits steal it to try and sell it, end up not being able to, and it rots in the cars they take. The Bandits also have a lot of townsfolks held hostage, along with at least one of the train conductors and his assistant. We stop the Bandits, we might be able to save everyone."

Ms. Bauer stood taller. "You let them have the goods, then all the town's people will be spared."

Lucy stared Ms. Bauer in the eye and moved closer. Her voice was hard when she spoke. "In all my years dealing with Bandits, I have never once known them to spare hostages. We leave them alone, they kill everyone in town and might kill the conductor. They don't care if the train leaves again. We do."

Ms. Bauer looked away from Lucy's hard glare, and Lucy turned to Roger.

"You in?"

"Is it just us?"

"No." Rose spoke up. "If you go talk to Harvy at Harvy's Goods and tell him I paid for your help, he'll tell you who to talk to."

Lucy and Roger nodded, then Lucy looked at Roger again. "So?"

He looked at Lucy then at Rose, then back to Lucy. "Did she really hire you?"

"Yes." The lie slid easily off her tongue. Lucy felt justified in lying about this as she planned on helping Rose for free anyway. Contracts in situations like this were just a formality and usually filled out after the fact. Her payment would be the death of the Bandits and getting the train rolling on time.

Roger shrugged. "All right. What's the plan?"

Lucy smiled as she launched into her plan.

⊱⊰⊱⊰⊱⊰

As soon as Harvy, a squat man with a no-nonsense attitude, understood why Lucy was in his store, he sent his helper to fetch a few other people. It took no time to get people gathered and on two rooftops. Roger found the other conductors asleep on the train and told them to stay put. He then found Lucy, Harvy, and Bell, on the rooftop of the saloon, waiting for the Bandits to strike. Bell was a quiet woman with wide hips and sharp eyes. There were three others on the rooftop of the hotel, but Lucy had a hard time remembering their names. Besides, they weren't here to make friends.

They had already disabled the elevators to the train, to force the fight up here. The train tunnel was cramped and dark. There were too many chances for friendly fire. Up on the surface, they could see when the Bandits moved toward the station and hopefully stop them before they got too far. Also, though the moon was waning, it was still almost full and lit up the night beautifully.

The group of four were seated with their backs against the low wall that surrounded the roof. Over the edge, they could see the entrance to the station. It was midnight, and tempers were running hot. Everyone was tense and wanted an end to this situation, but no one knew what time the Bandits would strike. The seven were sleeping in shifts, to get a little shut-eye. Lucy was the only one who wasn't trying to sleep. She wasn't tired yet.

At half past, according to Bell's watch, the town seemed to grow even more quiet. Lucy paid attention and realized it was because the music from the saloon and hotel lobby had stopped. The restaurant a little farther down the street also stopped their music.

Lucy whispered to her group. "Heads up, stay sharp."

Harvy carefully signaled the people on the other side of the roof, and everyone came to attention. As planned, Lucy went to the fire escape and used it to move to a storage room one floor down. She carefully walked through the room to the door and listened for a moment. Not hearing anything, she opened the door. When she saw no one in the hall, she eased out the door and moved to the stairs. She kept an eye on the hallway and tried to listen for sounds from downstairs. The plan was to try and get all the Bandits to leave the saloon and hotel and lock the doors behind them so they couldn't hole up and take more hostages.

When she couldn't tell what was going on, Lucy plastered a satisfied look on her face and swaggered down the steps. Once she could see that the place was clear, she nearly ran to the door. Her back against the wall, she looked out and made sure the way was clear, closed and locked both doors, then moved to the back. Just as she arrived, she heard gunfire.

Lucy dove to the ground in the back room and pulled her guns out. Or rather one gun. Her other she had left with Rose, who needed it to protect Jasper and Ms. Bauer. With her gun in hand, Lucy looked out the back window and saw the Bandits outside. She locked the back door, then turned and looked out the window next to it. A barrel against her lower back stopped her from shooting out the window. She raised her hands slowly.

"Who are you?" said a shaky voice.

Lucy recognized Gerald's voice. "I'm Lucy. A Hired Hand." *The sound of a gun being cocked is always louder when the gun is being aimed at me*, Lucy thought.

"Who hired you?" the shaky voice asked.

"Rose."

The gun was lowered. "Oh."

Lucy turned and regarded the man. "Can I shoot the Bandits now?"

Someone banged against the back door. "Open this door!"

Lucy holstered her gun quickly, grabbed the bartender's revolver and checked the cylinder. "You with us or them?"

"You. Us. Not the Bandits!" he said in a confused voice.

She went to hand the gun back to him. "Do you know how to use this?"

He looked terrified. "In theory."

Lucy put the gun in her off hand and unholstered her gun. "Go hide."

He ran, and Lucy moved again to a better location to see out the window. Someone still pounded on the door, eager to be let back inside. She could just barely see him through the window. It was brighter outside than inside. He was just out of view from her angle, and she didn't think she would be able to hit him. Therefore, she sighted out the window and fired at the Bandits who were coming back to the saloon. Many were already down, but more were left.

When the man at the door heard the shots, he ran. It was easy to hit him in the back. He went down with one shot. Lucy fired all twelve rounds, then turned and sat with her back against the barrel to reload. One of the first things Cecil taught her was to calm down while loading a gun.

Take your time. Remove all other thoughts from your mind. If you're distracted, you will drop bullets. You can't afford to do that in a shootout. This litany ran through her head in his voice, calm, cool, collected. It helped her to reload quickly and effectively. Both guns full again, she carefully moved to look out the window. As soon as she could, she fired, and more Bandits scattered to avoid being shot.

She stopped firing and moved to look out the window and hide herself. They weren't running in the direction of the hotel. They were running away from the town. She surmised they had a camp nearby and headed to the front of the saloon. She found the bartender in the worst hiding place. He was cowering under the bar, back facing the front doors. If anyone came in shooting, he would probably be hit. She pushed her thoughts aside and ran to him. She startled him completely, and he yelped.

"Are there any horses nearby?"

"Um, um, um . . ." he stammered.

She looked him dead in the eye. "Hey!"

He startled again, and his eyes went wide but he looked in her eyes.

"Horses?"

"No, they took them all."

"Damn. All right. You're going to go to the roof and tell Roger they're headed to a camp and Lucy is following them. Can you do that?"

The terrified look didn't go away.

Lucy pulled back as she heard a commotion on the steps.

"Lucy!"

She stuck her head up and saw Roger.

"They're leaving town," they said at the same time. Both nodded.

"Bartender is here, but he's terrified. Bandits took all the horses."

"They didn't take mine." Bell said from behind Roger.

"How far away?"

"Other side of town. I kept them hidden."

"Go get what you can. We're going to start after them. Can you track?" Lucy was holstering her gun and the bartender's. She liked having two guns.

"I've got a bloodhound."

"If I give you my bandana, will your dog be able to track us?"

"Any item of clothing will do. He's well trained."

Lucy made a disbelieving noise. Well trained or not, some dogs didn't listen. She didn't know Bell well enough to know how the dog would react, but there wasn't much choice for clothing. No one else had extra, as far as she could see. That thought in her head, Lucy removed her hat, pulled off the bandana tied around her hair and handed it over. "Just make sure he doesn't jump on me when you join up with us."

"He won't." Bell stated as she took the large red bandana.

Lucy slammed her hat over her braided hair and tried to stay in the moment. She caught the barest whiff of orange from removing her bandana, and it made her want to smile. Instead, she made sure the hat was on securely and asked, "Where are the others?

"Still on the roof. They're going to make sure no one comes back," Roger answered.

"All right. Bell, go get your horses. Roger, let's go."

The trio moved toward the back door, and left the saloon. Bell went one way and Lucy and Roger went the other. The pair were able to follow the Bandits' footsteps for about half an hour before Bell, Harvy, and a third person showed up with two extra horses. As soon as Lucy saw his turban, bushy beard and mustache, she remembered his name was Ranjit. Her attention immediately went from him to the bloodhound, who came right up to her. It didn't bark or jump on Lucy when it saw her, but it did growl a bit.

"Jackle. Heel."

The dog stopped growling and moved to Bell's horse. Roger and Lucy quickly mounted, and Bell handed Lucy her bandana. Lucy stuffed it into a pocket to take care of later.

"Can we follow the tracks?" Harvy asked.

"Should be able to. Moon's bright." Roger answered. "We were having a pretty easy time."

"Can we use the dog?"

"We don't really have their scent," Bell answered. "I'm going to send him home."

Lucy nodded, and Bell instructed the dog to go home. Jackle moved away, and the humans did their best to follow the tracks the Bandits left.

ELEVEN

Lucy pulled her horse up short and stopped it quickly. Roger reined in next to her, which caused the others to stop as well. "What's going on?"

"I see a flickering of a fire in the distance."

There was silence as the others looked. Roger spoke first. "I don't see it."

She spared him a disdainful glance, then addressed the others. "Bell, Harvy, Ranjit? Do you see it?"

"I do." Bell's voice sounded confident.

"Nope, don't see it, but I don't track, Bell does." Harvey answered quickly.

"Maybe. Not sure." Ranjit was silent for a moment. "Yeah, I see it. You think that's them?"

"I would bet on it. It's about the right distance from town," Lucy stated.

"What's the plan?" The familiarity of Roger's tone of voice was a sharp contrast to the fact that Lucy didn't know the area well enough to be in charge.

"Bell, what's the land like here? Any prairie dogs to worry about?"

"Animals tend to stay away from this side of town. We're above the train tracks. The vents are around here, but they're obvious even in the dark. The land's flat otherwise."

Lucy nodded. "Bell, want right or left?"

"Left."

"I'll go from the right. Roger, Ranjit, Harvy, wait about thirty seconds, then go straight at them. Questions?"

The others stayed silent.

"Go."

Lucy angled her horse to the right and heard another horse move off as well. About thirty seconds later, when she was closer to the fire, she heard the other four horses start off. As she continued, she saw the camp was much closer than anticipated. Concerned noises came from around the low burning fire. Lucy drew a gun and urged her horse faster.

She arrived just as Bell did and immediately took in the situation. It was chaos. Some people were crying, some were cursing and screaming, and some were standing in front of others as if to protect them. Bell's voice rang out clearly as Ranjit, Roger, and Harvy rode up.

"OI! Calm down! Sierra! It's Bell. Talk to me!"

A woman at the edge of the group of about one hundred people seemed to snap to attention, stood, and faced Bell. Her voice was ragged but loud and clear.

"The Bandits shot five people and ran off."

Upon hearing that, Lucy saw Roger dismount and headed to Sierra. "I have training. Who's hurt?"

Lucy turned her horse into the darkness beyond the crowd and tried to scan the horizon for movement. The others could handle the townsfolk.

She moved her horse slowly beyond the reach of the fire and waited a few minutes as she ignored Roger's voice. He was calling to her. He knew she could help, but the Bandits were still out there. Once she realized she couldn't see any movement, even with the bright moon lighting up the desert, she turned back to the camp.

Bell came to her as she dismounted. "I'm going back to town. Some of these people need a wagon."

"How many can move on their own?"

"Most of them."

"How in the world did the Bandits get these people out here? Rose said they took most of the town, but I didn't believe it."

"They did it slowly. They kidnapped people on the outskirts first, then came for the ones in town."

"No one noticed?"

Bell shook her head. "Most of these townsfolk are farming families. Most of 'em come to town once every two weeks or so."

Lucy nodded and looked around. "Let's round people up and get them moving. Is the wagon in town or somewhere else?"

"I have one at my place, but I can ride through town to get there, if needed."

"Make sure the Bandits didn't ride back that way. Sometimes they do."

"Sure." With that, Bell moved away, and Lucy went to Roger. Though she knew how to patch herself up in the field, she wasn't that good with wounds. She usually did a quick job and got herself back to a doctor as quickly as she could. She could try and help, though.

ༀ☙ℭ☙ℭ☙ℭ

Sometime later, after patching up who they could, the group was on their way. Two people hadn't survived being shot. Harvey had volunteered to stay with the bodies to make sure the coyotes and other predators didn't eat them.

Lucy walked next to the horse Bell lent her, leading it. On the horse was one of the shooting victims. The man, whose name she didn't remember, grumbled loudly about being able to walk. Lucy ignored him the best she could and watched the others around her. She preferred to be on a horse, where she could see more, but the gentleman had been shot. Having him walk was not advisable. She wasn't sure he was better on the horse, but he was too slow on his feet and refused to be left behind. She felt better though, when she heard the distinct sounds of a wagon approaching, probably a little faster than necessary. Soon, she saw Bell driving a wagon hitched to two horses. She stopped her horse and waited for Bell to arrive.

"Did you push the horses?"

"Maybe a little." Bell's voice suggested she knew what she was doing.

"Other than the hurt people, was there a reason for that?"

"The Bandits didn't come back to town, if that's what you're asking." Bell looked around quickly. "Where's Harvy?"

"He stayed that the campsite. Two people didn't make it."

Bell nodded. "All right. Let's get people loaded."

Lucy nodded and pointed to the man on her horse. "Start with him."

"I don't need to ride in a wagon! I'm perfectly capable of walking!" His voice was indignant.

Lucy looked at Bell. "He was shot in the leg. He fell when he tried to walk on his own. Got on the horse with help." She then turned to look at the man, caught his eye, and stated in a calm voice, "If you can walk, dismount on your own."

The man bristled. "Well . . . I . . ."

"You're not walking and holding us up. Get in the wagon." Lucy's voice gave no room for argument.

"She's right, Walter. You can't walk if you've been shot in the leg. Let her help you down and into this wagon." Bell sounded as if she had dealt with his stubbornness before.

Instead of saying anything, he crossed his arms and sulked, but when Lucy reached up to help him down, he let her. They got Walter into the wagon safely before getting others into the wagon as well. There were people with small children, and older folks who needed assistance. Luckily, Bell had grabbed a larger wagon, and they were able to get quite a few people settled into the back. Some of the parents opted to walk to leave more room for the children. Once all were situated, Lucy and the others mounted their horses and headed back to town.

It took a while, since there were still people walking, but they were able to get back before the sun came up. Once all were unloaded at the hotel, Lucy turned to Bell.

"You awake enough to go back and get Harvy and the bodies?"

Bell shook her head. "I need someone to ride with me, or maybe I need coffee."

"I'll get Roger to go with you. Someone should stay here and keep watch. I don't think anyone is."

"You think they're going to come back?"

"Yes."

Bell seemed to be waiting for something more, but when Lucy didn't say anything else, she shrugged. "Even Bandits have to sleep. Come with me. You can keep me awake since you seem so perky."

"Lucy!"

She turned at the sound of Roger's voice and spied him as he came out of the saloon with Mrs. Bauer and Rose. She didn't move but waited while the trio approached.

"We're heading to the hotel to try and get some sleep before the sun comes up. They did shoot the conductor but not his assistant. Since all the conductors have assistants, we have enough to get the train going. They want to leave as soon as the cargo wagons are unhitched. He's wiring a message to the home office to report."

Lucy nodded. "Someone should stay on watch."

Roger stood silently for a moment, then shook his head. "We all need sleep. I can't imagine you're still awake."

"Bell has to go out to get Harvy and the others. I'll either go with her or stay in town and keep watch. She needs someone to keep her awake."

"I'll keep watch."

All turned to Rose. Lucy looked down at Rose's hands to see that her gun was still in the young woman's hand. The barrel was pointed down, finger off the trigger. She looked relaxed with it in her hand. Lucy looked back into Rose's eyes and held them for a moment as others around her spoke. She ignored all except Rose. The young woman held her gaze readily. She looked alert. Lucy nodded.

"You know this town well?"

"I grew up here. I'm better in town than out there. I'll go on a roof like you did."

"You're going to the hotel roof. Roger will tell you our room number. If you see the Bandits approaching, you run to his room and you wake him up. Got it? I don't want it to be only you firing at them."

She looked about to argue, then shut her mouth and nodded instead.

"Good." She turned to look at Roger, who nodded, then turned her head to Bell. "I'll come with you."

Bell nodded. "Leave the horse at the saloon. I'll get him home later"

Lucy nodded, dismounted, and got on the wagon.

෫෪෫෪෫෪

The sun was up by the time the bodies were in the doctor's back office. Lucy needed sleep, but that uncomfortable tingle still played with her spine. Once Bell was all set, though, she left and found her way to the hotel's roof. When she opened the access door, she could see Rose, who nodded at her but kept moving. Lucy went to her as the young woman walked around the perimeter of the roof.

"Anything?"

"Just Bell's wagon."

"I don't like it."

"Roger thinks you're sleep deprived."

"Most nights I'm up watching Ms. Bauer. He's the one that's sleep deprived." Lucy's voice was matter of fact. No emotion came through.

"Why do you think they're going to come back?"

"They came for the cargo. They didn't get it."

"Do you think they went through an access tunnel?"

"Are there any tunnels around here, or is it just vents?"

"Vents."

"I was talking with Bell on the way out and back. We were practically on top of the rail tracks. I didn't see any newly dug access tunnels. Neither did she. When Bandits decide to steal cargo, they don't change their minds."

"Maybe our show of force convinced them to stop their plans?"

She gave a harsh laugh. "A show of force usually makes them try harder. It's like they're trying to prove they're not afraid."

Rose frowned. "Sounds useless."

"That about sums up Bandits."

This time she laughed. Lucy joined her. When they stopped laughing, they also stopped walking. Rose spoke first. "I need sleep."

Lucy nodded. "So do I." She unholstered the gun she'd taken from the scared bartender earlier. "Here. Give me my gun and take this one. I like mine better."

Rose smiled and traded guns. "I should have a holster."

"You should." She holstered her gun and looked around. "Let's both get some sleep. I'll just hope I'm wrong about the Bandits coming back."

Rose nodded, and both women went to the roof access and down to the rooms. Lucy stopped at Roger's door as Rose left completely. She knocked softly and Roger opened almost immediately. He looked terrible.

"Did you sleep at all?"

"An hour, maybe two. I'm too used to being up early." His voice was groggy.

"Is she still sleeping?"

"Yep. Ms. Bauer would like to be woken up when she's had more than four hours of sleep."

Lucy raised an eyebrow.

Roger rolled his eyes. "No, I don't know when she fell asleep. She means I should wake her when she's been in her room for four hours."

Lucy shook her head. "She should set an alarm."

Roger laughed softly. "She says I'm her alarm."

Lucy snorted laughter.

"Oh, ha ha." The sarcasm was thick in his voice.

She gave him a sly smile, but before he could say anything, he indicated the room.

"You going to sleep here?"

She shook her head. "I'm used to the train. I want to check on Lance, too."

Roger nodded. "You going to come up before the train leaves?"

"If I wake up in time."

"Wait, how are you going to get down there? We disabled the elevator."

She gave him an incredulous look. "You think that's going to stop me?"

Before he could ask further questions, Lucy turned and left.

TWELVE

Lucy woke after a few hours, feeling groggy. She hadn't slept enough, and her dreams left her confused. Since Roger wasn't down here, she figured the townsfolk either hadn't gotten the elevator going again or it wasn't late enough to leave. She rose from her cot, put the chair in front of the door to block it, stripped, and washed up. She wanted a real bath or a shower but that wasn't available most places. She did what she could with the wash basin and dressed quickly.

Once dressed, she moved the chair, left the room, and went to Lance's stall. He was fine and had plenty of food, but she fussed over him anyway. Before going back up to the surface, Lucy walked the length of the train. Nothing was out of place. She sighed and headed to the elevator. She pushed the "up" button, and heard a ding. A smile came to her lips as the clanking of the machinery indicated the car was headed down. She nodded to the elevator operator as the door opened.

"Hello." It was the man she recognized from the other towns, but he wasn't wearing his uniform. She looked him up and down as she entered the car. "What happened to your uniform?"

"It has bullet holes in it. Mixxie's fixing it for me, but it won't be ready until we're already on our way."

"Sorry about that."

He closed the door and got the elevator going, then turned to look her in the eye and shrugged. "I wasn't wearing it when it happened."

She nodded. "That is something to be thankful for."

"It's the best thing to be thankful for," he said as he turned back to his work.

"True." She smiled and settled in for the short climb to the top. As he let her out, Lucy tipped her hat to him and went on her way.

Her first stop was the saloon. She asked for and was given the location of Rose. Lucy thanked Gerald and went to the hotel kitchen, where Rose was washing dishes. Lucy strolled in like she belonged there, and no one questioned her place. She nodded to Rose when the young woman looked her way.

"Hello."

"Did you sleep much?"

"No."

Before Lucy could say anything, Rose turned to her and looked her in the eye.

"I want to be a Hired Hand. Can I Apprentice with you?"

"Not at this time. I'm in the middle of two jobs, both of which have me on the train. Can't teach you a lot of things on a train." Lucy saw hope fade in Rose's eyes, and she frowned a little. "You have time to learn a few things, though."

"You're the first Hired Hand I've met that I liked. You know how many have passed through this town? About one every time the train comes through. Both directions. Sometimes it's the same ones; most times it's not."

"Look, I'm coming back in three or six months. We'll talk then."

"Sure." Rose turned back to her work.

Lucy looked at Rose and took in her stance; she had written Lucy off. Lucy continued talking anyway. "I need you to do me a favor."

Rose gave her the side-eye but didn't stop working.

"I need you to convince the town to keep a look out for the Bandits. And if the town doesn't listen, I need you to watch for them." When Rose still barely glanced her way, Lucy folded her arms and said one last thing. "Consider it your first Assignment."

Rose stopped completely, a plate in one hand, brush in the other. She slowly looked at Lucy. "Oh."

"I was serious. I can't Apprentice you now, but I'll be back in three or six months."

Rose placed the dish and brush in the sink and turned off the water. She turned fully and looked at Lucy. "It sounded like you were brushing me off."

"Nope. Just need time."

The young woman was silent for a moment, then opened her mouth and took a long breath in. She spoke slowly, as if thinking about her words. "Why do you think we need to watch?"

"I don't trust that they won't be back." Her answer was sure and quick.

She watched as Rose thought about her words, her eyes skittering about the room. Finally, Rose looked back into her eyes. "Ok. I'll do it."

"Good. I want to talk to you privately, then. About things you should think about until I get back."

"Ok." Rose grabbed a hand towel and wiped her hands clean as she called out to someone. "Rob! I'm going out for a bit."

"You got here late this morning, and now you're leaving early?" A tall man moved closer from around the other side of a shelf. "Who do you think you are?"

"Your best dishwasher. I'll be back."

Lucy snickered as she nodded to Rob, then followed Rose out to the back of the hotel. Once outside, she looked around. "Let's go for a walk. This is for your ears only."

"Ok." Rose stated as they headed out into the desert. It wasn't too hot, yet.

"Word will get out that you're going to be a Hired Hand. People are going to start asking you to do things for them. You are not to take any jobs until you've signed the Apprentice paperwork."

Rose's eyes grew wide. "There's paperwork?"

Lucy smiled. "Yes. A lot of it. It keeps things legal."

"Oh."

"Also, make up rules to follow when you're a Hired Hand, and figure out which ones you're willing to break."

Rose frowned. "I don't understand."

"Hired Hands have a Code of Conduct we must follow. Most are obvious; some are not. Most rules we follow, we make up ourselves. Are you willing to kill someone for money? How far are you willing to travel? What job is too small? What job is too big? Think about it. Then write them out and look at the list every day. Then, think about what would make you break your own rules. Then realize that at some point you might be forced to break your own rules. Not because someone is paying you a lot of money, but because life has thrown you into a situation that has forced your hand."

"Oh."

"I know, it's a lot. But you have time."

"I didn't know …" She didn't seem to know how to finish her thought.

"How would you have?"

That seemed to surprise her too. Rose smiled. "Ok, fair point." She was silent, but as it looked like she had something on her mind, Lucy didn't speak. Finally, Rose asked, "Why can't I take a job yet? Is it just the paperwork?"

Lucy shook her head. "You need to learn to say no, to set boundaries. Someone at some point will ask you to do a job you don't want to take. If you learn to say no now, it'll be easier when it comes up. This is your town, your home, your people. You're not going to want to say no to them. Learn how."

Rose stood still as she appeared to absorb all the information Lucy gave her. She then nodded slowly. "Ok."

"Speaking of the Code of Conduct, request one from your sheriff. They're the only ones who can request one for an Apprentice if the Teacher isn't around. You tell your sheriff to say Hired Hand Lucy Marsh, number 25-2.09-03-2072A asked for it. Can you remember that?"

Rose shook her head, reached into her pocket, and pulled out a small well-worn piece of paper and nub of a pencil. When Lucy gave her information again, Rose wrote it down in tiny script on what looked like the last speck of blank space. That situated, Rose looked at Lucy.

"What about the Bandits?"

"I'm pretty sure they'll be back. I want this town prepared for it."

"Why do you think they'll be back?"

"I just do."

Rose looked to be waiting for more information, but spoke when none came. "Ok. I was hoping for something more so when I talk to the town council next week, they'll listen."

"All you need to do is point out that since it happened once, it can happen again."

The young woman nodded. "Oh. Yeah."

Lucy gave her a little smile. "You need to think about things like that too. And remember, the simplest answer will probably work in most cases."

It was Rose's turn to smile. "Unlike all the information you just gave me?"

Lucy shrugged as she smiled. "Sometimes long answers are necessary to help teach."

The women smiled at each other, before Rose sighed heavily. "I wish I could go with you now."

"Why?"

"I want to leave this place."

"Is that why you wanted to be a Hired Hand?"

"Yes." Rose's answer was quick.

"Me too. But there are other jobs you can do that'll get you traveling."

"I don't want to be stuck to one job, so the train's out."

Lucy nodded. "I thought the same thing."

A happy smile came to Rose's lips. "I feel like we might have a lot in common."

"We might. We'll end up finding out."

The smile grew on Rose's lips and lit up her eyes.

"Got any more questions?"

"Is there any paperwork I can do on my own?"

"Your Teacher has to ask for it and provide codes."

Rose looked crestfallen. "Oh."

Lucy laughed. "I'll be back this way before you know it."

"Yeah, but I don't want to wait."

"Being a Hired Hand, you do a lot more waiting then you realize. Get used to it."

"Anything else?"

Lucy looked off into the desert over Rose's shoulder and thought about it for a long time, then nodded. "Learn to meditate. It'll help you rest when you can't sleep."

"Is that a book thing?"

"Well, my Teacher Cecil taught me, but you can find it in books."

Rose's eyes lit up. "We have a roving library that comes through on a regular basis. They're about due."

"I think I've seen those. At least the Bandits leave them alone."

"I've heard the Bandits sometimes borrow books from them."

Lucy smiled but didn't comment on that rumor. "I have nothing more. Any other questions?"

Rose shook her head. "No."

"Let's get you back. I need to get to the train."

The women smiled and headed back to town.

₧₧₧

After saying goodbye to Rose, Lucy went back to the train and found Roger in their room. "Where's Ms. Bauer?"

"She found two other women to play cards with. She's in the dining car, enjoying herself."

"I'm surprised you're not with her."

"I need to clean up, and I told her that. I'll be quick enough."

"You didn't get enough sleep." It was a statement, not a question.

Roger shook his head. "I did not."

"You sound like your dad did when he was too tired. Like you're watching all your words to make sure you don't yell."

He paused in gathering his clothing, sighed heavily, and nodded. "Yep."

"You *are* tired." That earned her a glare. It didn't phase her much, but she did change the subject. "Do you know when we'll be on our way?"

"Couple hours. It's taking longer than they thought to unload the cargo, not sure why." He sat on his cot as Lucy sat on hers. "It's lucky the Bandits didn't find all the conductors."

Lucy nodded. "It's like they didn't even think about it."

Roger licked his lips, which made Lucy take note. When Cecil did that, it meant he was about to bring up a tough subject. "A couple of the townsfolk said you were pretty adamant that the Bandits were going to come back."

"They will."

"How can you be so sure? I mean," he shook his head, "you always seem so sure about the Bandits when we've talked in the past. Why do you think you know what they'll do?"

Roger had asked that question before. In the past, Lucy ignored it or found a way to bypass the question. As she stared at her longtime friend, she decided. It was time he knew the truth.

"You ever wonder where I was those three years you and Cecil couldn't find me?"

Roger sat silently for a moment before moving and placing his back against the wall. He stretched out his legs, and got comfortable, as if he knew a good story was coming.

"You never told my dad this story, did you?"

"No. And you're never to tell a living soul."

Roger touched the HH pin on his right lapel and nodded. It was a solemn oath. Lucy nodded.

"I spent those three years with a few different Bandit groups." She watched as he kept his words to himself. "I went north, as too many people knew me down here. I went as far north as I could before it got too cold, and I joined a Bandit group. When they became suspicious of me, I left and joined another, then another. I went to five in total."

He stared at her for a moment, then asked, "Why did you do it?"

"My whole childhood, I was told that the Bandits were misunderstood. That they were always welcomed to come back into society. That we should open our hearts and arms and allow them back into the fold. Then I went Above and started seeing their actions, and I wondered if they really were worth taking back in."

"What did you find out?"

"They don't treat each other well. As a new person, when I found my way to a Bandit camp, no one welcomed me. No one taught me anything. It was a 'learn on your own, fight for survival,' situation. If there was food, you had to fight for it or go hunting on your own. They don't run from fights unless it's part of the plan."

"You only saw five camps." The skepticism was thick in his voice.

"And they were all the same. Every single last one. There was one camp that had recently stolen a train's cargo car. They had planned to sell the food in it to a nearby town. When the town refused, the Bandits let the car sit in the desert. The food rotted and attracted animals, which they used for target practice."

Roger looked away. Lucy knew that would hit hard with him. He was an animal lover. She was sure he had some cats or dogs, or both, at home.

"They're all the same, Roger. One camp, some young people from Under showed up. They wanted to be Bandits. It was a group of six. One was shot for taking soup from what they thought was a communal soup caldron. Two ended up leaving that night. Three stayed, but two of them were dead by the end of the week. The one who survived turned just as hard as the rest of them as soon as he could. He even shot one of the people who came with him."

She stared at Roger. When he didn't say anything, she continued. "The Bandits that took over Bend have a plan. They're not done. They will be back."

He shook his head. "I still don't think you can know that. People are different."

"Individuals are different. Groups are not."

He stared at her for a moment, then shook his head as if to clear it. "Look, you still can't convince me you know they'll be back. And the train is leaving shortly anyway."

She shook her head in annoyance. "We'll find out on our way back."

"True. Now if you don't mind," he pointed to the wash basin, "I'd like to get cleaned up."

She stood. "I figured you'd get washed up in the hotel?"

"This is quicker. And I'd rather stay down here unless she needs anything."

Lucy shrugged. "I'm here. I can go into the dining car too."

He looked to be thinking about it, then shook his head. "We already checked out of the hotel, so that's out. This is quicker, anyway."

Lucy nodded. "I'll be in the dining car. Best place to sit if I can't be anywhere else."

Roger nodded, and Lucy left the room. She ended up in the dining car, the one with the gambling table on the top level. After surreptitiously checking on Ms. Bauer, Lucy ordered some food and a coffee and sat down at a table by herself. There was an old newspaper, which she read through. It was last month's paper, but it was something to do.

THIRTEEN

The rest of the train ride went without incident. It took twelve to sixteen hours to get from Bend to Sacramento, depending on how fast the conductor chose to go. The original city had largely been spared by the first Bombardment, as the meteorites landed to the northeast of the city. The original Bombardment, the terror that started it all, happened in the early spring. Due to the mild weather, the citizens of Sacramento were able to walk out of the city when traffic came to a stop. It was rumored that by the time the second Bombardment hit the next day, most of the citizens were to the west of the city. No one was sure how many survived, but many of the population went back to the city, to the underground areas, and started to rebuild. Sacramento was one of the first cities to have an Under. It helped that parts of Sacramento Above was built on old Sacramento.

As the train pulled into the station, Lucy shook her head. She had been here a few times, and each time, it was the same. The station opened into a mini city, full of lights. She didn't understand how a city could dare to produce so much heat. The towns Above stayed at around two hundred people. If a town had more than three hundred people, it was Bombarded.

People figured out it was due to the amount of heat produced by the people and the buildings. Sometimes, if a vent from the Under released too much heat, it was Bombarded.

Looking out the little used window of her room, Lucy shook her head again. It was so bright she could see people laughing and talking on the station platform. That was another thing; this station was huge. It had multiple tracks and multiple platforms, like train stations of old. Beyond the station was a small city, of well over five hundred people. They emptied the cargo cars and distributed the goods as needed to other trains. The trains led to more underground cities around here and the West Coast. It was like they were daring the Aimers to find them.

A knock on the door brought her attention around. She nodded to Roger. "We all set?"

"We are." He held out a bag of what she assumed was money. "Twenty gold."

She shook her head. "I don't need that much. It wasn't that hard of an Assignment."

Roger frowned. "You fought off Bandits. You protected her like you were hired to do. You deserve it. Don't argue."

She laughed a bit. "All right." Lucy stood, walked the short distance to her friend, and took the bag. She hefted it a bit before stashing it in a nearby saddlebag. "You off now or are you going to wait until the others have disembarked?"

"Ms. Bauer wants to get going as soon as possible. I've been tasked with hiring a car or seat, whichever is more readily available, on the next train that takes us down the coast. She has offered to pay you to come with us."

Lucy shook her head. "I'm looking for three people. I don't know where they went, and I'd rather be under the open sky rather than, well, Under."

He nodded. "All right. Maybe we'll run into each other again."

She smiled and held out her hand. "We always do."

They shook hands as they nodded to each other, then Roger left. Lucy took a few gold coins out of the bag and placed them in various pockets, hidden and obvious. Then she rearranged the things in her saddle bag to hide the rest of the gold, grabbed her saddle bag, and went to Lance's stall. He was prancing nervously, probably due to the increased noise. She soothed him a bit, then put his blinders on and opened the side of the car to let him out. There was already a young man outside the car putting the plank in place.

"Hello!" came his excited voice. "I'll have this in place in one moment!" She watched as he fitted it into place and turned to her. "All set, ma'am!"

"Did you know there was a horse in here, or did you guess?" She knew the Rail would have wired ahead that there was a horse in the stall, but she liked to see what the young workers would answer.

He smiled. "The Rail told me, ma'am!"

She smiled and led Lance out of the car. She then slipped her hand into a pocket, grabbed a coin, and held it out to the boy.

He immediately shook his head. "We can't take tips, ma'am."

Lucy smiled. The young ones always followed the rules. She looked around, and when she didn't immediately see anyone else who worked for the Rail, Lucy turned back to the boy. "Who's going to tell?"

When he looked even more bothered, she nodded, let the coin drop, and moved Lance to the ramp that led up to the platform. She positioned herself and saw when the boy looked around, bent down, and quickly picked something off the ground. People were well paid, but she always felt that wealth needed to be evenly spread. Everyone could use a little more money. And twenty gold was a lot. She could afford to spread it around.

Satisfied, Lucy led Lance to the freight elevator and waited in turn to go up. As most people didn't want to ride with a horse, she ended up being alone in the elevator with the operator and Lance. Lucy stood near the operator, as it really was the best place to stand with a horse around.

"You're not who I expected."

The woman, who sported one large braid down the center of her head, gave Lucy a quizzical look. "Oh, right. Most of us ride the trains. Not here. We get too busy, and the trains often leave when we're still needed. Not the main train, of course, but the smaller ones."

Lucy nodded. "So, you work for the station?"

She nodded. "Yep. Three years now. Steady work. Good pay."

"I've been trying to figure something out, if you don't mind me asking questions?"

"Go ahead." She looked back at the panel, but her face held a friendly smile.

"How do you all keep the temps down in this place?"

"I don't know how it works, but it's water cooled. Pipes or something."

Lucy, who understood a bit more of the technical side of things then she liked to admit, stared at the woman in wonder. Cooling a place like this with water in pipes was not a small feat. Before she could say anything more on the subject, the elevator stopped. As the door slid open, she thanked the operator and walked Lance out. She immediately found the exit, walked outside and, despite the people around her, paused.

Most cities Above were buildings made of wood, with glass windows and very little adornments. Sacramento Above was built in the remnants of Old Sacramento. The train station entrance was built of wood, but the place across the street, which had a few stores, was housed on the ground level of an old concrete and steel building. Two stories above the street, the building stopped, and she could see the girders sticking out from the top. Lucy figured that was on purpose. There was no reason to have that unless to show off that it had been bigger. Lucy shook her head and headed to the saloon farther down the street. There were three in a row, with the names of the establishments displayed proudly on brightly painted signs hanging above the doors.

The Haughty Gentlemen was painted green, *Estell's Gazelles* was a deep rose, and *Mora's Choice* had a rainbow for its background. Even if a person couldn't read, it was fairly easy to tell where to go for your preference of Escorts. Lucy tied Lance up to the post in front of *Estell's Gazelles*, but only because it was the middle one.

"Hello."

Lucy turned at the sound of the gentle voice and smiled to the woman on the boardwalk in front of her. She nodded. "Ma'am."

"How can I help you today?"

"Looking for a few things. I need to send a wire, I'll need a place to lay my head for later, and I need information."

The woman, who wore a short red skirt and a black bikini top, crossed her arms as she looked Lucy up and down pointedly. Lucy saw the look, reached up, and tapped the right lapel of her coat near her HH pin. The woman nodded, and her large curly brown hair bobbed. "Post office has the wire, but the sheriff's office has one too, if it's for official business. And the sheriff is pretty open with information. If you offer to buy her a coffee, she'll take the rest of the afternoon to talk your ear off."

Lucy smiled. "What's her name?"

"Macy. She almost never wears her badge though." The woman pointed down the street. "Sheriff's office is that way. You can ask for Macy, but she's the tiny one with the blue hair." The woman blinked and looked away. "Wait. Is it blue?" She seemed to be talking to herself, then turned back to Lucy and rolled her eyes. "I have no idea if it's still blue. Woman changes her hair faster than I change boyfriends."

Lucy laughed. "All right. Sheriff Macy it is."

"And what about tonight? You want a companion?"

"Yes, but I haven't decided on what type of Escort I'm looking for. I'm not picky."

"Since the east train just came in, your choices might be slim, so if you're not picky, that might be helpful."

"I'll keep that in mind. Lance ok here?"

"How long you staying in town?"

Lucy shrugged. "Until I have all the information I want."

The woman rolled her eyes. "It's always the same with you Hired Hands." She turned her head. "Arthor!"

A boy popped his head out of the doorway. "Yes, Becky?"

"Take this woman and her horse to the stables. She'll probably be here tonight."

He came out fully, walked to the edge of the boardwalk, and jumped down. There were stairs, but he ignored them completely. He took Lance's reins and nodded to Lucy. "This way, ma'am."

"Much obliged." She turned to the Madam. "I'll see you later. Thank you much."

Becky nodded, and Arthor led Lucy and Lance around the back.

Once Lance was situated in a stall, Lucy walked back to the main thoroughfare. Her first stop was the post office. It was normal for the post office and sheriff's office to have a telegraph. In general, the ones in the post office were for everyone's use, whereas the ones in the sheriff's office, as Becky stated, were for official business. There was a line at the post office, but once at the front, Lucy gave her name and her number and waited to see if there were any messages. If someone wanted to get a hold of her, all they had to do was wire the message to the main HH office. It would be held there until the Hired Hand wired in for the messages. Though she hadn't told Grace this information, Irene knew how to get a hold of her, and had on a few different occasions. With no messages waiting, Lucy headed for the sheriff's office.

It was easy to find the sheriff's office, as there was a large sign on the front of the building with a star on it. Lucy walked in as if she belonged, and the noise immediately stopped. There were four people in the small building, all dressed in subdued tans, suggesting a uniform. Three were at desks and one stood with her arms held out as if showing how large an object was. The person standing had to be Sheriff Macy. She was a petite woman, with short, bright blue hair. Hair dye wasn't entirely hard to come by these days, but it wasn't cheap. The more artificial the color, the more it cost.

All the people in the office stared at Lucy. She wasn't surprised by this. She was an unknown element in a sheriff's office. Also, she probably looked out of place. Her hat was still on her head, and she wore a large leather coat that fell to her ankles. She wore chaps over her jeans. Her leather vest and button up shirt completed an outfit that screamed horse rider, if not Hired Hand.

Lucy caught Macy's eye. "Sheriff Macy?"

"Yep. Who's asking?"

"My name's Lucy. I'm a Hired Hand." Though she let most people figure that out on their own, with sheriffs and deputies, she declared it right away. It saved a lot of hassle. "I'm looking for some information and was told you might be able to help me?"

Macy put her arms down, and the people at the desks went back to looking as if they were working. "Why me?"

Lucy grinned. "I'm assuming ma'am, that since I didn't tell Becky what type of information I needed, she felt it best to have me talk to the sheriff to see what I would do."

Macy grinned back, and a couple of the others snickered. "Because if you were looking for information on an assassination, you wouldn't come here."

"That's my assumption."

The sheriff looked at one of the men in the room. "Sounds like Becky." They nodded to each other, then Macy looked back at Lucy. "All right, what do you need?"

"Well, I was wondering if we could go somewhere for coffee and food? It feels like lunchtime."

"That's a great idea! There's a coffee shop up the road that has the best coffee in town. They also have sandwiches. Occasionally they have pastries."

"Sounds great." Lucy smiled, showing off her whiter than white teeth.

Macy looked at one man in particular. "You have the office. We'll be at Leslie's if you need me."

One of the men nodded but didn't say anything. Macy grabbed her hat off a desk, placed it on her head, and walked toward the door. Lucy held the door open for her and headed out after the sheriff.

FOURTEEN

ow long will you be in town?"

The women were sitting at a table outside, in Leslie's Garden. The coffee shop and a few other establishments had access to this courtyard via their back doors, and it was lovely. There was a pond in the center, with flowers and trees all around. There were tables and benches and a small walkway that went all the way around the place. It wasn't large, but it was peaceful. Lucy spotted a few people sitting by themselves, reading or simply being. She took a deep breath and settled into her seat as the sheriff did the same.

"I'll be here at least one night. Mostly to give myself some time to relax."

"Not trying to catch a train?" Macy stirred her coffee carefully, as if she wanted something to do rather than needing to mix its contents.

"I prefer riding my horse, Lance. I can only take so much Under."

"Let me guess, you live Above?"

Lucy nodded. "In Meridune, Arkansas."

Macy shook her head. "I have an old map or two in my office," she said in such a way as to suggest "a map or two" meant many. "And I've been trying to memorize the states names, but I can't recall where Arkansas is."

"Well, it doesn't help that a lot of state borders from Before changed after we became the Broken States."

"Did Arkansas keep its borders?"

"Some of it, but a lot of new cities formed After, including Meridune. We're one of the cities on the East/West Train, though. I can point it out on a map and tell you of any other cities you might not know about."

Macy raised her large plastic mug in acceptance. "I would appreciate that." She took a sip of her coffee. "So, what can I help you with?"

"I've been hired to find three men so I can talk to them. The first two I'm looking for may be a couple. They were going to open a pet shop and sell animals changed by the Red Rock."

"Got names or a description?"

"Two well-dressed men. One might prefer purple. About the same height, and both had beards when my employer saw them. One had a deep voice."

"The only couple we've had around here like that were Watsom and Maxine. Maxine had a deep voice and loved the color purple."

Lucy frowned, about to say no. Then something Grace said popped into her mind and her eyes went wide. "I wonder if that's why . . ." she shook her head and looked back at Macy. "Go on."

Macy smiled and continued. "Maxine's voice sent chills down my back. I love deep voices. And her dresses were gorgeous! Almost all were royal purple. They had a pet shop that sold mutated animals. They might have stuck around if the Howler pup hadn't bitten someone."

Lucy allowed herself to be momentarily distracted. "Howler?"

"Yeah," Macy nodded, "those two-headed beasts that howl too

much."

Her eyes opened wide. "Two-headed?"

Macy stared at her. "You've never seen one?"

"No. I've heard them, never seen them. It always sounds like a pack."

Macy shook her head. "Nope. I mean it's usually two or three running around together, but because they each have two heads, it sounds like more."

Lucy leaned back in her chair. "Well, I'll be damned. Two heads, huh? What's the rest of it look like?"

"They're about the size of a coyote, with the same spindly legs, but are stocky as heck. You ever seen pictures of the old types of dogs?"

Lucy shook her head. "I'm more interested in the animals we encounter now than in what used to be."

Macy shrugged and plunged on anyway. "Well, to me it looks like a cross between a bulldog and a coyote, but with two heads. Thick body, spindly legs, color of the desert." She put her arms out and hunched over like she was showing off muscle. "Just stocky as heck. Probably to keep its heads up."

Lucy smiled. "All right. Maybe next time I hear them, I'll try and get a peek."

"Just be careful. The couple that had the pet shop thought they domesticated the puppy. As soon as it had a chance, it bit a customer, with both mouths. The bites were bad. People were upset enough to start talking about running the couple out of town. I calmed the townspeople down but asked the couple to leave. We don't need trouble like that."

"What happened to the person who was bitten?"

"Once the Howler got its teeth in Herbert, it shook its head and ripped open the wounds. He's got bad scars, but at least there was no infection. I think if someone got bit by a Howler out in the desert, it would get infected. They seem to eat carrion, but will hunt as well."

"I'll continue to keep away from them then."

"Probably smart."

Lucy was silent for a moment as she thought about the couple. It sounded like it could be the people she was looking for. "You don't know where the couple went, do you?"

Sheriff Macy shook her head. "I think the only train in town that day was heading toward San Francisco."

Lucy gave a slight smile, and Macy noticed.

"What's the smile for?"

"I've always found it interesting that the cities on the East and West Coasts insist on keeping their old names, whereas many cities in the middle call themselves whatever they want."

"I think it has to do with how much of the old city was kept. Here, we were able to rebuild Above and Under the remnants of the original city. So were San Francisco, Seattle, and Portland. I hear places on the East Coast were able to do the same. You said Meridune was built After, but was it built anywhere near an old city?"

Lucy shook her head. "It grew up around a train station."

"There you go. If there's a history, it's kept."

Lucy nodded. "Makes sense. Never really thought about it before."

"Happens sometimes. We get so used to how things are that we don't feel the need to think things through."

"I try not to fall into that trap, but yeah, that's humans for you."

Macy smiled. "Yep." She paused then turned the conversation back to the issue at hand. "The next train to San Francisco, if you're interested, is in a few days."

"I'll ride out tomorrow. It's a good ride on a horse, and I should beat the train."

"Whatever drives your progress."

Lucy smiled and took a sip of her coffee. It was good and had a nice deep flavor. She then frowned. "I haven't gotten my sandwich yet, but I feel I have all the information I need."

Macy looked around and pointed out the long line at the counter. The shop's wall that faced the garden had several large windows to allow people to see inside and out. As the sun was behind the building, it was easy to see inside the restaurant. "They're busy. Close enough to lunch to have a crowd. They'll bring your sandwich soon. I could tell you more about anything you want. I do a lot of reading in my spare time."

"Is there a lot of that? I saw three other people in your office."

"One of them is my deputy. The two others are deputies from Under. For some reason, the office here became the default one to send reports from. The deputies from Under and a few towns around come here when things need filling out."

Lucy frowned. "Isn't it more efficient to file things from their own towns?"

"We have a post office hub."

Lucy nodded in understanding. Mail would be dropped off at the hub, and couriers would run the mail to other nearby towns, often Above and Under. "Still sounds like there might be too much to do around here to read much."

"It comes and goes." Macy took a long drink of her coffee, set it down and sighed contently. "We go months without an incident and then BAM! Someone gets bit by a Howler and we have too much to do."

Lucy smiled and nodded. As a server delivered their food, Lucy grinned. "What, other than the Howler, is the strangest animal you've ever heard or read about?"

Macy's eyes became big as the ladies thanked the server and picked up their food. "That's a heck of a question. Hmmmmm, you ever hear of a platypus?"

Lucy shook her head as she dug into her warm grilled cheese and ham sandwich with tomatoes. There were thick cut potatoes on the side.

"When it was first discovered back in the late 1700s people thought it was a hoax. Of course, this was an age when animals didn't mutate much. Oh, and did you know that back in the 1900s people made up an animal called the jackalope?"

Lucy's eyes went wide. "The jackalope existed previously?"

Macy nodded. "As a completely different creature. It was kind of a joke. Couple hunters that also knew how to do taxidermy put antlers on a jackrabbit. It took off as local mythology and spread around the States."

"Was it supposed to be dangerous?"

"Not like the ones today."

Lucy nodded as she thought about the terror that was the jackalope, shuddered a little, then turned the conversation to something better. "So, tell me about the platypus."

Macy grinned and started the tale.

ଔଔଔ

The next morning, Lucy left Sacramento with a smile on her face. Sheriff Macy had been a wealth of information on old and new animals, and was a pleasure to talk to. It was Fiona who kept the smile on her face, though. The Escort knew how to use their body and wasn't afraid to do so. Lucy licked her lips and looked at the road in front of her. She needed to concentrate on her ride. There were plenty of animals and humans that took advantage of unwary travelers.

She didn't have a plan in mind, only to go south toward San Francisco. She would probably stop at all the small towns she came to and ask about the pet shop. Macy told her that the store didn't have a name other than "Pets." She would look and ask for the store by that name and see if anything, well, bit.

Lance snorted and drew her attention back to the task at hand. Her horse knew her well. Whenever her thoughts wandered, she tensed a bit and Lance felt that. He would snort, as if to let her know she was needed in the here and now. She patted his neck, held his reins better, and let him move a little faster. She never urged him into a gallop unless it was necessary. With a long road ahead of them, speed was not needed. Lucy sighed, pulled her compass out, referenced it one last time, and headed off.

ℤℤℤ

The covered wagon passed them slowly as Lucy kept Lance still. They were on the side of the road. She didn't like having a wagon at her back, therefore when she realized they were going the same way and it was moving slightly faster than her, she pulled over to the side of the road.

She had been on the road three days now and visited two towns. No pet shops, no Maxine and Watsom. It was only a couple of towns though, and she wasn't discouraged. There was no reason to be, yet. The wagon passed her quickly enough, and she waved to the young kids sitting with their legs hanging over the back. The young girl caught her eye, waved back, then looked extremely happy.

"Lucy? LUCY!" She jumped up as Lucy recognized her. "Dad! Stop the wagon! It's Lucy!"

Lucy grinned as Gia raced into the wagon. The young man was waving happily now, but she doubted he knew who she was. She last saw the Ricci family five years ago. They were Scavengers who sold to towns and Bandits alike. Though Lucy had opinions on selling to the Bandits, she knew that Scavengers did what they had to in order to survive. It was either that or be killed.

The wagon slowed and stopped as Gia and Madeline jumped down from the wagon and ran to Lucy. She dismounted and hugged mom and daughter.

"Hello. Haven't seen you all in a long time."

"Mama?" said a young voice next to Lucy.

Lucy looked at the young boy. "You were five the last time I ran into your family. It's ok if you don't remember me." She held her hand out to Joe. "I'm Lucy."

The ten-year-old hesitated, then looked at his mom, then looked back to Lucy. He took her hand and shook it. "Hi. I'm Joe."

Lucy smiled. "Hello." She took her hand back and grabbed Lance's reins as Antonio came around the back of the wagon. "Antonio. Well met."

"Lucy! Travel with us." It wasn't a question.

She smiled. "Where are you headed?"

"I don't know the name of the town we're approaching, but the Orators are heading there too."

Her eyes opened wide in happiness. "I haven't run into them in a year! I'll gladly come with you."

Antonio smiled. "Good. The kids like to be around you."

She smiled. "Can I tie Lance to your wagon?"

"Of course!" Antonio shook Lucy's hand, then turned back to the wagon. "Say your hellos quickly. I want to get to town before sundown."

The rest of them agreed to Antonio's words and got Lucy and Lance situated. They were underway in less than five minutes, with Lucy sitting between Gia and Joe.

FIFTEEN

That night, the Ricci family, along with Lucy, sat in a field on a blanket, facing a quickly built stage. It was a warm night, and an impromptu outdoor theater could accommodate far more people than an indoor auditorium. The Orators started with a play written by one of their members. It was short but wasn't bad. It earned the actors a round of applause. Next was a play depicting history. Lucy had seen this one but encouraged the kids to pay attention. It was a sketch on how the first Bombardment came about.

Politician Olin Misk of the Most Efficient Department of the Government strutted across the stage, his voice larger than life. There were other actors on the stage, standing all in a group, with a sign that read House of the Senate. They were all nodding as Misk spoke.

"We've run out of resources! The Opposition won't let us dig any farther into the Earth! So, we'll send miners to the asteroid field and mine those! The asteroids aren't owned by anyone, so we'll own them all! It'll make us the richest nation in the world!"

Most of the House was nodding, but one actor stepped out of line and faced the audience. "But sir, we can't send people into space! We don't have the tech! We can't live in space! How will we mine?"

"I've secretly been building spaceships that will take electronic miners into space! It'll make the United States great again! We'll send AI into space to mine our asteroids!"

The House went nuts. The audience booed the actors as they left the stage. A child wearing a sandwich board ran out once the stage was clear, screaming his head off.

"Extra, extra! AI Miners turn against humanity! Read all about it! Asteroids heading to Earth from the AI Miners!" The child held his hands out as a person dressed as an asteroid ran at him from offstage. The boy screamed as the asteroid actor snatched him up and ran offstage with him. The audience booed the scene loudly, but also applauded, as the actors had done well.

Lucy let out a humorless chuckle as Gia leaned closer to her and whispered into her ear.

"Was it really that simple?"

"From what I can piece together, that was an oversimplification of the beginning of many failures." She spoke as quietly as Gia had, but people still shushed them. Gia and Lucy pulled apart and continued watching the Orators. Next was the news, which ran through a lot of information Lucy had picked up along the way in the past year. Many people in the audience didn't know that another person had stepped up as ruler of the Broken States. It was a Bandit on the East Coast this time, but he had quickly been subdued by the local authorities. That brought a laugh from the audience.

Every few years, someone tried to call themselves the ruler of the Broken States. Sometimes King, sometimes President, sometimes Emperor, but it never stuck. No one seemed to want that anymore. The states, sometimes cities, were far more content ruling themselves. There were some rules all areas Above and Under followed, but it was mostly about how money worked. People wanted to be able to use the same currency in the Broken States. The rest of it, people weren't that interested in. People wanted to rule themselves and weren't too keen on a central government. For now, the Broken States would stay broken, with locals capturing or even killing anyone who tried to be "king."

Once the news was conveyed, an actor came out and spoke to the audience. Her voice rang out well above the crowd. "Good evening, folks! Welcome! Tonight, we have a scene from a book found by a Scavenger."

Gia leaned over. "I hate this part. I always want to know more."

"You want to go for a walk?"

Joe decided this was the right time to speak loudly. "Mom, can I have something sweet?"

Lucy leaned over to the Riccis. "I saw a candy shop in town earlier. Let me take the kids."

Madeline looked at her kids, who nodded enthusiastically. "All right, but if they get to be too much, bring them back here."

Antonio blew kisses at Lucy and the trio headed away from the stage. The way into town was lit by torches. There were some guards along the path as well, to keep any animals away. The stage had been set up about three minutes from town, in someone's fallow field. As they walked, Lucy took deep breaths. The air smelled different. In and around Meridune, it smelled dry and sandy, with the undertone of the Red Rock that prickled the nose like nothing else on this planet did. Here, it smelled of trees and, oddly, green growing things. She looked around a bit, but the darkness revealed nothing. When the trio arrived in town, Lucy immediately noticed the trees growing next to the boardwalk. She made note of it as she steered the kids to the candy shop.

As they entered, Lucy instructed the kids, "Get what you want, but don't spend all my money. If the candy is more than five pennies, you get my ok." The kids nodded, and she pointed toward the counter. "What do you two want to drink?"

"Hot chocolate!" Gia stated excitedly.

"Berry milk!" Joe said with equal excitement.

Lucy smiled and nodded. "All right. You two look around, figure out what you want, and I'll get the drinks."

"Thank you!" They said as one and went about their business.

Lucy smiled and headed to the counter. There were a few people in line, but not many, and she was soon giving her order. "One hot chocolate, one berry milk, and what is an iced coffee? As in, how cold is it really?"

The woman behind the counter gave Lucy a slightly frustrated smile. "Well, we brew coffee, grown in the town's greenhouse, by the way, allow it to cool down, then add it to cold milk. We're trying for ice, but you know how it is."

Lucy nodded. "I'll take one, but yeah, generators for cold storage make a lot of heat."

The woman shook her head. The beads in her hair made a nice clacking sound. "It's not really that. It's that as soon as we get one generator going, everyone in town wants their own and then we have a heat problem."

Lucy looked surprised. "That's . . ."

"An annoyance we're working on. We can get the drinks started for you, but are you getting anything else?"

"Kids are getting candy."

"When they're ready, you can pay and pick up your drinks."

"I'll pay for the coffee separate. I don't want to wait."

The woman smiled. "I understand that." She looked to the man who had just come from the side room, presumably the kitchen. "Get me another iced coffee please, Sebastian."

"Sure, ma!" He set down a tray of drinks and ran back into the other room.

The woman turned to Lucy and told her the cost. By the time the exchange of money had occurred, Sebastian was back with a plastic tumbler. Lucy took the drink, thanked them both, and went to find Gia, who stood in front of a wall of gummies. The shelf wasn't floor to ceiling, but it was impressive. The different shapes and colors were in large glass mason jars.

"I want one of each."

Lucy pointed out the price, which was listed on a card near Gia. "Get a medium bag. It's not too bad."

Gia smiled. "Thank you. Joe's by the rock candy."

Lucy nodded and went to Joe, who was near a roll of candy dots on wax paper, not the rock candy. He smiled at her nervously.

"Mom and Dad don't like me having a lot of sugar too late at night. They say it keeps me up."

She leaned down to make it seem like she was sharing a secret. "Then don't eat all of it tonight."

Joe laughed and covered his face with his hands as if embarrassed. "I didn't think of that."

"Get a medium bag of candy." When he looked at her oddly, she held up a finger. She moved to the section of wall next to him, grabbed a medium bag off the shelf and handed it to Joe. "This size. It's priced mostly by what you can fit in it."

"What about rock candy? That won't really fit."

"That's a different size. You know how to read prices right?"

Gia came over at that moment and answered for him. "He does. He reads better than I did at his age. He's just used to Dad telling him everything."

"I am not!" came the singsong denial.

Gia stuck her tongue out at her brother.

Lucy shook her head and looked at Joe. "Figure it out, young man, and if there is something you don't understand, ask Gia or me."

He rolled his eyes, then went to a different part of the store, where the taffies were.

Lucy took a deep breath as she realized how many varieties there were in the store. "I don't think I've seen a shop like this in a long time, if ever."

"We come here once a year. They have this all the time."

"When I see variety like this, I worry about how much heat it all takes to make."

"Not enough to call a Bombardment. And I think they've figured out how to hide the heat by cooking almost in the open air, away from town. They'll probably tell you if you ask."

"Well, if they're amicable to questions, I have a different one for them." She looked at Gia. "You have what you want?"

Gia held up the very full bag. "Yep. I love gummies. I can only get them here."

Lucy nodded. "Let's go help your brother out."

"He doesn't need help."

"He hasn't chosen one thing. I want to sit down and enjoy the night air. There's a sign at the counter that says they have tables out back." Lucy's voice reflected her happiness.

"You sit a lot."

"Yes, but sitting on a horse is not the same as sitting in a chair."

Gia rolled her eyes. "Fine. Let's go help the booger."

Lucy laughed, and they headed over to Joe.

ᏏᏣᏏᏣᏏᏣ

The night air felt fine on her skin. Lucy removed her coat, draped it on the unused seat, and sat next to Gia. Joe had already run off with a group of kids his own age. His candy and drink were on the table, waiting for his return. Lucy saw Gia looking around from her seat across the table and gave her time to look. They were outside, in an enclosed courtyard. Lucy could tell the back entrance to the hotel was across from the candy store. There were a few other store entrances, but there was nothing to give away what they were, as there were no windows or signs. There were also a good number of tables, most with two or three people sitting at them.

"Lucy, did the Orators tell the truth on how this all came about?"

"From the information we were taught in school and what I've been able to read from very old newspapers, yes. I have to assume it wasn't as simple as what they showed tonight, but it was probably close."

"I've seen bits and pieces and read different history books, but it just doesn't make a lot of sense."

"Why not?"

"Why would we put that much faith in machines?"

"I have no idea, Gia. I don't know if we'll ever know."

Gia nodded, took a sip of her drink, then set it down and looked around. "There's a lot of people out here."

"Probably due to the Orators."

"Is it too many?"

"Shouldn't be." Lucy frowned. "What's on your mind, Gia? You know what causes Bombardments."

She shook her head. "I guess I was just thinking about when you traveled with us. I miss that."

"You miss that because you had a confidant."

Gia smiled. "Yes."

"Anything on your mind?"

Her face changed from contemplative to curious. "Actually, you said you had a question for the candy store, but then you didn't ask any. What did you want to ask?"

Lucy nodded slowly, leaned back in her chair, thought better of it, and looked behind her. When she saw that there was someone rather close to her back, Lucy shifted the chair and then leaned back.

"I wanted to find out why it's so green. I think I was here about ten years ago and it was a desert!"

"No, it was never a desert!" came the voice from behind her. Gia and Lucy looked at the man, who had a large smile on his face. He nodded to them both and tipped his straw hat. "May I continue?"

"Sure." Lucy stated with enthusiasm.

He shifted to look at them a bit better. The woman he was sitting with, Lucy noticed, rolled her eyes and picked up her book. Lucy turned her attention back to the man.

"We were never a desert. Out here it's always been dirt. It did get really dry, but we never had sand. When we were able to find the water table, we started irrigation. That brought back the trees and flowers!"

Lucy frowned in thought. "I thought the Red Rock was hurting the dirt?"

"In some areas, especially where the Bombardments happened, but not here. We weren't hit. All we needed was water."

"That's lucky."

"You're telling me! I have a farm. We're growing good quantities of food and can ship some off to areas that need it!"

"Including Under?" She knew that some places Above didn't like to ship Under, for reasons she couldn't discern.

"Absolutely! I'll sell to anyone."

The woman across from him made a loud noise.

"Oh, um, almost anyone." He gave Lucy and Gia a somber look. "We don't sell to Bandits."

Lucy and Gia nodded, then thanked the man for the information. He seemed about to say more, but the woman at his table made a noise again, as if annoyed, and he bid them goodnight.

SIXTEEN

Once settled back in her chair, Lucy heard the woman tell the man it was time to go. The couple left the area, and Lucy settled more fully into the seat. She didn't mind getting the information she wanted but knew his type. He was apt to talk their ears off. At times, Lucy looked forward to people like this, but tonight, she already had company.

She decided to start easy, as Gia still looked like she had a lot on her mind. "It's a nice night."

"It is. Do you know how long the Orators will be?"

"It varies. Your parents might take advantage of the free time, though."

"Good." She fell silent and started to look through her bag of candy, but Lucy could see she was deep in thought.

"You're old enough to Apprentice. Have you thought about what you're going to do?" Lucy knew she hit a sensitive topic when Gia went still. Though she was still looking into the bag of candy, Gia's eyes went to her hands, which slipped under the table.

"No."

Lucy shook her head. The girl was old enough to know the truth. "Did you know that when you lie, you look at your hands and start cleaning under your fingernails?"

Gia went completely still for a moment, then she looked up at Lucy. "Oh, wow."

"It happened when I traveled with you. Your parents know you do that too."

She rolled her eyes. "Oh, wow! No wonder they knew . . ." Gia hid her head in her hands. "I can't believe that."

"Take a minute, then answer my question, ok? Maybe I can help you through your thoughts."

Gia nodded and took a few minutes to gather her annoyance around her. When Gia's hands dropped back to the bag of candy, Lucy knew she was ok to talk.

"I don't know what I want to be, really, but I know I don't want to be a Scavenger."

"What does that mean to you?"

Gia sighed and leaned back in her chair. "I want to live in a town. I don't want to move from place to place, never having anywhere to call home. Dad says all the Broken States are our home, but I want a bed to sleep in every night. I want to wake up in the morning and open drapes and see the same thing every day. I don't want to roam anymore."

"That's a big decision."

"I haven't told my parents yet. I just keep saying I don't know."

"Have you picked a town?" Lucy grabbed her drink and took a long slow sip. It was starting to warm up, but it was still good.

"I think so."

"Did you know that hotels are great places to Apprentice if you don't know what to do?"

Gia sat up and looked at Lucy. "Really? Why?"

"When you Apprentice at a hotel, you get to learn from all the positions they hire for, not just one position. You can learn from the front desk clerk, the kitchen staff, and everything in between. With most other Apprentice positions, you get stuck with one."

"Oh." Gia leaned back in wonder.

"Here's some advice: start at a hotel. Unless you really hate one of the positions, stay in each for six months. It'll give you a good taste of what happens on a regular basis."

"What about if I hate all of it?"

"Have your parents told you much about how Apprenticeships work?"

"Not really. I don't know if either of them know. All my grandparents were Scavengers, and my parents learned from them."

"With an Apprenticeship, every six months, and at the end, you talk to your Teacher or Teachers. They have a list of questions that are geared toward helping you see what you liked and didn't like about the position. Then they look the answers over with you and help you to determine if you should stay or move on. And if you want to move on, they can help you determine what would be best to try next."

Gia's eyes were wide and gleamed with hope. "That sounds like what I need." The hope faded quickly. "How am I supposed to tell my parents?"

"I don't know, but I would suggest you tell them sooner rather than later, or you may find yourself a Scavenger for life."

The young woman sighed heavily and started playing with her drink. "I know."

Joe ran up to the table, stopping all talk. He sat heavily in a chair. "Hi!"

Gia shook her head. "Where did you come from? I didn't see your group playing."

"Terry's parents have a store on this block. Their basement is set up for kids to play in." He grabbed his drink and guzzled it down.

"Woah! Slow down!" She grabbed the drink carefully out of his hands. "You're going to make yourself sick."

"I didn't get anything sweet! I'm tired and hot. Give me that back."

"If you two don't settle down, I'll take you back to your parents now." Their voices were starting to get shrill, which Lucy disliked.

The kids both looked at Lucy, then settled back in their chairs.

"Sorry, Lucy."

"Yeah, sorry."

"Your sister is right. Drink it slow or get some water."

Joe nodded and took his drink back. This time, he drank it slowly. When he put the glass down, he looked at Gia. "How come Mom and Dad aren't coming to find us?"

"Are you tired?" She ran her hand through his hair, a gesture Lucy had seen Madeline perform many, many times.

"Yeah."

"We'll go look for them after you two finish your drinks, if you want to finish them. They need the glasses back, so you can't take them with you."

Joe looked at his half-finished drink. "I don't know if I want any more. It's good, but my stomach is already starting to hurt."

"You can leave it, it's ok." Lucy stated before Gia could say anything.

Joe looked surprised. "Are you sure? Mom hates it when I do that."

"Well, it's my money and I said it's ok."

Joe gave her a grateful smile but still took another drink. They gathered their things. By the time they were ready to part, he had finished most of the drink and proclaimed that his stomach did not hurt. Gia rolled her eyes at him, and they left the courtyard.

ଽ୦ଓଽ୦ଓଽ୦ଓ

The Orators had packed up by the time the trio reached the field. As soon as Joe saw his parents, he ran off, which gave Lucy another moment with Gia.

"Don't forget what we talked about. And give your parents a chance. They love you. They want what's best for you. And they never struck me as the type of people who wouldn't allow their children their own lives."

"It's hard, though. I'm thinking about a town that's on their route, but that means I won't see them much."

"It'll give you time to figure out how much you miss them. It might make you change your mind, or it might make you appreciate them more. Give yourself that chance, Gia."

They were almost at the Riccis' blanket now, and Gia stopped to look at Lucy. "How come you know so much?"

"It's amazing what people will tell a Hired Hand. I had one client hire me specifically to advise them on what to do with their life. Also, I do a lot of observing. You learn a lot by watching people, especially if they're talking to other people."

Gia giggled. "I'll keep that in mind."

The ladies smiled at each other, then continued to the Riccis. Lucy bid them goodnight, gave hugs all around, and left the family alone. They needed their time.

Lucy woke early the next morning and found where the Riccis were staying. Antonio was awake but made shushing noises and pulled Lucy away from the wagon. He gave her a hug and patted her on the back.

"Gia said you advised her about life last night. Thank you. We knew she wanted to Apprentice, but she wouldn't tell us where. Last night, she did."

"She would have come around eventually without me."

"But now she can start. Thank you."

"You're welcome."

"I have something for you. Wait here."

Lucy tried to stop him, but Antonio was quicker than she was and slipped to his wagon. She was too far away to see what he was doing, but eventually, he came back and handed her a brown leather bundle. She took it and her eyes went wide.

"What's this?"

"Something I've been keeping for you on the off chance we ran into each other again. It should fit."

Lucy found the edges of the bundle, grasped it, and allowed the rest to fall away. It was a light brown leather coat that looked a lot like hers. It looked to be her size and closed with buttons, just like the one she had on. It looked brand new, and in fact, still had faded, plastic tags on it.

"Where did you find this? It looks brand new."

"It was buried under a lot of other things that people had overlooked."

"For eighty years?"

"We Scavengers still have jobs for a reason. I can't tell you how many times I've found usable items in places that have been thoroughly picked over, including by me."

"Antonio, I can't-"

"Don't finish that sentence. You can and you will. I can't tell you how many times you helped us out, including last night. Take it as payment for all those times."

Lucy gave Antonio a steady look, which he returned. She finally nodded, as did he. "All right. Thank you, Antonio. Mine's getting a little worn in some places."

"You are welcome." He held his arms out. Lucy draped the coat over one arm and embraced Antonio.

They let go, and he helped her get rid of the plastic tags. She slipped on the new coat and found that it fit perfectly. Lucy smiled, took everything out of the pockets of her old coat, then handed the old one to Antonio. Scavengers were the best people to give old clothing to. They always knew what to do with them.

Once the new coat was on, Lucy said goodbye again. "Give Madeline and the kids hugs and tell Gia good luck, all right?"

"I will. I'll send word to Meridune once Gia is settled, so you know where she ends up."

"I would appreciate that."

"Of course. You're family, Lucy."

She smiled, gave him one last hug, and went on her way. Lucy wanted to travel with the Riccis, but they were headed southeast, and she was headed southwest. Lucy went back to the hotel, mounted Lance, and headed on her way.

SEVENTEEN

Lucy's first stop in Stockton was a horse ranch. She had been traveling for more than a week now and had visited more towns than she could remember the names of. Before going to Stockton, she'd led Lance down a steep hill that shifted and crumbled as they walked down it. Since then, Lance had developed a limp. She was worried for her horse, whom she needed. Though many towns between here and Sacramento had figured out irrigation, much of the land in between the cities was arid and hot. Too hot to be without a horse. In the last town she visited, there had been signs for a horse ranch, aptly named Four Legs. The signs stated the ranch was near or in Stockton.

At the last town, Lucy didn't pay much attention to the cute painted signs of smiling horses, but once Lance started to limp, she remembered and started looking for more of their signs on the road. Now, as she stood in the front yard of the place, she tied Lance to the post outside the house and patted his neck. He neighed in a sad way. Lucy knew something was wrong with that sound. He never complained about anything.

Lucy moved toward the front door, but it opened before she climbed the steps.

"Morning!" The young girl's voice was open and friendly. "Welcome to Four Legs Ranch. How can we help you?"

There were hurried footsteps from inside the house, and a man appeared. Though most of his face was covered by a thick beard, it was obvious by the shape of the man's eyes and the high hairline that he was the child's father. "Now, Catrina, what have I told you?"

The little girl rolled her eyes dramatically. "But you were busy!"

"Go inside, little miss!"

She huffed dramatically and stomped back into the house.

Lucy looked at the man and raised an eyebrow. He looked her over, let his eyes stay on her right lapel for a few seconds, then held out his hand.

"I'm Max. This is my ranch. We've had some trouble with Bandits lately. How can I help you?"

She took his hand. "I'm Lucy. Lance started limping about a mile from here. I need to make sure it's not serious. I looked at his leg, but I couldn't see or feel any injuries."

"Take him to the barn around the side." He let go of her hand and pointed to her right. "My wife and eldest are there and can take a look. We're all trained."

Lucy nodded, tipped her hat, and turned back to Lance. She untied his reins and led him around the right as Max went back inside.

To the right of the house sat a large, new-looking barn. There was a fenced-in field behind it where horses were running or walking around. Some were standing or lying down as well. The main door to the barn was open, and she could see stalls, more horses, and a few people. A young man, who also had a high hairline, smiled and broke away from the group to come talk to her.

"Hello, I'm Charlie. How can I help you?"

"I'm Lucy. This is Lance. He's got a limp, and I don't know why."

Charlie reached for the reins, and Lucy placed the leather in the young man's hands. As Charlie walked Lance in a small circle, he asked questions.

"When did it start?"

"About a mile away from here, near the last town I was in."

"A mile, which direction?"

"Northeast. I don't remember the name of the town. We were coming down a mountain. I was walking him, and he slipped. He caught his balance, but then he started to limp."

"The terrain is a little different in each direction you come from. North is more gravel from the old asphalt roads. It's easy to slip up." Charlie stopped walking, then hunkered down to touch Lance's leg. When the horse didn't make a noise, he stood. "I'm going to take him into the barn and take off his shoe. I want to take a better look at the hoof."

"That's fine. I'm actually looking for information on someone too. Mind if I ask you?"

He turned and looked her over. Like his father, Charlie looked at her right lapel. He nodded, then looked into her eyes and nodded again. "Yep. Come on."

She followed as he led the way into the barn. "I'm looking for a couple who may own a pet shop around here. They would be selling Red Rock mutated animals. Have you heard of anything like that?"

As he secured Lance in a stall, Charlie frowned. "I can't remember if I heard about a pet shop selling mutated animals, but a new pet shop did open about a month ago. It's on the other side of town from us." He turned to Lucy. "Mind taking his saddle and bags off? You can put them in the chest." He pointed to a chest at the end of the stall. "I'm going to get tools."

Lucy nodded and went to work as Charlie moved away. The chest was large enough to accommodate the saddle and the bags, with plenty of room to spare. She moved everything off Lance except his bridle and reins. By the time she was done, Charlie was back with tools. Without being told, Lucy moved out of the stall and kept silent as Charlie went to work on Lance's shoe. Though Lance did neigh in a way Lucy hadn't heard before, he stood still and allowed Charlie to do as he needed. Once the horseshoe was off, Charlie hissed. Lucy didn't like the sound.

"I'm sorry, Lance's hoof is split. It's bad, too." He looked into her eyes. "You're not going to be able to ride him for a while."

"Damn." Her hand went to Lance's head and patted him softly.

"It'll heal up," Charlie said in a comforting way.

"Sure, but those can take a while to heal. I need him now. I can't wait."

Charlie looked at the group of people that were still outside, then back to Lucy. "Ma can give you a better estimate on the time it'll take to heal, but she's busy right now. The shop isn't that far away on foot, even though it's on the other side of town. It takes about fifteen minutes to get there."

"How's the heat around here though?"

"It's not too bad right now. We're getting into the cooler months."

"Is there a path? I'm not from around here."

He grinned. "I figured. There's a dirt road from here to town."

Lucy nodded, then shook her head in disbelief. "I haven't been without a horse in a long time."

He gave her an odd look. "It's just across town."

Lucy gave him a mock angry look. "I don't go anywhere without Lance."

Charlie smiled. "I get that. Ma'll tell you more later. We have a bunkhouse here if you need a place to rest. We offer dinner too, all for a modest price."

"Does the bunkhouse have a bathroom?"

"Three separate rooms with tubs and running water. No extra charge."

She smiled. Her last real bath had been back in Meridune, about three weeks ago. She wanted a real scrub down, and needed to braid her hair again. "Sounds like a plan to me." Lucy looked at the chest with her belongings. There was a lid leaning open against the wall. "My stuff safe here?"

Charlie stood, took a few steps to the chest, lowered the lid, locked it with the key in the lock, and handed Lucy the key. "It's safe."

She smiled. "That's a nice service."

"We're one of the largest horse vets in the area. We know how to keep horses and humans safe."

"I like that." Lucy sighed, looked at Lance, and placed a hand on his back. "You be good to them, all right?" She looked at Charlie. "I'll be back later. Thank you for taking care of Lance."

"Welcome. Dinner's at six."

"Thank you!" With one more wistful look at Lance, Lucy set out.

☙◌☙◌☙◌

The walk down the road was pleasant but felt lonely. Though Lucy did walk on her own two feet when she was traveling, it was usually beside Lance. He wasn't very vocal, but she missed hearing his gentle breathing and occasional neigh. Lucy shook her head at her own annoyance and paused. She was at the edge of town. It looked like most towns in the Above: wooden structures, boardwalk, dirt road. The stores had signs advertising their function, and there were some people walking about but not many.

On the other side of town from where she stood, she saw the sign for the pet store. "Watsom's Inferno Pets." Lucy sighed heavily at the name, then startled as a sound interrupted her thoughts. She looked to the left, into the alley beside her, but didn't see anything. The odd squawk came again and drew her attention to the ground.

The rust-colored animal flopped around on the dirt street, its wings flapping half-heartedly, as if trying to fly. Lucy moved closer and peered at it. There was enough light in the alley to see that the animal had no eyes but had a beak. The body ended in tentacles. She realized it was struggling to breathe.

Lucy's head drew back in disgust as she grimaced. She watched it flop around for a short moment, then stepped forward and brought her heavy heel down on the poor thing's head. There was a crunch of skull, and a final squawk cut short by death as Lucy ended its life. She shook her head, then turned and glared at the pet shop. She moved closer to the nearest building, where a patch of weeds served to clean her boot off.

Lucy hated the mutated animals. Most that survived were aggressive, like the Howlers. Most didn't survive, though, and ended up like the thing on her boot: sightless and unable to breathe. Why anyone would want to try and sell the animals was beyond Lucy's understanding.

Boot clean, Lucy started toward the pet shop, scowling in annoyance. As she neared, she saw a group of two adults and three times as many kids walk off the boardwalk and into the pet store. It stopped her cold. There was no way she was going into the shop behind a large family. She wouldn't be able to talk freely if the shop was full. Lucy's eyes moved to the store sign next to the pet shop, and she smiled. "Helen's Good Eats" made her stomach growl.

Anger pushed aside for hunger, she moved to the restaurant. It was crowded, and Lucy realized it was lunchtime and she'd barely had any breakfast. Some of the patrons looked her way, but she ignored them and moved to a free stool at the bar. The bartender acknowledged her with a nod. It was busy, but a moment later the woman was in front of Lucy, a smile on her face.

"Welcome! New in town?" The voice was friendly, but had an edge to it, as if she had put up with enough in life and wasn't going to take any more shit.

"Passing through." Lucy smiled at the bartender as the woman looked her up and down. Her eyes seemed to rest on her right lapel. Lucy liked when people did that. It meant they knew what to look for and how to act toward Hired Hands. Despite how popular Hired Hands were, some people didn't know the rules, didn't know that if the pin was obviously displayed, they were on the job and weren't a threat. Only Hired Hands who didn't show their pin were trouble.

"I'm Helen." She held out her hand. Her nails were short but well cared for with red nail polish. The polish matched the lipstick and red wire-rimmed glasses. Lucy was impressed. People didn't do their nails or wear make-up unless they had a lot of money to buy the products or could make it themselves. She had a feeling this woman took great care to make the products herself.

Lucy took the woman's hand and shook it. "Lucy."

"What can I do you for?" Helen stated plainly as she took her hand back.

"Do you serve breakfast all day?"

"Sure do. I can get you a menu, if you want?"

"No thank you. Eggs, meat, cheese, and bread. Don't care what type of eggs, meat, or cheese your cook uses."

Helen gave her a smile. "Well, that's fun!"

Lucy smiled. "I like surprises."

"All righty then. Anything else?"

"Coffee. Black. And information if you have time for it."

The woman smiled, and it lit up her brown eyes. "Let me get this order in. I can probably talk for a moment or two."

"Thank you."

Helen smiled, turned, and headed to an open space in the wall. "Give me a number three!"

"Sure, Mom!" came a higher pitched, masculine voice from the kitchen.

Lucy watched as Helen poured a cup of coffee and brought the larger mug over. It was a plain brown ceramic mug that looked like it could be used as a weapon, as it had thick walls. Helen set it down in front of Lucy and smiled.

"What information are you looking for"

"What can you tell me about the pet shop next door?"

"They sell the mutated animals. They seem to do well. My son wants to get one of the animals, but he hasn't decided on which one, yet."

"Do the owners come over here much?"

"Maxine does! I love her style! She's always dressed in purple and has the best outfits! She sews all her own clothing."

Lucy nodded as she sipped some coffee. The liquid slid past her tongue and down her throat in a warm cascade. She smacked her lips. "Good coffee. Do you know where the couple came from?"

"I think they said east, but almost everyone is from east of here."

Helen laughed, then turned when she heard her name being called. "I'll be right there, Marge!" She turned to Lucy. "Enjoy the coffee. Refills are free. Food should be up soon."

Lucy nodded and watched as Helen went off to take care of other customers. She didn't have a chance to say anything else to the bartender, as Helen was too busy to talk. Her food arrived about ten minutes later and took most of her attention. The omelet was thick with meat and cheese. There was fruit on the side, and toast. Though her first bite was full of cheese and meat, she couldn't identify what she was eating. That didn't surprise her with the cheese. A lot of towns made their own cheese, and all of it tasted different. The meat was gamey and sweet but didn't taste like anything she remembered. It was tasty, though, so she didn't think much about it as she devoured her food.

About halfway through breakfast, a conversation to the right caught her attention. She didn't want it to, as it was about the Bombardment, but the people were talking loudly.

"I tell ya! I bet once we're able to get up there, it'll be aliens!"

The group, about four of them, were all dressed alike in dusty jeans and T-shirts of various styles. From the tans on their arms and the dirt on their lower legs and boots, Lucy guessed farmers. Most had beards and wore either straw hats or leather cowboy hats, like hers.

"Gerard, you tell us that crazy theory one more time, and I'll wallop you!" This came from a person who was shorter than Gerard. They had their fist in the air, almost threateningly. Gerard didn't flinch.

A calmer voice added their opinions. "Come on, Bruce, you've had a rough day. Don't fight with Gerard because of it. And Gerard, you really have got to stop this talk. Everyone knows we did it to ourselves. We sent those damned AI machines to mine the asteroids, and they decided to do their own thing."

"But that doesn't make any sense! I read up on this! We programmed them not to harm us. We programmed them to mine. That's it. They didn't have the intelligence to think for themselves!" His voice was getting louder as if he wanted everyone in the bar to hear him.

Lucy shook her head in disbelief as the rest of the group told Gerard to stop. The man with the calmer voice spoke again and encouraged the others to change the subject. Lucy silently thanked the man and went back to her food. She had heard all kinds of theories on the subject and had to admit aliens taking over the AI miners was the most outlandish one. She smiled, mentally added that to her list of conspiracy theories, and finished her breakfast.

EIGHTEEN

Once she was done with her food, Lucy walked over to the pet shop. As the door opened, a bell sounded overhead.

"Be with you in just a minute!"

The deep baritone voice sent a shiver of pleasure down Lucy's spine. She moved into the store and listened as the owner, presumably, spoke with another customer. Lucy wandered the shop and looked in the cages, terrariums, and aquariums. The animals were all shades of red, to blend in with the Red Rock that fell from the sky and changed the landscape. Since the Red Rock was still in isolated places, and the animals were not, it only made them easier to see.

Lucy stopped at a terrarium and watched the lizards. These didn't look too mutated, except they were a rust-burgundy shade. As she observed them, though, one opened its mouth and breathed a bit of fire. She drew back from the glass, glad the thing couldn't breathe fire on her.

"That's our most popular animal. We call it a dragon, but the official name is Fire Lizard. It may look fierce, but it's harmless."

The baritone voice cascaded down her spine again, and she turned to greet its owner. She smiled at the woman in front of her. This had to be

Maxine. She wore a royal purple hat that fit tight to her head and had wide straight sides that fell almost to her eyebrows. There were purple and gold feathers on one side, and a veil that fell over one eye. Her suit was also royal purple and looked brand new. The jacket was tight-fitting against her modest chest, made larger by the frilly white shirt. There was a gold flower in her buttonhole that matched the feather in her hat. Her pants were straight and tight. Her shoes were dark brown work shoes that didn't quite match the outfit. Shoes weren't always easy to find, though, and you took what you could get.

It took very little time to assess the woman, and Lucy had her hand out quickly. "You must be Maxine. I'm Lucy. I was hired to find you and talk to you."

Maxine had been extending her hand in response to Lucy, but she quickly withdrew her arm with her words. "Hired?"

Lucy tapped her right lapel below the HH pin. "I'm a Hired Hand." When Maxine looked terrified, Lucy said it again, "I was hired to *talk* to you. I promise."

"I'm sorry. It's been . . . there's . . ." But it didn't look like she knew what to say.

"You don't have to explain anything to me, ma'am. Do you mind if we talk privately, though? This is a little personal. I would like to talk to your partner too, if he's here?"

"Watsom's out searching for more animals. He won't be back until tonight."

"Do you mind talking to me alone, then? I can at least see if you're the couple I'm looking for."

"Oh!" She looked surprised. "I suppose so." She looked at her watch. "I can lock the door and say I'm at lunch. I haven't had a chance to eat yet.

You can wait for me by the counter. It's in the back."

She went to the door as Lucy walked to the front counter. Lucy heard the door being locked as she looked at the counter. It was cluttered with various brochures about mutated animals. She picked one up and flipped it open quickly. There were hand-drawn pictures and a lot of text inside of it. She placed it back as Maxine showed up.

"You can follow me to the back," the woman said as she walked through a doorway into the backroom.

Lucy followed her and sat in the offered chair, opposite Maxine. Lucy had expected a desk, but there wasn't one. There were, however, shelves of empty cages, both glass and wired.

"Expecting to get a lot of animals?"

"Watsom's been capturing more and more animals lately. We wanted to be prepared."

Lucy nodded.

"So what is this about?" Maxine sounded worried.

"I was hired to find a certain couple that used an Escort in one of the towns on the train west. Did you and Watsom come from the east a couple seasons ago?"

"We did."

"Did you frequent any saloons?"

"We . . . partook of some saloon services along the way, yes."

Lucy nodded. "Have you been tested for the Red Death?"

Maxine's eyes went wide. "Yes! Both when we left and when we arrived. We're both negative."

Lucy nodded again. "Good, good." She paused, licked her lips, and leaned forward in her chair. "Do you remember a town called Meridune?"

Maxine frowned. "Is that one of the towns along the railroad?"

"It's Above, but yes."

"I don't know. I'm not great with names."

"How about the people you slept with along the way, do you remember any of them?"

Maxine blushed. "Though we were interested in the services, we didn't learn their names."

"If I may ask, why didn't you and your partner just get a room to yourself?"

Maxine sighed heavily. "That's . . ." She seemed to think about it, then shook her head. "I don't really want to talk about that."

"No worries. None of my business anyway. I do need to ask, though, did you . . ." She paused and wondered how to approach the subject. She assumed this was the right couple, but she didn't know fully. Lucy decided to plunge on. "Did you or your partner . . ." an old word popped into her head, "consummate . . . with any of the women?"

Maxine looked confused and shook her head. "I don't know what that word means?"

Time to be blunt, Lucy thought as she pursed her lips. "Did either of you ejaculate inside any of the women?"

Maxine's eyes went wide. "Oh! No. We . . . no, that's not what we prefer."

"All right."

Maxine looked curious now. "May I ask what this is about?"

"You and your partner hired an Escort that ended up pregnant and with the Red Death. She's pretty sure neither of you got her pregnant, but she wasn't sure about the Red Death."

Maxine placed both her hands over her heart. "The poor dear. What's her name?"

"Grace."

Maxine seemed to think about it for a moment, then shook her head. "I don't even remember that name. I feel bad about it now."

Her low baritone voice sounded even lower filled with sorrow. Lucy felt the woman was telling the truth. She described Grace, but it didn't jog any memories. She tried one more tactic. "Might have been kids toys in the room."

Maxine snapped her fingers. "Grace and Gracie!"

Lucy gave a slight laugh. "Yes."

"I do remember her but only because I almost fell on top of Grace when I tripped over a toy. Watsom caught me, but it could have been terribly embarrassing."

Lucy had a genuine smile on her face. "They've seen worse."

"Sure, but I don't like doing things like that."

Lucy laughed. "Most people don't."

They both sobered, and Maxine looked sadly at Lucy. "I'm sorry that happened to her. Is the baby going to survive the Red Death?"

"We don't know."

"So she's trying to find the person who gave her the Red Death and the person who got her pregnant?"

"Yep. She thinks it's the same person though."

"Oh, well . . . well that just doesn't sound very promising for either of them."

"It's a tough situation."

Maxine started to fidget with some stray lint on her suit. "May I ask more questions?"

"You can, but please keep in mind, some information is confidential."

"Ah. Well, then," she frowned, "what does the word 'consummate' mean? I've never heard it before."

"It's an old term. From the way back before the Bombardment, before most of that history. It's a word used in literature to mean the groom fucked his bride and made their marriage legit."

"Oh."

Lucy smiled, showing off her large white teeth. "I read a lot."

"Ah. Hmmm. Interesting."

Lucy smiled again, then stood. "Well, I have my information, so I'm going to head out." She held out her hand to Maxine. "Thank you for your time, ma'am."

Maxine stood and shook Lucy's hand. "Thank you too. I'm sorry if I was afraid of you to begin with."

"No problem." She let go of Maxine's hand. "We get that a lot. But here's a tip: always look at a person's right lapel. That's where the HH pin is supposed to go. If you see it, you're safe."

"And if I don't see it?"

"That means it's a regular person. Hired Hands on duty are required to wear their pin."

"But what if they've been hired to kill or kidnap someone?"

"Sorry if this startles you, but if they're going to kidnap you, you won't see them until you wake up in their custody. If they're hired to kill you, you'll never see them."

Maxine's eyes were wide. "Oh."

Lucy tipped her hat to Maxine. "Have a good day."

With that, Lucy let herself out of the pet shop.

ജ്ഞങ്ങജ്ഞ

Lucy made her way back to the Four Legs Ranch, mentally crossing the couple off her list. They weren't the ones who got Grace pregnant, and they weren't the ones who gave her the Red Death, which meant she was now on an even wilder chase. Deter said he was headed west to mine, which narrowed the search a bit, but not by much. The mines out here took up a large area. She wasn't sure why. For a long time, the story was that the scientists in the Under were studying the Red Rock.

Slowly, rumors came that Scavengers and scientists were looking for technology lost during the first Bombardment, but that didn't make much sense to Lucy. Most of the tech, as far as she understood, had been above ground and therefore destroyed by the first Bombardment. There were also rumors of cities being built under the ocean as a way of masking heat. Lucy didn't know much about tunneling, so she didn't know if it was even possible to build under an ocean. She hoped to find out more the farther south she went but wasn't sure that would happen. Information on the mines was usually found in the Under, and she didn't like being Under. Wide open spaces were her thing.

Most of the mines were farther south than Old San Francisco. There were some in operation in cooperation with Mexico. Lucy had heard rumors of collaborations in that area but wasn't sure how much was rumor and how much was hope. She mentally shrugged and let her thoughts go as she found herself back at the ranch. She turned her steps to the barn and saw Charlie just inside, mucking out a stable.

"Hello," she called out when she was close enough.

Charlie turned and nodded. He then turned his head and yelled into the barn. "Ma! Lucy's back! That's Lance's owner."

"Coming!" came a voice from farther in.

Charlie turned back to Lucy. "She'll be right with you. Lance is still in the stall. Ma walked him a little bit, but he started limping, so she brought him back in and gave him a low dose of pain relievers."

Lucy nodded, but before she could say anything, a woman in jeans and green T-shirt came out of the barn's gloom. Her hair was tied back in a bun. Her shoes were quiet on the dirt floor. She held out her hand as she approached.

"Lucy? I'm Kiera."

Lucy nodded as she took Kiera's hand and shook it. "Pleasure. I was told you could tell me more about Lance?"

Kiera let her hand go and nodded. "I can't tell you too much more. Hoof's split. Charlie said you seemed to understand that type of injury can take a while to heal. Really not much we can do but wait."

"I get that, but I'm on Assignment and it's time sensitive."

Lucy watched as Kiera's eyes went to her right lapel. She nodded, but her voice sounded sad. "The best I can do is offer you another horse."

Lucy shook her head. She didn't want another horse but knew it might come to this. "Damn. I got him three years ago. I like keeping them a bit longer than that."

"I'm sorry."

Lucy sighed. Kiera did sound sorry at least. "How much is it going to cost me, anyway?"

"Not as much as you might think. Lance is in good shape, and he's young. Once this hoof heals, we'll be able to either use him or sell him. We're not losing anything. A fair trade might be possible."

Lucy's eyes went wide. She hadn't expected this. "Oh. That changes things a bit."

"Feels a bit better?"

She nodded. "Yeah."

"Do you want to come look at the horses we have? If you can stay here a few days, you can figure out, of the ones we can trade, which one suits you best?"

"I like doing that. I can spare a few days if you know someone in this area who knows the mines? I'm looking for someone."

"I work mainly with horses. My husband might be able to tell you who to talk to."

"Well, I'll take that chance." She felt a little more optimistic about this entire situation. It would be even better if she didn't have to settle for a bad fit with a horse and could get information on the mines.

Kiera nodded and pointed toward the field to the side of the barn. "Most of our horses are in the field. Let's go take a look."
Lucy nodded and followed Kiera to the fence.

NINETEEN

Kiera and Lucy stood by the fence and watched the horses in the pen. There were probably a dozen or so. Most were brown and tan, like Lance, but a couple were black or white. One was black and white, like a cow. Its head was black, as was its mane and tail. Its body was black and white. It was beautiful, and full of spunk. It bucked as it moved across the field.

"That's a feisty one." Lucy observed with a little disdain.

"That would be Bucky." When Lucy snickered, Kiera continued. "He did that as soon as he could stand. It made him stumble, but once he was upright, he did it again."

Lucy frowned. "Must be a handful when he's being ridden."

"That's the odd part. He doesn't do it if he has a saddle on him, even if there isn't a rider."

Lucy nodded as she watched Bucky move across the field. She shook her head as she realized he was heading to them. Her frown came back when Bucky neared the fence, as he turned and seemed to catch her eye.

"Oh, no." Lucy's eyes went wide, and her voice sounded annoyed, even to herself. It wasn't the first time a horse had chosen her but, in the past, she had wanted the horse that chose her.

Bucky neighed, shook his head as if showing off his well-cared for mane, then pranced off a bit. Kiera laughed as Bucky turned and pranced back, as if showing himself off.

"He likes you."

"Nope. I want a brown and tan horse. Standard colors."

"Bucky's a good horse. I think he wants to be out of this pasture."

As if understanding Kiera was talking about him, Bucky moved closer to her and placed his head near her. She started to stroke the bridge of his nose. "He's a good horse, like I said. Young too. Only two. He's fully trained with a saddle and reins. Picks up on command words fast. You can teach him what you're used to using, if you don't want to learn what we trained him with."

Lucy reached out and stroked Bucky's nose as well. He made a satisfied noise and seemed happy to be touched, but she shook her head. "I really do have a preference for a brown and tan horse."

"Sometimes the horse chooses the owner."

"Though that is true, I've only looked at the horses for a few minutes. Let me take a few days to decide."

Kiera nodded. "Of course, you're the customer. Come on, I'll have you meet a few more horses."

Lucy nodded, gave Bucky one more pat, and followed Kiera into the pasture. While she walked around, she realized that Bucky was always a few steps away.

☙ଔ☙ଔ☙ଔ

Four days later, Lucy found herself outside the small town of Jose, which was south of what used to be San Jose. She only knew this as she had passed the city limits sign a few miles back. Yes, the green had mostly flaked off, and the "San Jose" lettering was more gray than white, but the metal looked to be in good shape and didn't have bullet holes or rust in it. By now, most old road signs had been taken down for their metal. She was amazed the sign was still there.

Jose was the first town in a long line of mining towns. There were a few along the coast, though, that were more for beginners. Max had informed her that this was one of them. She hoped to get information on Deter but knew it would not be as easy as finding the pet shop. For one, there were more mines than pet shops.

Lucy sighed and urged Bucky into a steady walk. She still marveled at the fact that she had made the trade for this horse. He was young and stubborn when able to walk freely, but once that saddle was on him, he knew how to control himself. He was a good horse, but she missed Lance. Brown horses made more sense in the desert, as they were better camouflaged. Piebald coloring like Bucky's did well if there were shadows and other alternating colors.

Back home, in the real desert, there weren't too many variations in color. But Bucky had insisted. Anytime she tried to ride another horse, Bucky stepped in and nuzzled her, to the point of gently pushing her away from the other horses. Kiera thought it amusing but did put Bucky away so Lucy could try out other horses. Thing was, she wasn't happy with any other horse. None of them seemed to connect with her as much as Bucky did. Therefore, despite what she wanted, she was here, with Bucky.

Lucy chuckled as those thoughts went through her head. So far, Bucky had proven himself. She was sure he would continue to be a good steed. For now, though, she turned her thoughts to the town ahead of her and watched as it grew closer. Soon enough, Lucy found herself in front of the tavern. She dismounted, tied Bucky's reins to the post, and headed inside to what she knew would not be her last tavern.

꙰ꙮ꙰ꙮ꙰ꙮ

Lucy sat heavily on the barstool, and tried to remember how many taverns and saloons she had been in recently. She left Jose what felt like yesterday, but was probably more like two weeks ago. It had been a long, slow road full of the same type of people and the same questions. The towns ran together and the names were a mystery. As the bartender of this newest tavern came up to her, Lucy tried a smile. The place was nearly empty, but it was midmorning. It was possible the townspeople were working.

The bartender nodded at her. "You look like you've had a rough morning. Need some breakfast?"

"Yeah. Whatever you have that resembles eggs, cheese, and meat. I'm not picky, as long as it tastes good." Her voice sounded dull, even to herself.

The woman looked at Lucy. "You sound like you've had a rough road too."

"You know where Jose is? The town up north?"

The woman nodded as she indicated the coffee pot behind her. When Lucy nodded, she grabbed a mug and poured Lucy a drink. "I've heard of it. It's where the mines start. A lot of people moved through there to get to here."

"I've been making my way south. I started in Sacramento, at the train station, and have been working my way down for . . ." Lucy stared off into the distance, "I really have no idea how long we've been traveling. Well," she corrected herself, "my horse and I." Lucy frowned. "What month is it?"

"It's halfway through August."

Lucy's eyes grew wide. "A month and a half then."

"That's a long time to travel, but then, I don't like to travel." The mug was placed in front of her, and the bartender pointed over her shoulder. "I'll get your order in. Did you need milk or sweetener for your coffee?"

Lucy shook her head as she picked up the cup and drank half of it down before tasting it. "That's good coffee. I like it black."

The woman laughed. "I can tell. I'll be back."

Lucy nodded, and the bartender went through a door, presumably to the kitchen. Most taverns had windows people yelled through, but this place seemed a bit bigger than others she'd visited. The woman was back quickly. She placed her arms on the bar top and looked at Lucy.

"Name's Bea."

"Lucy."

"What brings you by, Lucy?"

"I'm looking for a miner. Maybe you can help me?" Lucy set the empty mug down and watched in happiness as Bea turned, grabbed the coffee pot, and refilled her mug.

"I can try. We get a lot of them."

"Sounds like he's from Deutschland, has a name that's close to Deter, but hates the nickname."

Bea set the pot on the burner and shook her head. "That's not a lot to go on."

"I know."

"Why are you looking for him, if you don't mind my asking?"

"I was hired to find him to ask him some questions."

Bea nodded then shook her head. "One of my brothers is a Hired Hand. The kinds of jobs he gets," she shook her head, "I could never do it."

"And I could never sit behind a bar and be nice to people."

Bea laughed. It was a rich laughter that told volumes. "Oh honey, I'm only nice if they're nice to me. The instant they're assholes, I kick 'em out."

Lucy laughed. "Good."

They shared a smile, then Bea took a breath. "The best place to see miners, outside of mines, is the dining hall. A lot of mining camps have them. And, since the towns always try and get the miners out into the fresh air at the end of the day, they're all above ground."

Lucy's eyes lit up. Most of the mining camps were underground but had towns Above. Since she preferred to be Above, a dining hall would make it easier for her to see and talk to the miners. She frowned. "You're the first person who's told me about that. Do all towns have them?"

"No. It started south of here, I think in Mexico, and it's slowly creeping its way north. More and more places will have them, I think."

"All right. Good." Lucy was relieved. It irked her to think she might have missed something like that in the other towns.

"It does mean you'll have to stay until dinner."

"That's all right. Is there a room available anywhere? I don't think I saw a saloon or a hotel."

Bea shook her head, and her blond curls scattered. "They're both Under."

"Damn. I prefer being Above."

Bea looked her up and down. "I can lend you my bed."

Lucy frowned in disbelief. "That's generous."

Bea shrugged. "I'm not using it right now." A soft look came into her eyes. "And if I help you, then maybe someone helps my brother when he needs it."

Lucy nodded once. "I get that. All right. I appreciate the offer."

"You can stable your horse around back, if you like. The dining hall is that way too. It'll be a couple more minutes for your breakfast. I had to wake up the cook. Dad's a bit old."

"All right. Much obliged. I'll be back."

"You bet."

Lucy nodded again then went to take care of Bucky.

☙ℭ☙ℭ☙ℭ

That night, Lucy found her way to the dining hall. Bea told her they started serving at 5:30, so she went at six, to give people time to settle and eat. Dinner smelled great, but she couldn't tell what it was by the smell. There were scents of grilled food, but everything mixed in the air. She arrived at the hall and got in the short line. The people around her mumbled to each other, but no one said anything to her. She didn't mind, it gave her time to look around.

The hall was just that: a long room with many tables and benches that ran the length of it. The room was filling up fast, but she could still see people standing in another line just inside the door. The line wound around the room to a window in the far wall. There were plates being passed to the people in line, who would then be ushered to an empty seat at a table. It seemed rather organized.

"Next!" said a voice at the front of the line.

Lucy looked and saw a boy about ten behind a pedestal. She moved forward. "Hi."

"Employee number?" He didn't look up.

"I'm not an employee," she said, congenially.

"Employees only. Next!"

Lucy added a touch of authority to her voice. "I'm not moving until you address me fully."

That worked. The boy looked up at her with eyes wide. "Um . . ."

"Name's Lucy. I'm a Hired Hand. I have a question for you or someone in charge."

The boy yelled over his shoulder as he stared at Lucy. "John!"

A man in clean shirt and jeans broke away from a group of people and came right over. He looked Lucy over, seemed to realize something, and held out his hand to her.

"I'm John. Is there a problem?"

She took his hand. "I'm Lucy. I'm a Hired Hand. I was trying to tell him I'm looking for information."

"Trevor's my Apprentice. It's his first week."

She gave a grin. "And you didn't teach him about Hired Hands on his first day?"

John chuckled. "Ah, no. We don't often get many here, well, that announce themselves."

Lucy nodded but didn't say anything.

John turned to Trevor. "I want you to take a good look at Lucy, Trevor. See the pin on her right lapel? The HH stands for Hired Hand. Do you know what they are?"

"We kind of learned of them in the Under."

"A Hired Hand is someone you can hire to do almost anything, as long as they agree to the price. If someone comes in with a pin like that and wants information, it's up to you to decide if you're going to help them. You don't have to."

Lucy nodded in agreement.

Trevor looked at both of them as if confused.

"Why don't you go outside with Lucy and see what she wants. I'll take care of the workers."

Trevor frowned. "It's my decision?"

"It is." John looked at Lucy. "Will you tell him why?"

"Sure will."

Trevor thought about it for a moment, then nodded and followed Lucy out the door. They moved to the side of the building, and Lucy took a seat on a bench next to a small garden. Trevor stood near the bench but didn't seem interested in sitting.

"You don't seem comfortable with this. Do you want to tell me why?"

"We were told to always tell adults the truth."

She nodded with understanding. "I grew up in an orphanage in the Under. They want us to tell *them* the truth, but how is that always possible, when they don't always tell *us* the truth?"

She could almost see him looking into himself as she spoke. It was one of the reasons she'd decided to leave the Under as soon as she could. The people who ran the orphanage, and the professors meant well, but a lot of time, they told half-truths to appease the kids and make the day go smoother. Lucy understood that; what she didn't like was the fact that too many lied about the Above. Once she was able to get out and see it for herself, she knew she had to leave the Under.

She could see Trevor had figured out the same thing. Instead of telling him any of that, she waited for him to decide to speak. Until then, she moved her eyes to the small garden and looked at the flowers. It was a tiny garden but had five different types of flowers, all different colors. It looked like a rainbow in the ground. Lucy took a deep, careful breath and inhaled the scent of the flowers as Trevor sat down next to her.

"Ok, what is it you want to know?"

TWENTY

Lucy turned to Trevor. "I want to know if a man with an accent works here. The only real information I have on him is that he hates the nickname Deter."

Trevor's eyes popped open. "I know who you can talk to!" He stood. "Come on."

Lucy smiled as she stood and followed Trevor back into the dining hall. She tried to follow as he moved quickly to the other side of the building. He was faster than her, therefore she watched where he went and moved at her own pace. She saw him talk to someone who looked her way and nodded to her. Lucy moved carefully through the crowded hall and stopped in front of Trevor. She nodded to him.

"This is Bixley. He can help you."

Lucy stuck her hand out to Trevor. "Thank you, sir. You listen to John, ok? He seems like the kind of Teacher that will lead you in the right direction."

Trevor nodded as they shook hands. "I think so too, which is why I chose him."

Lucy grinned, and Trevor left the area. She turned to Bixley, who gave her a steady look.

"You looking for Deter?"

"Yep."

"He isn't here anymore, of which most of us are glad."

"Why?"

Bixley looked at her right lapel. "You looking to kill him?"

She shook her head. "I wasn't hired to."

"That's almost too bad."

"Oh. That's interesting." Intrigue sparked in her voice.

"He has a short fuse, especially about his name. When he was here, we had two Dieters, one Dietrich and two Dierdras. The first time we called for Dieter, he yelled that it wasn't his name. We weren't talking to him. We were talking to one of the actual Dieters. He kept mishearing his name, which became almost amusing when we called for one of the Dierdras. It was like he was looking for a reason to get upset."

"Seems like a handful."

"Yeah."

"How long was he here?" Lucy turned her head as she felt a tap on her shoulder. The man next to Bixley was standing and indicating his seat.

"I'm leaving. Take it if you want before they fill it."

"Thank you," she said as she sat. Turning back to Bixley, she saw he was waiting on her.

"He was here about three months, then left when the recruiter came from down south to get people for harder jobs. Pays more."

"Do you know where, other than 'down south'?"

Bixley tapped the person on the other side of him on the arm. The person turned and regarded both Bixley and Lucy. "Where did the recruiters say they were going?"

Lucy sat with her back against the table. She relaxed a bit more and leaned into the table. It wasn't comfortable, but the people around her seemed to relax more when she did it. The person on the other side of Bixley looked at Lucy.

"Why do you want to know?"

"I was hired to find him and talk to him."

The person nodded. "Near Temple. You know where that is?"

Lucy shook her head. "I'm not from around here, and I don't find myself on the West Coast much."

"You got a horse?" Bixley jumped into the conversation again.

"Yep."

"You'll want to head to Parson, catch the train down to Temple. It's too far on a horse. The animals get more aggressive the closer you get to Temple. The Red Rock there is thick, and it's mutated a lot of animals. More than around here."

"I do carry a gun," Lucy stated with a bit of bravado.

"When's the last time you rode a horse through that area?"

Lucy leaned back just a bit more. "Oh, probably ten years ago or more."

"Trust us. Take the train."

"I hate the Under."

"Do it anyway," Bixley and the other person said at the same time.

Lucy held her hands up in defeat. "All right. What direction is Parson?"

"West about three miles, and the train runs regularly."

"So does the train west to east, but it's not frequent," she stated plainly.

Bixley laughed. "True. The train to Temple runs south twice a day."

"That is frequent. I can't believe that happens."

"We figured out how to hide the heat of the trains better. Something to do with cold water and pipes. We dug the routes for the pipes. The water's being pumped in from the ocean."

Lucy frowned. She couldn't remember the last time she saw the blue of the ocean. "Isn't the ocean a bit far?"

"Not for the pipes."

When no other explanation came, Lucy decided to change the subject. "What time does the train from Parson leave?"

"Morning and noon."

"Safe enough to get there in the growing dark?"

The people around her looked at each other, and Bixley turned back. "Probably safe."

Lucy nodded, then held her hand out to shake the people's hands. "Thank you much for all the help."

The people shook her hand, then Lucy stood and left. She found Bucky, untied his reins, and mounted. Lucy pointed Bucky to the road and walked him at a slow pace. At the side of the road, right before the town line, was a post with arrows pointed toward different towns. She located the one that said, "Parson" and pointed Bucky in the right direction. Once she was away from the town, she set him at a good pace, hoping to reach the next town before the sun went down completely.

꽁꽁꽁

Temple looked like almost every other town she had ever been in. The buildings were made of wood planks, with mismatched store signs, some form of boardwalk, and a dirt road running down the middle. The people dressed as they liked, with shorts and shirts with short sleeves being the prevailing look. Most people also wore hats to keep the sun off their faces. Unlike other places, everyone who could walk seemed to carry a gun on their hip.

Next to her, Bucky neighed. He'd been great on the train but did complain a bit in the freight elevator going up and down.

She patted him on the neck. "I know. I'll find a good place where you can run a bit, I promise."

He neighed again as if he understood. She felt he did and moved them both toward the tavern. She tied him to the post, patted him on the neck again, and walked into the tavern. It was dimly lit and since it was midday, full of people. She went to the bar, but it was a few minutes before she even tried to get the bartender's attention. Once she did, the tired-looking man shook his head.

"Sorry if I missed you earlier. It's a madhouse."

"I could tell. That's why I didn't flag you down right away. I'll take a coffee and a menu if you have one."

He nodded and moved away. She watched as he served a few other people new drinks before coming back with a large mug of coffee and a chalkboard full of writing.

"Need anything with the coffee?" he asked as he set the board and the mug down.

"Nope." She pointed to the first item on the menu. "I'll take that."

"It'll be a while."

"I can wait." She kept her voice light and friendly.

He nodded gratefully and moved off again.

⁗

The place was empty now, and Lucy sat with her mug of coffee and an empty plate in front of her. Zach, she learned the bartender's name from another customer, ran around the place, clearing tables. Someone else had explained that his servers were down with colds. The servers were sisters and lived together. It left Zack without help. On the few occasions he did have time to check on her, she let him know she could wait. And she could, but her patience was running thin.

While waiting, Lucy took all the plates from the bar and stacked them up at one end while he took care of the last customers. Now, as he cleared tables, she shook her head and started clearing the tables close by. She cleared three tables before he came over.

"Please stop." His voice was downtrodden.

She looked into Zack's eyes. "Why? I'm trying to help."

"Look, if you're here about the money . . ."

"I'm not here for you."

He stumbled over his next words before he grew very quiet. She watched as all his worries left him. Zack pulled a chair out and sat down heavily. "Oh."

Lucy pulled out a chair as well. "I'm Lucy."

"Zack."

"I'm looking for a miner with an overseas accent who hates the name Deter."

"It's probably better if you ask the other miners. There's a mining office here. Beth-Ann will talk to you."

"Where's the office?"

"Three doors down to the left on the other side."

Lucy stood. "Get yourself better help, and whatever trouble you're in, get out of it."

"I keep telling myself that."

Lucy nodded and left the tavern.

ಙಐಚಐಚಐಚ

Some weeks later, Lucy found herself in yet another town, in yet another recruiting office. They all looked the same: a small room with a counter about halfway into the room and space behind the counter. This one, though, had one occupied desk in the back. A woman with gray hair tied back in a bun and round wire-rimmed spectacles sat at the desk. She was behind a typewriter, a neat stack of papers to her right and a messy stack to her left. Lucy rarely saw so much paper. It was hard to make and expensive. The stack, though, was yellow. Therefore, she wondered if the woman had purchased a box from a Scavenger.

Lucy stared at the woman from across the counter, but the woman didn't notice her. She stared at the typewriter, her fingers clacking away at the keys. It was fascinating to watch her, and it gave Lucy a minute to catch her mind. She didn't remember the name of the town she was in and realized she was lost in a brain fog. She gathered her thoughts and hit the bell on the counter. It dinged and the woman looked up.

"Oh! I didn't see you there. I'm sorry if you were waiting long."

"It's fine." But it really wasn't, Lucy realized. She needed an end to this journey. Too many towns, too many offices and dining halls, and too many roads to count. And not enough beds to sleep in. "I'm looking for a miner. His name is Dietrich. He hates the name Deter, and he has an overseas accent. Overseas as in from Deutschland."

The woman blinked at her a few times before answering. "How many times have you said the same exact thing?"

Lucy let her head fall backwards in frustration as a heavy sigh escaped her. Was her voice showing that much to this stranger? She brought her head back up and stared at the woman. "Too many times."

"Hm. What do you need him for?"

"I was hired to talk to him." She tried to fix her cadence, to sound more relaxed, but the look on the woman's face made it obvious she failed. Then the woman smirked.

"Talk to him, not . . . um . . ."

"No, not kill him," Lucy interrupted curtly.

The woman hid her mouth with her hand, and her eyes went wide. "Oh. He's not liked much, is he?"

"No, ma'am," Lucy stated. She didn't stop the tiredness from showing this time.

"Well, that's interesting and unfortunate for him." She picked up the stack of papers to her left and took a few minutes to neaten the pile. When she was done, she moved over slightly and placed her hands on the desk, her fingers folded. "I'm afraid he left us yesterday."

"Well at least I'm closer. Do you know what mine he went to?"

"He's not heading to a mine. A woman, I think it was his relative, showed up to take him home."

Her mind, which was overworked, stopped and the fatigue hit her hard. "What?"

"He's headed back east. With his cousin or sister, I can't remember which."

Lucy tried to rein in her emotions but failed. Her voice reflected her exasperation. "You have *got* to be kidding me."

"Oh dear, you look like you're going to collapse. Why don't you come back here and take a seat." She indicated the seat across from her.

Lucy thought of her options, realized she didn't know what they were, and headed to the chair. She sat in it heavily and took off her hat to fan herself with it. She was flush with anger at the situation. "I can't believe it."

"Well, um . . ."

Lucy eyed the woman wearily. She seemed rather nervous. "Did you leave something out?"

"Well, it *is* possible I know where they are."

Lucy glared at the woman. She then took a deep breath, gathered herself together, and sat up a bit better in the seat. "All right. What do you want?"

"Well, um . . . I'm a writer, and I'm writing a book about a couple who meet and . . ." She looked into Lucy's eyes. "Well that's not important right now. What is important is that there is a minor character who's a Hired Hand. I've wanted to hire one of you to tell me stories so I can make this character more three dimensional. He's a bit flat right now."

"And?"

"And if you stay here and answer some questions for me, I'll tell you where they are," she said almost sheepishly.

Lucy stared at the woman. "When's the next train east?"

The woman waved her hand away. "Oh, it's not for couple weeks."

Lucy stared at the woman for a moment as the answer sunk in. The last time she asked what month it was, she had been told August. If the train was due in a couple weeks, that meant it was halfway through September. She rubbed her face with her hands and decided. "Ok. If I stay and talk to you, will that put me in jeopardy of losing them again?"

She stared at Lucy for a moment, then shook her head. "They weren't planning on leaving the area for a few days."

With that information, Lucy knew she could leave and search the town for herself, but . . . "Got coffee?"

She pointed to a pot behind her, as a smile threatened on her face. "Just brewed a fresh pot."

Lucy looked around but didn't immediately see any signs of a kitchen. "How about some food?"

"Tell me what you like to eat, and I can get you something from next door."

Lucy pursed her lips as she thought about her options. After a moment or two, she nodded. "All right. Sure. I'll answer your questions. Please keep in mind there are some things I might not be able to tell you, like names and dates and things like that, but sure, I'll answer your questions in exchange for information on Deter."

The woman clapped her hands and nearly squealed with joy. She jumped up. "Cups are next to the pot. Do you like steak? They have steak. It's real good."

"Sure." It had been a while since Lucy had steak, real steak. Lots of places had chopped steak, but it wasn't as good. She took what she could get.

"Great! I'll be right back. If anyone comes in, let them know I'm at the hotel getting food."

"Sure," Lucy stated as the woman ran out. "If I see them."

She said the last to an empty room. As the sound of the door closing faded, Lucy put her feet up on the desk, put her hat on her head to hide her eyes, and placed her hands on her chest, under her breasts. In an almost reclined position, Lucy took a nap.

TWENTY-ONE

ucy and Annette burst out laughing. "He really did that?"
A wide grin broke out on Lucy's face as she remembered the incident in question. After Annette returned with a tray of food, they had discussed how all Lucy's stories would be treated. Annette swore never to reveal where she learned her information and to never use the real names of the people involved. Then, they introduced themselves. Annette had admitted not wanting Lucy's name, at first, to help with anonymity. Once they established rules, though, Lucy introduced herself and Annette followed.

"I can't believe that happened." Annette's face was awash with delighted disbelief.

Lucy grinned again. "It happened. I can't prove it happened, as it was part of a job, but it happened, and it was hilarious."

Annette fanned herself with some papers; her face was flushed. "Ok. So that was the funniest story. Now do you have any, oh how to put it," she scrunched her nose, "cute stories?"

Lucy frowned, thought for a moment, then said, "I think so." She reached forward for her last bite of bread. She scraped it across her empty plate, in case any juices were left, and popped it into her mouth. After a moment of thinking and chewing she nodded and sat up straighter.

"I don't remember how long ago this was, but I was riding through a town near home when someone screamed my name. I turned to the boardwalk, and Miss EmmaJean is standing on the boardwalk, hands on the railing, face barely peeking over the wood, staring at me. I stopped Lance, dismounted, and walked on over. EmmaJean pointed to a cactus that was right next to the building. On top of the cactus was a tiny kitten, meowing forlornly."

Annette stared at Lucy, her pencil stopped over her paper. "You rescued a kitten from atop a cactus?"

"Yep. I wasn't sure how it got there; some of the needles were larger than the kitten. But I didn't just rescue the kitten, I taught EmmaJean about Hired Hands."

"Oh!" Annette perked up. "That's great!"

Lucy smiled. "I thought you might like that. EmmaJean was about ten. I've known her family for a long time. Her grandma, and at the time her dad, made rock candy."

"That's fun to make. I used to like watching it form."

"It is fun and keeps kids occupied, but they're the best. They make all kinds of colors and flavors. Marissa once made coffee rock candy."

"That sounds amazing!"

"It was. Had a nice, strong flavor, wasn't too sweet." Lucy frowned. "I don't know how they managed that, but I bought a few of those."

"I would have as well."

The women shared a smile, then Lucy continued. "EmmaJean's mother . . ." Lucy squinted off into the distance, then shook her head. "I don't remember her name. Doesn't matter, her mom was standing right there when EmmaJean got my attention. She tried to get EmmaJean to leave me alone, but the little girl turned to her mom and said, 'It's her job to help!' Her mom and I exchanged glances, and I nodded. Mom relented after that.

"So what did you do?"

"EmmaJean was old enough, so I looked at her mom and said something like, 'I'd like to teach her how to hire me, is that all right?' Mom said sure, and I turned to EmmaJean."

Annette sat up straighter. Anytime Lucy talked about the rules of Hired Hands, Annette wrote things down word for word.

ಊಗಊಗಊಗ

Some years prior

"EmmaJean, how are you this morning?" Lucy looked the little girl in the eye.

"I'm sad! Can you help me?"

"Well, that depends on you. You know you can hire me to take care of jobs, right?"

"Yeah. That's why I want you to do this for me."

Lucy shook her head. "That's not how it works. You're old enough, I think it's time you learned how to hire a Hired Hand."

"Ok. Can I hire you?" Her words came quickly as if she wasn't listening.

"EmmaJean, if you want to hire me, you have to follow the rules. First, you have to tell me what exactly you want me to do. You can't just point at the problem."

"Oh." She seemed to shrink back into herself.

A despondent mew came from the top of the cactus in the silence.

EmmaJean took a deep breath. "Lucy, can you get my kitty down from the cactus?"

"Thank you for stating the job. Now you tell me what you're going to pay me to do the job. It can be any amount."

"Oh." The meow came again and this time, EmmaJean looked up, moved to the street and looked up again. She stared at the kitten, then looked at her mom. "Mom?"

"I'm sorry, EmmaJean, you can't ask someone else to pay for you." Lucy's voice was stern. Her gaze wasn't on EmmaJean, but on the little girl's mom.

"Listen to Lucy, EmmaJean."

With a troubled look on her face, EmmaJean stuck her hands in the pockets of her dress. She looked surprised, then withdrew her hands. In her right was a stick of bright orange rock candy. EmmaJean looked at Lucy and held out the candy.

"'amma made this for me. It's my favorite flavor. Lemon orange, with more lemon than orange. If you get my kitty out of the cactus, I'll give it to you."

Lucy stared at the rock candy. She loved Marissa's rock candy. It was the best she'd ever had. It was obvious, though, that EmmaJean had licked some of the sugar already. A little water would clean off any germs and lint. She nodded.

"All right." She moved closer to EmmaJean. "I accept those terms, Miss EmmaJean." She stuck out her hand. "Now we shake on it."

EmmaJean moved her rock candy to her other hand, took Lucy's hand, and shook it.

"If I complete the terms of our agreement, you'll give me that candy, exactly as it is now." She said the last as the little girl was subconsciously moving the candy to her lips. With Lucy's words, she stopped, looked at it, sighed heavily, and looked back to Lucy.

"Well then you better get my kitty down, 'cause I don't know how long I can hold back."

Lucy burst out laughing. EmmaJean's mother came to the little girl's side. "I'll keep it safe for Lucy. You don't want to renege on your deal, dear. That's not a good thing to do, to anyone."

"Yes, Mom," EmmaJean stated in an almost annoyed voice. She handed the candy over as Lucy nodded.

"All right. I'll be back," Lucy stated before she turned on her heel and headed for the general store.

꩜꩜꩜

The present

Annette looked at Lucy. "So did you get the rock candy?"

"Yes. Her mom kept it safe for me. She asked if I wanted a new one, but I told her that would be against the rules too. I washed it off and enjoyed it as I rode the rest of the way home."

"How was the kitten?"

"It was stuck. A couple of the needles were sharp enough to . . ." she paused and looked at Annette. "Do you want to hear this?"

"I'm not squeamish."

"All right. A couple needles had punctured through three of its paws."

"Oh, the poor thing!"

"Yeah, once I figured that out, I stayed on the ladder until someone else could run up a pair of pliers. It was safer to pull the needles out of the cactus than to try and remove them from the kitten while it was still stuck. It tried to fight me, but I wrapped my bandana," she tapped her head, "around it to calm it. Then I pulled the needles and climbed down. EmmaJean wanted to take the kitten, but I insisted it needed to go to the vet. Then I showed her why. EmmaJean screamed."

"Oh, no. I don't blame her."

"Yeah, she was distraught, but once we were at the doctor's office, she calmed down enough to help. I grabbed my bandana, took the rock candy and left."

Annette blinked a few times, then looked over her notes. "You didn't tell her all of how to hire you, did you?"

"I didn't, but she wasn't going to listen once that kitten was in her hands, and since I didn't plan on logging it as a job, I figured it didn't matter. The next time I went through the town, I was able to sit with her and her mom, and we talked about it better. She knows what to do now."

Annette nodded. "That was a fairly cute story, except for the needles in the paws."

Lucy looked regretful. "We don't get a lot of 'cute' stories."

"I get that." She sighed. "I have one more set of questions."

Lucy nodded. She felt she knew what was coming.

"Have you ever killed anyone? I mean, have you ever been hired to kill anyone, like as an Assassin?"

Lucy decided to ignore the first question. "I have been hired to kill people, yes."

Annette settled her back against the chair more fully. "How many times?"

"Three times."

Annette looked at the paper in front of her and fidgeted with the pencil in her hand.

"I can tell you the procedure for that, in case it comes up in your book."

The woman frowned slightly as she nodded. As she didn't seem ready, Lucy stayed silent. Finally, Annette took a deep breath. "Sure. I would like to know the procedure from a Hired Hand's side of things."

"As I think I told you at the beginning, when we accept a job, we have to fill out paperwork. We can start the job as soon as the paperwork is filed, except when hired as an Assassin. When that happens, we have to wait for the paperwork to come back stamped. It can take up to three months to come back."

Annette's eyes were wide. "Three months?"

"It's sent in an envelope. Sealed with wax. It's taking a person's life. We have to get the ok before we can proceed."

"I guess that's better than having people hire you every day to kill someone random."

"That's probably why they make us wait. I've been hired five times as an Assassin, but two backed out before the paperwork came back."

"What did you do?"

"Wired the home office that it was cancelled."

Annette nodded, her face awash in contemplation.

After a few minutes of silence, Lucy cleared her throat. That brought the woman back.

"I'm sorry. I was lost in thought."

"I know. If I may, I would like to tell you one other thing that you probably wouldn't think about, when it comes to killing for hire."

Annette's eyes went wide. "I'm sure there's a lot but go ahead. I appreciate any advice."

"When I was training to be a Hired Hand, my Teacher and I talked a lot about assassination jobs. He told me that I should take my entire Apprenticeship to think about whether or not it was something I could actually do. Then when I took my first assassination job, he told me not to take any jobs once that one was done. Take time to be with myself and only myself and really think about how I felt about killing someone."

Annette nodded. "Good advice. Did you take it?"

"When I take an assassination job, I don't do any other jobs. Once it's done, I go sit with myself for a month and see how I feel about it. It's best to really think about the act and to decide if it's something I would want to do again."

The women stared at each other over the paper crowded desk for a few minutes before Annette cleared her throat and looked down at her hands. "That was all fascinating."

"Did you have any other questions?"

"No, but now I wish I could talk to you again. I feel like I'm going to have so many more questions once this all settles in my mind."

"Sorry." Lucy didn't exactly sound sorry.

Annette looked up and sighed. "Was this really that terrible?"

"No, this was fun, but I don't want to stick around here long enough for you to figure out your book and characters."

"That's fair."

"You can hire one of us for any reason. Another Hired Hand may talk to you."

Annette crinkled her nose. "I like the spontaneity of this meeting. Also, what do I pay for a service like this? That's what's stopped me in the past."

"You can offer any type of payment, including a copy of your book."

"Oh, I didn't think of that."

Lucy smiled.

Annette nodded, then sighed. "I suppose that means you want your information."

"Yes."

Annette pursed her lips. "They're staying at the hotel next door, under her name."

Lucy stood up. "What's her name?"

"Ms. Adelia Bauer."

Lucy had been reaching for her hat, which was on the desk. She paused and stared at Annette in disbelief. "Say again?"

"Ms. Adelia Bauer. She's with a man . . ."

"Dressed in mostly black. Goes by the name of Roger?" There was a sharp edge to her voice. It was so sharp, Annette shrank back.

"Um . . . yes."

"Son of a . . ." She slammed the hat on her head and stormed to the door and out.

TWENTY-TWO

Lucy's anger widened her usually long stride. People on the boardwalk moved out of her way. Before she could enter the hotel next door, though, a voice echoed in her head. *Don't approach a target while angry.*

Cecil's calm voice carried through her body and pulled her steps away from the hotel door. She moved past it as more of that memory surfaced.

∞⬥∞⬥∞⬥

Some years prior

"Why not?"

Lucy looked up from the cooking fire into Cecil's eyes. This was their first night together as Teacher and Apprentice. He had caught a rabbit, gutted it, skinned it, and skewered it with a long piece of metal. There were supports at two ends of the fire, opposite each other, that looked to be able to hold the long thin metal rod the rabbit was on. It was Lucy's first time at a campfire. Her last Teacher made sure to spend each night in a town, at a saloon. They had avoided sleeping in the open, to the point of staying in a town if Darrell didn't wake up on time to get to the next town in one day. Lucy had spent many days sitting around saloons talking to the Escorts while Darrell drank the time away. When Cecil took her out of town on their first day together, she felt a lot better about being a Hired Hand's Apprentice.

"If you approach a family member or friend with anger on your mind and you confront them with that anger, what happens?" He added some spices to the spit rabbit.

Lucy frowned. She wasn't sure she liked rabbit, but there wasn't much else out here. "I don't have much family, but I guess once the argument is over, we can apologize?"

"Sure. What do you think would happen if you approached a stranger angrily?"

"Um . . ." She scrunched her nose in thought. "I don't know."

"Sure, you do. What would you do if someone approached you and they were angry right away?"

"I wouldn't like that. I wouldn't want to talk to them."

"Exactly. So if you approach a target, either one you're going to kill or one you're going to talk to, and you're angry, what do you think'll happen?" Cecil moved his big bulk closer to the fire and set the spitted rabbit on the supports.

"They'll leave? Maybe fight me?"

He nodded. "If you're trying to talk to them, they'll either fight you or run away. If you're trying to kill them, you'll miss. It can get messy if you miss."

"I don't think I want to kill anyone."

Cecil sighed as he put away spices and cleaned the knife he'd used to gut the rabbit. "Don't be too quick to make that decision. A lot of Hired Hands think they'll never kill, then they do. But we'll talk more on that another night. Tonight, I want you to remember: don't approach a target with anger in your mind. Clear it out, approach calmly. Allow logic to guide you. Don't approach a target with anger. You get one chance to meet them, in whatever capacity you're meeting them. Make it count."

ဆဣဆဣဆဣ

The present

Lucy stood at the end of the boardwalk now, her head clearer. *Don't approach a target while angry.* Every night for a year, he gave her the same speech, until she was sick and tired of hearing it. There were quite a few times she wanted to yell at him for repeating it over and over. There was a time or two that she did yell at him. When she did, he smirked, as if proving his point. It had saved her a few times over the years. She knew it saved her today.

She knew two of the three people she would be encountering, but the one she needed to talk to, she didn't know. Approaching them with a look angry enough to scare passersby was not recommended. If Roger saw her approaching with an angry look, he might pull his gun. She didn't need that. Also, she wasn't angry with them, she was angry at the situation.

In the back of her mind, her emotions still raged. She wanted to address all those thoughts too, but excuses for anger would only, well, make her angry. Lucy knew it was important to let those thoughts go. Yes, she could have cut her trip short if she had asked Ms. Bauer or Roger what they were up to, but that wasn't her way. She rarely asked for information if it wasn't part of her job. It kept her out of trouble.

Along the way, she had asked a few of the miners Deter's last name, but most hadn't bothered to remember. The mining offices were upfront about not giving out that information. She had a feeling even Annette would not have given her Deter's last name. It was part of their policies to keep their workers safe.

Lucy sighed, then took a few deep breaths. She felt calmer now, more in control. Her anger still gnawed at her like a hungry dog, but it was easier to push aside. Life did what it wanted, no use being angry about it. She took a deep breath, then turned and headed back the way she came and looked around a bit. Across the street, she saw a sign for the postal service, which advertised it had a telegraph.

A small laugh escaped Lucy. She hadn't checked for messages since Sacramento. It was best to find out if Grace had left her a message before she found Deter. With that thought in mind, Lucy headed to the post office to check her messages. Then she would head to the hotel. Whether she had a message from home or not, it would be nice to see Roger again.

ဆၢထၢထၢ

It was loud inside the hotel. It made Lucy realize that this entire town had a lot of people in it. The boardwalks were crowded. Most of the tables in the lounge were occupied. It felt like there were a lot more people than was safe. She frowned and looked around the room. She immediately saw Roger, but he wasn't facing her. Lucy moved through the room, her eyes not on Roger but on Deter. She still noticed when Roger saw her. He stood when she approached their table.

Ms. Bauer barely glanced at her. Roger nodded in greeting, but there was a frown on his face. Lucy nodded to Roger, then looked at Deter.

"Hello, sir. My name is Lucy. Is your name Dietrich?"

"It is." His thick accent made Lucy wonder why Ms. Bauer didn't have an accent. She filed that away as "none of my business" and moved along.

"Sir, I'm sorry to ask this, but I do need to make sure you're the person I'm looking for. Does the nickname 'Deter' bother you?"

He stood quickly, and his chair slid back a few inches. Ms. Bauer stood as well and placed a hand on his arm. She spoke to him in their native language, which seemed to calm him. Dietrich grumbled a response to Ms. Bauer, then sat down. The others followed suit, except for Lucy.

"It is not a preferred name for me."

"Sir, I'm a Hired Hand, and I was hired to find you to talk to you. Is there somewhere we can talk in private?"

He immediately frowned. "I think here is safer."

"The information I need to convey is rather private sir. You may not want anyone to hear it."

Roger cleared his throat. The three others turned to him. "Sir, if she was hired to kill you, she wouldn't be here talking to you. That's not how it's done."

The look on Dietrich's face conveyed his nervousness. "Well . . . I . . ." He looked at Lucy, then at Ms. Bauer, then at Roger. He looked back at Ms. Bauer when she placed her hand on his arm again.

"I'll come with you, as will Roger. It'll be fine."

"This really may not be something you want someone else to hear, sir." Lucy didn't want to have an audience for this information.

Dietrich shook his head. "I think all together is good."

"We'll use my sitting room." Ms. Bauer offered.

Lucy gave up and nodded. "All right."

Ms. Bauer, Dietrich, and Roger stood up from their table. As they moved away, another set of people almost immediately took their seats.

☙ ❦ ☙ ❦ ☙ ❦

When they reached the room, Ms. Bauer spoke to Dietrich in Deutsche. He nodded and immediately went to the bar and made everyone a drink. Lucy declined and waited for all those gathered to settle. Though the room had seating for four, as the chairs were close to the exit, Lucy chose to stand. If things went sour, she would be able to leave quickly.

Once the others were settled, Lucy looked at Dietrich. "Do you remember being in a town called Meridune when you came out west? It's one of the train stops."

He shook his head. "I didn't learn the names of the towns."

Lucy looked at Roger for a second before settling her gaze upon Dietrich. Ms. Bauer had taken the seat right in front of Dietrich, which was across from the door. It meant Lucy saw the back of her head. Lucy looked away, licked her lips, and spoke again. "An Escort in Meridune asked me to find you."

His face went bright red, and Lucy could tell he was looking at Ms. Bauer. "Ah. Oh. I . . ."

When Ms. Bauer said nothing, Lucy caught Dietrich's eyes again. "Are you certain you don't want to talk with me privately?"

He threw his hands up as if exasperated. "I think she knows the worst of it now."

"Don't be too sure."

He looked shocked. "What else could there be?"

"Sir, do you have the Red Death?"

He looked down at his hands. Ms. Bauer gasped and started talking in Deutsche. Roger looked rather uncomfortable. After a few minutes of back and forth between Ms. Bauer and Dietrich, he finally answered.

"I had to test before mining. I test positive, but don't show."

"Do you know how long you've had it?"

He looked rather sheepish. "I test before I leave home. I have it but doesn't show."

"You infected the Escort."

"No, no, impossible. It doesn't show on me."

"It's a sexually transmitted disease." Roger's quiet voice cut through the room. All three people looked at him.

"Vat?" Dietrich seemed confused, but it might also have been anger. Lucy wasn't sure.

"I learned last week, through the Orators. The scientists and doctors finally figured out that it's a sexually transmitted disease. Even if you don't show sighs, you can pass it on to someone if you sleep with them."

"No foolin'?" Lucy's voice was soft as well. If it was sexually transmitted, that meant Gracie wouldn't have to be as careful around her mom.

"The doctors in town can verify."

"Still!" Ms. Bauer's voice was not to be denied. "Can she prove it was him? How many other men did you have to track down?"

"Two. And they didn't ejaculate anywhere near her." Lucy wasn't going to mince words. Ms. Bauer sounded as if she wanted to blame Grace for her disease. That wasn't going to happen on Lucy's watch. Sure, Grace's job was to sleep with a lot of people, but Escorts . . . Lucy's thoughts paused, and she turned her attention to Dietrich.

"You said you knew you had the Red Death, but you still slept with

Escorts?"

All other voices stilled.

Roger reached out and placed a hand on Lucy's arm. She turned her attention to him. "Nothing on the books says he can't, Luce."

Lucy frowned as she tried to remember all the rules around people with the Red Death and then realized she couldn't. There were too many, and at the same time, too few, as it had been hard to pinpoint all the problems with the disease. Maybe now it wouldn't be as hard.

"All right, point taken, but I'm still angry about it." She took a breath. "There is another thing, but I want you to understand. There are circumstances that prove what I'm about to say is true."

All three gave her annoyed looks. Lucy felt she wasn't really making much sense but plunged on anyway.

"You got her pregnant. You're going to be a father."

☙ℰ☙ℰ☙ℰ

Lucy leaned against the wall outside of Ms. Bauer's room. Before she could get too comfortable, the door opened and out stepped Roger. He closed the door and sighed just as heavily as she had.

"She chased you out too?"

"When she told you to get out, I didn't realize she meant both of us."

They turned to the door as loud arguing could be heard. If it were in English, Lucy was sure they would be able to understand what was being said. She frowned and turned to Roger. "Do you know what they're saying?"

"No. You know me with languages; I have a hard enough time with ours."

Lucy laughed. It was a long-running joke between them that Roger used the language as he wanted. Lucy noticed he had gotten better since working for Ms. Bauer though. "So you have no idea what's being said?"

"I know '*nein*' is no and '*ja*' is yes."

Lucy frowned a little. "That doesn't help."

"It does in certain situations."

She shook her head. "Do you know how long they're going to be in there then?"

"No idea. They would argue a bit before he left the house, but the length varied depending on the subject . . . I think. They never told me what they were arguing about."

"That is not helpful."

"Sorry. I'm the help. What do you expect?"

"You don't eavesdrop?"

Roger looked shocked, then he busted out laughing. He placed his hand on her shoulder and shook his head. "You had me there."

Lucy smirked. "So what now?"

"I'm going to my room. She knows to find me there."

Lucy nodded for a moment, then looked at Roger thoughtfully. "Do you know if there's a doctor in town?"

"I would think so. Why?"

"I want more information on the Red Death."

"Who hired you? I don't recall if you said."

"Grace."

He shook his head. "I don't know that name."

"She has a young daughter. If they can hug . . ."

"Gotcha. Well, I'm in room 306 when you're done. Feel free to stop by."

"Thanks."

"Yep."

Lucy turned and headed back down the steps to find out if there was, in fact, a doctor in town.

TWENTY-THREE

Lucy?"

"Yes." She looked at the older gentleman as he walked into the small room. She had been sitting for only a few minutes but took in her surroundings the moment she was led in here. There was an examination table, a small desk, and two chairs. The small desk looked more like a side table.

He didn't look her way yet. "I'm Dr. Salizar. I see you didn't provide a last name. It is customary to do so."

"I gave my ID number. That's all that's necessary when it's part of a job."

That got his attention, but all it did was make him look at her right lapel. "Ah." He looked into her eyes finally. "What information were you looking for?"

"A friend told me that the Red Death is a sexually transmitted disease. Is that true?"

He studied her for a moment as he leaned back in his chair. Dr. Salizar was a portly, older gentleman, with graying hair and mustache. His deeply tanned and wrinkled skin betrayed his love of outdoors.

As she studied him, he seemed to study her. They looked each other in the eyes after a moment, and Dr. Salizar picked up her folder. "How much do you want to know about the Red Death? We're allowed to tell people all the Under lab found out, but most people don't want specifics."

"Give me all you know. If I don't understand, I'll ask questions."

He nodded. "It's a blood-borne virus, like herpes. You heard of herpes?" When she nodded, he continued. "If someone has an open sore, and you touch it, and then touch say, your eyes or your mouth, the virus can get in that way, but mostly, it's sexually transmitted."

Lucy frowned. "If it's sexually transmitted, how come the sores don't start around the genitalia?"

He shook his head. "The scientists don't know. They're still looking into it."

Lucy nodded, then leaned forward in her chair, her arms over her knees, her hands intwined. "So if my client, an adult, has a young child, they're ok to hug?"

"As stated, it's still advisable not to touch open sores."

"But if mom's all covered up?"

"If mom is covered up and child is careful and washes their hands right away, it should be ok. Kisses are not advisable as again, open sores."

Lucy nodded, then leaned back in her chair. "Is this information being sent to all towns Above?"

"Should have been. It's big news."

Lucy nodded, lost in thought. Part of her wanted to wire Meridune, make sure Grace heard the news. Dr. Middleton was old, but he was good. If this news was being shared with all the towns, then Grace probably already knew. Lucy frowned and looked at the doctor. "When did you all get the news?"

"About a week ago."

Lucy nodded. "So there's a good chance my hometown knows."

"Unless your doc is keeping the news quiet, which . . .?"

With the pause and the upward inflection, Lucy shook her head. "Nah, Middleton's good. There's been a time or two when medical news needed to be shared. He did it every time."

"Then the person in question should know, but I really can't say."

She cracked a smile. "I know. I'm just worried for my friend."

He nodded. "What about yourself?"

That elicited a frown. "I'm sorry?"

"Have you been tested for Red Death?"

"When I was a kid and at various times since, but not recently." Her eyes slid left and right as she thought about it. She looked at Dr. Salizar almost in surprise. "I was going to back home, then didn't. Job distracted me."

"We can take your blood. You'd have the results in a day."

She frowned. "It used to take longer."

He smiled. "The lab that does the testing is in our Under portion."

Lucy looked surprised. "Oh. I didn't notice a way down or signs."

"The way down is closer to the mine entrance, which is away from town."

She nodded, a smile on her face. "I should have figured."

Dr. Salizar smiled. "The town wanted it to be more hidden. Help people separate work from home type of situation."

"Interesting."

He smiled. "Do you want us to run the test again?"

She nodded. "It's about time I did."

"Any other tests?"

"I had a bunch of tests run six," she paused to think, "no, eight months ago now."

"How many people have you slept with since then?"

Lucy tilted her head back and thought about it. There had been Alice back in Meridune, and . . . Her thoughts stilled . . . was there . . .? Yes. She looked at Dr. Salizar. "Only two people since the last test. Both Escorts."

"I'll get the questionnaire, and the nurse will come in for your blood. It'll take a little longer to get all your tests run, but . . ."

Lucy held up a hand. "I know the drill. It'll be sent to my home doctor, Middleton."

"Yes. Any other questions for me?"

"Can't think of any."

He stood, held out his hand, and shook Lucy's when she reciprocated. "Glad you came in today. I'll send the nurse in."

"Thank you for your time."

They nodded to each other, and Dr. Salizar left the room. Lucy relaxed. She was happy to know that Grace could hold Gracie again. Part of her wanted to wire home to make sure they knew, but she didn't see a real need for it. She would leave it for now and place her faith in Dr. Middleton.

❧☙❧☙❧☙

Lucy headed back to the hotel, not sure what else to do. She meandered her way to Roger's room, noting the number of people in the streets and in the halls. It wasn't crowded, but there were more people than she was used to seeing in one place. Lucy wanted to understand, but more than anything, it made her want to leave. Lots of people meant more heat released into the air, which meant a greater possibility of Bombardment.

With the uncomfortable, yet familiar chill running up and down her spine, Lucy knocked on Roger's door. She could still hear Dietrich and Ms. Bauer arguing in the next room. The door opened, and Roger let her in.

She tilted her head toward the room next door. "You have any idea how long they're going to be arguing?"

He shook his head. "Sometimes when they sound like this, it lasts a few minutes, sometimes hours. Since I don't know the language, I have no idea if they're being friendly or not."

She shook her head. "You really should learn the language of the people you're working for."

"I've tried. It doesn't stick. Susie's getting the hang of the language though. She's a natural."

"She isn't around enough to help you on your jobs, but that's not important now." Lucy shook her head then changed the subject. "You don't happen to know why there are so many people in town, do you?"

Roger shook his head. "Nope. I think it has to do with the mines, but not sure."

She frowned. "I don't like it."

He shrugged. "What are you going to do about it?"

"Complain until we leave."

That elicited a laugh from Roger.

"For now," she waited until he looked at her with a listening expression on his face, "I'm going to dinner. Want to join me?"

"Can't. Until they're done arguing, I can't do anything." He frowned. "It's not really close to dinner, you know."

"No, but I could eat, and if I'm sitting in the dining room, it might give me an opportunity to find out why there are so many people here."

Roger nodded but didn't seem overly interested. "Let me know what you find out. I'll come find you if they sound like they're slacking off."

"Will do," Lucy stated quickly as she headed to, then out of, the door.

ဩ୧ဩ୧ဩ୧

Downstairs, the dining room was packed. Lucy didn't like it one bit. It felt dangerous. It was three in the afternoon. Most people should still be working. She wiped the worry from her face as a Hostess came to help her.

"How many?"

"One. I don't mind sharing if that's needed."

The older woman looked down at her list. "Looks like you're not going to get a choice. A four-seater is open." She looked up at Lucy. "If you sit there, and more people show up, you're going to get company."

Lucy smiled. "That's fine."

The woman nodded and led Lucy to her seat. "We have a choice of four soups and one entrée."

"I don't like tomato soup. Otherwise, I'm not picky."

"You got it."

"Why don't you have more choices?"

"There are enough restaurants in this town. If people want better choices, they go to one of them."

Lucy nodded and watched as the woman walked away. It was odd that they didn't offer more food, but Lucy wasn't here for the food. She was here for potential company. As she settled into her seat, Lucy plastered a friendly look on her face and waited. When her entrée arrived, she was finally rewarded for her patience. A knock on the far side of the table roused her from her meal. She looked up at the older gentleman and smiled.

"Mind sharing a table with a colleague?"

Lucy's eyes went to the man's right lapel, took note of the HH pin, and looked back into his eyes. He had nice gray eyes that had a network of wrinkles at the corners. His hair, white and thin, nevertheless looked soft and well cared for.

"Please take a seat."

Once settled, he held out his hand. "Robert."

They shook hands. "Lucy."

They both turned to look as a server placed food in front of Robert. Lucy looked at the newcomer and frowned in thought. "Ordered your food before you sat down?"

"They know me. I get the same thing every time."

She nodded. "Is this your hometown?"

"Born and raised."

"That's unusual for someone in our line of work."

"I tried moving away for a while but kept coming back. Gave up and called this home by the time I was thirty."

Lucy nodded and was silent as they both took a few bites of food.

"How about you? Where's home?"

"Meridune, but I was born and raised in Dallas Under."

Robert shook his head. "I don't know where Meridune is."

"It's on the East/West train line. We're about the last stop before the desert changes to forest out east."

"Is that the southernmost train?"

She gave him a curious look. "It's currently still the only train that heads east. Or did that change recently?"

"I heard the Rail's been trying to dig another train heading east/west, in a couple places to try and reach more people.”

Lucy nodded. “I think the Rail’s been trying for my entire life to do that. I don’t know if they’re ever going to succeed.”

“Why wouldn’t they?”

She paused with her fork halfway to her mouth. “You ever been north or in the middle of this country?”

“No. I tend to go south.”

“Too many Bandits the farther north you go, and in the middle as well.”

Robert frowned. “Why is that?”

“The weather is hard to handle during most of the year. Too hot in the summer, too cold in the winter. I’ve heard parts were better for growing Before, but now,” she shook her head, “the Bombardment ruined the land.”

“That’s rather unfortunate.”

“We have enough trouble with feeding people. We don’t need to expand further.”

“I suppose.”

They fell silent for a few minutes. Lucy took advantage and finished her entrée. It was some sort of pasta with sauce and meatballs. Simple and filling. She pushed her plate away and looked at Robert, who was still working on his plate.

“Mind if I ask you about this town?”

“Sure!”

“Is it just me or are there too many people here?”

He beamed with pride. “We think we have a good amount. At last count, we had five hundred residents!”

Lucy’s eyes opened wide in terror. That was double the recommended amount. "Five hundred?"

He made a gesture as if to wave away her worry. "Our buildings are being cooled by water in pipes. It's cooled in the Under, then pumped through the buildings."

This didn't sound like enough to Lucy. "All right, so it hides the heat of the people indoors, but what about outdoors?"

"You might not have noticed, but most people stay under the awnings in the street. The water is piped through those areas as well."

"Where is the water pumped from?"

"The ocean. Nice cool water."

The more he talked, the more unsafe it felt to Lucy. "How far is the ocean from here?"

Robert frowned. "A few hundred miles? Not sure, really, but it's all perfectly safe!"

Lucy looked at Robert, her eyes wide open in disbelief. "You're telling me this town is pumping water from the ocean hundreds of miles away and everyone is fine with that?"

He shrugged; the look on his face indicated he didn't see a problem. "It's been like this for a few years now. We've been told that as long as we stay at five hundred people, we should be fine."

"What happens if the pumps stop?"

"Oh, they do every six months for maintenance for about a half an hour. Usually at night when everyone is asleep and indoors anyway." He knocked on the table. "Haven't had an issue yet."

Lucy mulled this around in her mind, picked up her water glass and had a long sip to think. Done, she set the plastic tumbler down and licked her lips. "How do they keep count?"

Robert's eyes went wide for a moment. "Well, now. I know we have a census every year."

"What about between the censuses? I don't have a room in the hotel. I've just been wandering around. No one's given me the rules of the town or asked me if I've been counted."

He looked worried for a split second, then shook his head. "They have it figured out, even if I don't have all the answers."

Lucy nodded as if she agreed, but when she saw her server, she caught their eye and paid for the meal. The server tried to offer change, but Lucy gave a big smile and waved the thought away. "I have some business to take care of. You keep the change."

The server looked down at the gold coin in their hand, gave a happy smile, and moved away.

Lucy turned to Robert. "Thank you for your time. Enjoy the rest of your dinner."

"I didn't scare you, now did I?"

"Nope. You informed me. Thank you much." With that, Lucy got up out of her seat and headed out of the hotel. There were some things she was going to take care of before heading back up to Roger's room.

TWENTY-FOUR

Lucy's first stop was the ranch south of town where she'd boarded Bucky. He seemed happy to see her, if his neigh and head bob were any indication. "Hello, Bucky. Seems like we have a rough town here. We're going to see if we can't get out."

Her words were whispered to her horse; she didn't want to cause an alarm. The fewer people who understand there might be an issue, the better. She patted Bucky on the neck, then went to see the stable owner. She needed a wagon, another horse, and some information. When she tracked the owner down, the woman was too busy to ask too many questions.

"Your horse seems more than adequate for a wagon."

"It needs to be big enough for four people."

The woman nodded. "That makes more sense. I have an older wagon; nothing wrong with it, just looks old. For horses, I have a couple for rent."

"I'd rather buy. I don't know if I'll be back this way."

"Oh." She stopped looking through her paperwork, even as her assistant brought her more. "Danny, do we have a horse for sale?"

Danny, a man who looked to be about fifteen years younger than the owner, frowned, then shook his head. "Only if you feel like selling Mable or Brier."

"Can we afford to sell one of them?"

He looked at Lucy, then back to the owner. "That's your call, Ma."

"You always seem to know who needs horses before I do."

"Oh." A look of pride crossed Danny's face. It faded as he thought about things for a moment, then nodded. "Yeah, if the price is right, we can probably let Brier go. He's older," Danny looked at Lucy, "Just older than Mable, not old, and he's a good work horse, if that's what you need."

"She needs him to pull a wagon with four people in it. There will be another horse hitched," said Danny's mom.

Danny nodded. "Yep. We can sell Brier if the price is right."

"Thank you. Go get him ready, will you?"

"Sure, Ma!"

With that, Danny left. The owner looked at Lucy. "Sorry about that. He's my oldest and still doesn't have a lot of confidence. He knows as much as I do but somehow," she shook her head, "no confidence. I wonder what his Pa and I did wrong, but I can't go back and change things, you know?"

Lucy nodded but didn't say anything, as she felt it wasn't her place. "So how much for Brier and the wagon?"

The woman stood. "Why don't you come with me, and I'll show you both so you can haggle with knowledge?"

"Mighty kind of you."

The woman looked Lucy in the eyes. "I don't like ripping people off. Come on, follow me."

About half an hour later, Lucy was on her way to her next stop. She had asked for a ranch as far east from the town as possible that was easily accessible by horse and wagon. As she passed the town name on the way out, she glared at it. The town was named Taft. She felt it should be Daft.

The ranch she was pointed towards, Two Forks, was about twenty minutes away if the horses were going slow. As it was her first time there, Lucy didn't rush the horses. They arrived with the sun barely touching the horizon. A man stood at the gate, a deep frown on his face. From the wrinkles around his mouth and eyes, it was obvious this was his usual look and not due to her arrival. She nodded to him as she stopped the wagon.

"Evening. I'm Lucy. Do you have any lodging available?"

"Maybe. You come from town?"

She took note of the fact that he didn't give his name but let it pass. "Yep, but I don't live there."

He gave a hard laugh. "That's a surprise."

She looked him dead in the eye. "Too many people there."

They looked at each other for a moment as he seemed to understand she was not asking a question. After that moment passed, he nodded slowly. "Seems like most don't understand that."

"Seems like."

"Tell me your plans."

"There are three in town with me. If something goes . . . awry, I want to race out of there."

"Not sure if my place is safe from a Bombardment. It's not that far from town."

"It's a staging point. I want someplace to point my horses and wagon to."

He nodded. "And if the meteorites don't fall here?"

"Then my friends and I will need a place to regroup before we plan our next move. I'm sure two of the group will need to process the Bombardment. If it happens, that is."

He gave a harsh laugh. "It's a matter of 'when' not 'if.'"

"I feel the same way, but it may not happen today. I just want to be prepared. I will pay."

"I'm sure you will. Name's Mortimer. Come inside for a few minutes so we can talk a bit more. I want to know the type of person I might be housing."

"Thank you."

He gave another harsh laugh. "Don't thank me until I've said yes to the deal."

This time, Lucy laughed.

It was nearly ten at night when Lucy returned to Taft. The horses and wagon were housed at a ranch closer to town. It would make a quick exit to Two Forks easier. She had left the tack on the horses, just in case. As she made her way back into town, some of Lucy's fears felt justified. There were a lot of drunk people weaving their way from one business to another. Most were not staying under the wooden awnings that covered the boardwalk. It felt like a disaster waiting to happen.

Lucy made her way quickly into the hotel and up to Roger's room. As she knocked on his door, she realized that Ms. Bauer and Dietrich were still arguing. She shook her head and knocked louder when Roger didn't open quickly enough. When he finally opened the door, he looked disheveled.

"Sleeping on the job?"

"They've been arguing nonstop."

"How can you sleep through that? Invite me in."

He moved out of the way and let her inside. She started to pace as he closed the door and sat down on his bed. There wasn't much in the room: a couple beds, a dresser, and a wardrobe.

"If you don't have a place to sleep, you can share this room with me."

"I'm not staying in this town. Did you know there are five hundred people here?"

Roger gave her a blank stare. "How can that be true?"

"There's a system installed that pipes water through the buildings to cool them down. I don't know all the details, but a local colleague told me about it at dinner. He seemed to think it was great."

Roger stared at her for a moment, then rubbed his eyes. "Lucy, I was deep asleep. I need you to get to the point."

"The system hides up to five hundred people. They count their inhabitants once a year. I don't recall anyone counting me or asking if I've been counted or anything. When I arrived, there was a family of six disembarking from a wagon. They had all their belongings with them. They looked like newcomers. I don't think there's an accurate ongoing population count. And then there's the fact that, right now, there are a ton of people in the streets, carrying on like it's safe. They're not staying close to the buildings like they're supposed to."

Roger blinked a few times, then nodded slowly. "You're worried about a Bombardment."

"Yes."

"You have a plan?"

Lucy nodded. "And all the elements are lined up already."

Roger rubbed his hands together. "What do you need from me?"

"How long were you all planning on being in this town?"

Roger frowned and thought about it for a moment. "We leave in three or four days."

"I need everyone to be ready within five minutes if I say it's time to go."

He nodded. "That's not a problem for me." Then he shook his head. "You don't think you're being overprepared?"

"You know me. I always overprepare."

Roger opened his mouth to speak, then simply nodded.

"If I knock on their door, how upset will they be?" She indicated the voices coming through the wall."

"Does it really matter?"

Lucy thought about it, then shook her head. "No."

They looked at each other for a moment, then Lucy left and headed next door. She knocked loudly before trying the doorknob and finding it unlocked. She opened the door, but they were oblivious to her presence and continued the angry back and forth in Deutsche. Lucy shook her head, then shouted, "Hey!"

Both Ms. Bauer and Dietrich stopped and turned her way. Ms. Bauer looked perturbed. Lucy ignored her and looked only at Dietrich.

"Did you know there are five hundred people in this town?"

"*Ja.* Yes. It's cooled by pipes," he answered in a heavy accent.

There was a gasp from Ms. Bauer.

"I think there are more people here than that." She stepped into the room and closed the door. "Look, I prefer to be careful when my life may be at stake. This town doesn't feel safe. I need you both to be ready to leave at a moment's notice, if needed."

"Wait, you want us to leave?"

"No, I want you to be ready to leave quickly." Lucy looked at Ms. Bauer. "If I were to tell you that you have five minutes to pack before we leave, would you be ready?"

She frowned. "No. Who would be?"

"Can you be?"

Ms. Bauer looked at Lucy as if she were crazy. "I . . . I . . ."

"Ma'am, if your life depended on it, would you be willing to leave all your belongings behind?"

She looked shocked for a moment, then shook her head. "This is silly. This isn't happening."

"It could."

She shook her head again. "No, this is the musings of a madwoman."

Lucy held her tongue. "You're right, I may be mad, but my instincts have gotten me out of too many bad scrapes for me to ignore them."

Ms. Bauer stood taller. "We only ever remember the times our intuition is right."

"No, *you* only remember the times you were right." The women stared each other down for a moment, then Lucy turned to Dietrich, as if dismissing Ms. Bauer. "If we had to leave at a moment's notice, would you be ready?"

His eyes went to his cousin, then back to Lucy. "*Ja.* Yes."

"Good." She turned to leave.

"Wait." His voice seemed hesitant.

Lucy turned back. "Yes?"

"May I speak with you, about the woman?"

Lucy looked at Ms. Bauer, who would not meet her gaze, then turned back to Dietrich. "Sure. Do you want to get a drink?"

"Ja."

Lucy smiled.

Dietrich looked at Ms. Bauer, said some words in Deutsche and then pointed the way out to Lucy, as if to indicate they could leave. Lucy turned and headed out of the room.

ဢႢဢႢဢႢ

The bar area was crowded, but they were able to find a secluded spot in a back corner. They placed their orders and stood close to each other, to hear what the other was saying. The room was full of voices talking over the low sound of water running through pipes.

"I have questions."

"I'm sure you do. Her name is Grace, and she wants to talk to you."

"Do you know why?" He seemed more curious than anything else.

"She probably won't know what to say to you, other than introducing your kid to you."

"Ah. I see." He sighed heavily. "How does she know it is mine?"

"Do you know how people know they're pregnant? Don't look at me like that. I've had rough conversations with too many people not to have to ask."

He gave her a wide-eyed stare, then nodded. "I was taught menstrual cycle. They bleed every month until they are pregnant."

Lucy stared at Dietrich for a moment, then nodded. "Close enough. Grace was at her mom's ranch for a month before she slept with you. Her mom doesn't approve of her job, so when Grace sees her, she doesn't sleep with anyone. While at her mom's ranch, she bled. Then the day she returned to Meridune, three people purchased her time. There was a couple before you, who were far more interested in sleeping with each other than with her. After they left, you got her. You slept with her. She didn't take any other people that night. The next morning, she saw the first signs of the Red Death. Sometime after that, she found out she was pregnant."

He looked down at his drink, which had appeared during her answer. "The Red Death doesn't appear that quickly."

"It can, if a person gets sick a lot, which Grace does."

He looked as if he wanted to be angry, but he kept it in well enough. Lucy was impressed. Most accounts of this man were that he was quick to anger. "You don't believe me, do you?"

"It's hard to believe."

"Look, the baby will be born by the time the next train gets to Meridune. You were headed east anyway. Stop at Meridune and talk to Grace. That's all she wants."

He made a noncommittal sound in the back of his throat and took a sip of his drink.

"You're taking this better than you did earlier."

"I've had time to think. And yell."

Lucy took a sip of her coffee and looked around the room. There were too many people here, and she hated it. She looked at Dietrich and decided to ask him the same question she'd asked Roger. Maybe he had a definite answer. "When are you and Ms. Bauer set to leave this town?"

"Three days from now. Friday morning."

"Any way we can convince your cousin to leave now?"

"We have a coach ride to the train station nearby."

Lucy pursed her lips, an annoyed look on her face. "You didn't answer my question."

He seemed to shrink back into himself. "I . . ." He paused, thought about things, and answered. "I don't know. You would have to ask her."

Lucy looked down at their drinks, which were almost empty, then back up at Dietrich. "Let's finish our drinks and head back up to her room."

Dietrich raised his drink. They toasted silently, finished their drinks, and headed back upstairs.

TWENTY-FIVE

Again with this nonsense?" Ms. Bauer had her arms crossed, an equally cross look on her face.

"All right, if you don't want to leave tonight, what about tomorrow morning?"

That was met with silence. Ms. Bauer looked away from Lucy and started to pace between the furniture. The woman navigated gracefully between the chairs, walked to the side of the room with the windows, leaned against the desk for a moment, then turned back to face Lucy. Ms. Bauer held her gaze, then looked at Dietrich. They spoke a few sentences in Deutsche, then Ms. Bauer held up her hands.

"Fine. We can leave in the morning after breakfast, if there is a coach."

"I have a wagon with two horses."

There was a snicker from Roger, who leaned against the wall next to the door.

Ms. Bauer, Dietrich and Lucy all looked at Roger. Lucy with a smile in her eyes, Dietrich with a look that indicated he had no idea what to think, and Ms. Bauer with indignation. When he cleared his throat as if to hide his snicker, Lucy smiled. She hid it when Ms. Bauer looked her way again.

"A wagon?"

"It was what I could find on short notice. I'm leaving this town. It's not safe. I bought transportation that could take all of us and your luggage. If you want to stay here another three days, that's your problem, but Dietrich is coming with me. He's my Assignment, and I won't leave him behind or allow him to make a decision that may get him killed. Grace wants to talk to him. That means he stays alive."

"You didn't indicate this downstairs."

"Lucy only reveals information when it's necessary." All eyes landed on Roger. He pushed against the wall and stood tall. "I've known Lucy a long, long time. If she thinks it's dangerous, it probably is. We should leave tonight. If you refuse, we should definitely leave in the morning, before breakfast."

Before Ms. Bauer could voice her thoughts, Roger stepped to her and held out his hands. She hesitated, then placed her hands in his.

"I've worked for your family a long time now. Your uncle trusted me to keep you safe. Trust me to keep you safe now."

Lucy could see when Ms. Bauer gave in. Her entire body relaxed to the point of sagging.

"All right." Her voice reflected her defeat. "We leave in the morning."

"Thank you. I'm going to go sleep outside of the town. I'll be back in the morning." She pointed her finger at Dietrich. "Don't die."

"I could come with you?" He asked, as if afraid to.

She gave him a hard look. "I'm sleeping in Bucky's stall."

He didn't look deterred. "You said you have two horses?"

"This doesn't fit any of the things I've heard about you."

"I've been trying to change since I arrived in the west." Dietrich cleared his throat. "I have heard I am . . . a hard man to like."

Lucy opened her mouth, then closed it. She had nothing to say to him, therefore turned to Ms. Bauer. "And you? Anything to add?"

The woman looked to be thinking about it for a moment, then shook her head. "No."

Lucy nodded and looked at Dietrich. "All right. Let's go."

"*Ja.* I fetch my bag."

The others in the room waited in silence as he went to the bedroom. He came back a couple minutes later with a backpack. He slung it onto his back as he joined Lucy. She turned to Roger.

"See you in the morning?"

"We'll be waiting outside for you." A look of surprise blossomed on his face. "Wait! What happened to Lance?"

Lucy walked past him to the door. "I'll tell you in the morning. We'll have a ways to go."

With that, she stepped out of the room, Dietrich on her heels.

જીભ્લજીભ્લજીભ્લ

They were well away from the town before Roger turned to Lucy and indicated the horses. "Bucky's the black and white one, isn't he?"

"Yep."

"What happened to Lance?"

"Split a hoof bad enough he has to be pampered for too long."

"Wow. How did that happen?"

"He slipped on an old gravel road. After that, he wasn't walking right. I took him to a vet who diagnosed him. She lives on a horse ranch. They traded me, almost equal value, Bucky for Lance. I tried to get a horse that looked like Lance, but Bucky chose me."

"Wow, that's unbelievable. You've had Lance a real long time."

A small smile came to her lips, unnoticed. "Yep."

Roger looked forward. There was nothing sharing the road with them. "I can't believe after all this time . . ."

When he grew quiet, Lucy wondered if he finally clued in to the joke.

"Wait a minute." There was surprise in his voice. "How did you have Lance for over twenty years?"

She cracked a smile and turned her head to look at him but didn't say anything.

A glimmer of realization came to his eyes. "Wait . . . how many horses did you have named Lance?"

The smile grew wider and, this time, showed off her large teeth made brighter in contrast to her skin. "All of them."

Lucy turned back to look at the road, not that it was needed. There was no one out here.

"What?" His voice was raised.

She heard Ms. Bauer and Dietrich, who had been playing cards, stop their chatter. Lucy looked at Roger. "All of them were named Lance." She gave him a snicker. "Took you long enough to figure that one out."

He gave her an indignant look. "This was a joke to you?"

She made a noise and used the reins to urge the horses to walk faster. The road was hard-packed dirt and looked safe enough for the wagon. She then turned to Roger and shrugged. The look on his face was priceless. She smiled again, sheer happiness in her eyes, then turned back to concentrate on the task at hand, mostly to irritate Roger. He made indignant sounds and leaned back a little farther on the bench. There was nowhere to go, and he was obviously irritated with her.

Lucy smiled for a long time while Roger pouted. She hadn't called all her previous horses Lance as a joke, but once it became obvious that he, and others, didn't realize she'd switched horses but not names, Lucy went with it. She made bets with herself against who would come to the right conclusion last. Roger wasn't the last, but he wasn't the first either. For some reason, his confusion was the best, probably because she'd known him the longest. She smiled wider as the road continued under them. They would arrive at Two Forks within a few minutes. She hadn't told the others her plan but wanted to use Mortimer's place to do so. He seemed keen to leave the area too.

They turned a bend and saw his fence. She turned the wagon onto his road. "We're stopping here to talk to the owner. Not sure how long we'll stay."

"I thought we were going to the next town with a train station?" Ms. Bauer seemed annoyed.

"I talked to Mortimer last night. He was keen on leaving. We'll talk to him and see what he thinks. We're away from the main town. It's safe for a little bit out here."

They arrived at his yard. He was again standing at his gate. He tipped his hat when he saw Lucy. "Something happen?"

"I talked my companions into leaving early. We have a spot for you, if you want to come with us."

"Have you all had breakfast?"

"No."

He nodded. "Come inside. I'll make some quick food and pack as you eat."

Lucy looked at her companions. They all nodded and started to disembark.

The thick-cut farm bacon and fresh eggs went well with the fresh coffee and warm bread. They ate quickly and were on the road less than an hour after arriving at Two Forks. Mortimer sat with Roger on the bench while Lucy rode Bucky. Mortimer had hitched his horse up to the wagon, as it was a work horse and used to pulling wagons. Lucy was more comfortable riding a horse as she traveled anyway, to keep an eye out for trouble.

The plan was to head to the next town with a rail station which would take them to Sacramento. Ms. Bauer had some belongings in storage at the train station there and wanted to make sure to get everything back home. Lucy wasn't told what belongings were left in Sacramento and was a bit put off. At this point, they were close enough to Bend, they could have gone there instead of Sacramento. Lucy didn't fancy going to any town that felt too crowded. Also, all those towns were connected by the same pipe network. If one went down, she felt it was possible that all the pumps would go down. Lucy wanted to get as far away as possible from this area, as soon as possible.

There was a train that ran north and south twice a day; she had used it to get down in this area. With luck, they could get to the train station by nightfall. Lucy wanted to hurry and catch the noonday train but felt that was impossible with the wagon. She sighed and looked around. There wasn't much out here. Though the people were finally winning over the land and turning the red earth back into black soil, there still wasn't much growing. It was almost winter, though. Maybe the crops had already been brought in for the year. Even the trees, sad, stunted, and leafless, looked like they were struggling too much.

A burst of giggles from the wagon stopped her thoughts. Lucy looked over and from what she could tell, Ms. Bauer just won another hand of cards. Dietrich looked annoyed, but only a little. Ms. Bauer said something quietly to him, and Lucy couldn't hear it. Whatever the woman said, Dietrich gave a hearty laugh. It made Lucy smile. At least those two weren't a problem. She hoped that would continue.

ಬಂಬಂಬಂ

They made it to the train station by eleven, much to Lucy's surprise. Dietrich and Roger unloaded the wagon while Ms. Bauer went to secure train tickets. Once the wagon was empty, Mortimer took Lucy to the other end of the small town. There was a stable there, and he knew the owners. He felt they might buy the wagon and Lucy's extra horse. It was an easy purchase for them, but Lucy lost out on the deal. She put it out of her mind quickly, though. She still had most of what Ms. Bauer had paid her for the guard job. Mortimer sold his horse for less than it was worth as well, but didn't seem bothered by it.

Wagon and horses situated, Lucy and Mortimer wandered back toward the train station and headed down to the Under. Bucky was calm, but Lucy doubted it would last. He didn't like the Under much, but she'd never had a horse that did.

"You don't mind if I tag along still, do you?"

Lucy turned her head to look at Mortimer. "I don't see a problem with it."

They were on the train platform, waiting on the train with Bucky. Roger, Dietrich, and Ms. Bauer were seated at a café close by. Lucy and Mortimer stood with other passengers who had horses. They weren't allowed near the café. It made sense to Lucy, but others around her were complaining. Mortimer decided to stand with her, stating horse neighs were better than the chatter of people waiting for the train.

Lucy turned back to look at Bucky but still questioned Mortimer. "You going toward family?"

"Don't have any."

She gave him a slightly shocked look. Though his face was perpetually grumpy, he was a kind man and helped at every opportunity. Surely someone would have seen past the grump at some point in his life. "That surprises me."

He wet his lips and sighed a little. "It's a long story."

"We've got time, if you feel like sharing?"

He sighed again. "I had a wife. Caroline and I were married six years. She gave me three children. Hughy, Mara, and Tara. Our fourth child died during delivery and took Caroline with him. I raised the kids as best I could. Never saw the point in having another wife. The kids and the farm were enough to keep me going. Hughy died at the age of fourteen because he thought he could outsmart a Howler that was killing our chickens." Mortimer shook his head. "Damned fool ran off into the wilderness one day and never came back. His bloodied horse did though. Vet said it was Howler bites and scratches on the horse's body. Horse died the next day."

Lucy placed a comforting hand on Mortimer's arm but didn't say anything.

Mortimer sighed again. "Mara and Tara were twins. Tara married first. She died the same way her Ma did, in childbirth. Unfortunately, it was the first babe that killed her. Docs did the best they could to save her but couldn't. She bled to death, same as Caroline."

"That's terrible. I'm sorry."

He made a noise in the back of his throat, then sighed again. "Mara ran off after that. Said I was bad luck. She left me a letter and took a horse. I have no idea where she went. I didn't try to find her, as she wanted to be left alone. I hope to find out one day what happened to her, but," he shrugged, "I don't think I ever will."

"You could hire someone."

"To what end? She doesn't want me in her life. She made that plain in her letter. No, I hope to run into her one day, catch a glimpse, and just see her. She can live her life the way she wants. I just want a glimpse."

"I'm sorry."

He made the same noise as before. "Life's not always easy."

"That's for sure."

They fell into companionable silence as through the tunnel came the sound of an approaching train.

TWENTY-SIX

Lucy was woken from her light doze by an odd sensation. It felt like her stomach was doing a flip flop. Her eyes popped open as screams came from the train car. She instinctively reached out to steady herself, as she felt like she was falling. The noise, buckling wood, and the screeching of metal on metal as the train tried to stop came to her ears. It also sounded like things were falling and glass was breaking. Lucy barely had time to wonder what was going on before she was thrown into the seat in front of her.

Pain blossomed on her face as her nose connected with the seat back. Luckily, her arms were still up so she didn't hit as hard as she could have. Lucy leaned back in her seat and saw that the front of the car was higher than it should be, by quite a bit. She also realized the only light in the car was from outside the windows. She turned to Mortimer, who sat in the seat next to her, and placed a hand on his arm.

"Mortimer?"

"I'm all right, I think."

"Good." She took a breath and raised her voice. "Roger?"

"He went to the restroom." Ms. Bauer's voice, from the seat in front of Lucy, sounded pained.

Lucy carefully rose from her seat and walked a few steps to look Ms. Bauer in the eye. She caught Dietrich's eye as he stretched his arms above his head as if looking for injuries. At least he looked all right. Lucy turned her attention to Ms. Bauer. Her nose was bleeding.

"Other than that nosebleed, are you all right?"

Ms. Bauer raised a hand to her nose, her eyes full of disbelief. "I don't know. I don't even know how I missed that my nose is bleeding."

"We're all in shock." She looked up as the door at the lower end of the car opened and Roger stepped through. They looked each other in the eye and nodded to each other. Hired Hands were trained for things like this.

Lucy moved to the higher end of the train, took a deep breath, and spoke in a loud voice, not to be denied. "Listen up!"

That killed all the noise.

"I'm Lucy. I'm a Hired Hand. If you all listen to me and my associate Roger, we'll be able to get out of the car in an orderly fashion. A lot of injuries happen after the fact, when people are trying to rush around. So, let's take things slowly."

Lucy looked around the dimly lit car and saw that most people were in fact looking at her and paying attention. Lesson the first in accidents: act like you know what you're doing; people need guidance and want a leader. Be that leader.

She took a deep breath again. "Stay in your seats and see how badly you're hurt. Start with you. If you're traveling with someone else, make sure you know your own injuries first. Start with your head and face." She reached up to touch her head and realized her hat was missing. Lucy filed that away for later and touched her head and face, then moved to her neck.

"Next touch your neck, then move it around."

Lucy demonstrated and spoke as she moved her hands around her body. When she reached her knees she said, "You may not be able to touch your feet from a seated position. Just rotate them and make sure you're not hurt. Now that you're done with you, if you're traveling with someone, make sure they know their injuries too. If you're traveling with small children, check the eldest first, then have them help you check anyone younger. I know some babies are crying, but we're going to need everyone's help to get out. Now, if you're traveling by yourself, but there is someone in the seat next to you, check on them. I'll give you a few minutes to check on people around you, then I'll have more to say."

There was a general murmur as people talked to each other. Roger came up to speak to her softly.

"You seem like you know what you're doing."

"Your dad always taught me how to look like I did."

This earned her a laugh.

"Can you check the doorway to make sure we can get out?" Lucy kept her voice low.

"Already did before coming back in here. The accident threw the door open, and the way appears clear." Roger sounded confident, which calmed Lucy.

"Good. I'm going to talk to them again."

"Dead first?" he asked before moving away a step.

"Yep." Lucy looked around, saw most people were finished and took a deep breath. "All right. Is there anyone unresponsive?"

A man at the lower end of the car raised his hand. "I'm traveling alone. The woman next to me isn't responding."

Roger moved to the end of the train carefully. She watched as he moved to the pair, leaned over to the passenger, then stood tall and looked her way. She saw the minute shake of his head and nodded.

"All right. Now we need to find out if we can stand. We're going to do that one person at a time. Until I reach you, you will stay seated. Chaos causes injuries."

The people in the car all had their eyes on her. Lucy went to the row on her right and looked at the woman in the aisle seat. "Ma'am, are you by yourself?"

The young woman shook her head and laid her hand on the knee of the man next to her. "My husband and I are traveling together."

"Are either of you injured, as far as you can tell?" She looked at them both as she spoke.

They shook their heads and the woman spoke. "Bruises probably."

"All right. Ma'am, please stand. Once you can tell you're ok, you're going to start slowly toward the other end of the train. Keep your hand on the seats to keep yourself from falling." She looked to the man next to her. "Sir, please stay in your seat until she's one seat down, then start moving."

He nodded, and Lucy watched as they followed her instructions. Both seemed fine, even though the steep decline proved hard to walk. Once they were a few seats away, Lucy turned to the row on her left and instructed them in the same way.

₧₧₧

It took some time to get everyone out of the car. Lucy and Roger left last, and they could tell by the noise in the tunnel that most of the cars were probably empty now.

"What do we do with the woman?" Roger asked as he indicated the car's lone fatality.

"We wait until we find out if there are other corpses being brought out. People don't need to see her yet."

"All right. Then that's it."

"Good. I'm going to find Bucky."

Roger's eyes went wide. "I forgot about Bucky. I'm surprised you stayed this long."

"You know if I had rushed out of here to check on him, other people would have followed me, and they would have hurt themselves and each other."

They locked eyes for a moment, then Roger spoke. "Let's get out of here. I'm going to see if I can help some more."

Lucy nodded, and they left the car carefully. Once outside, Lucy moved quickly to the back of the train, and Roger went to join the others. It was a mess in the tunnel. There wasn't that much space, and no one really knew where to stand. Several of the passenger cars farther down the line had fallen on their sides. Lucy had to climb over them to find the last car, which housed the stalls. She breathed a sigh of relief when she climbed over a car and saw that the last two cars were upright. People looked shaken, but not injured, and someone had let the horses out. There was more space back here, beyond the train.

As she moved over the train and down to the horses, several people stopped her with the same question. "What happened? Is everyone else ok?"

Lucy looked back to where she had come and realized the light didn't help anyone see beyond the wreckage. She looked at the crowd in front of her. "People are up there. I'm here for my horse. Once I check on him, I'll go back over and find out what we need to do. I'm Lucy, by the way."

The crowd of people seemed to take that as an invitation to ask more questions. Lucy held up her hands and raised her voice. "I don't have any more information! I'm here to check on my horse!"

The people moved out of the way as she pressed forward. Lucy moved quickly to the horses and nodded to the older gentleman she had given Bucky to earlier.

"I'm here to check on my horse."

"Lucy. I remember. The horses all seem fine. You're the only one who's come back so far."

"People are in shock. I think they'll start coming back here when they realize they can." She was in front of Bucky now, who was neighing and tossing his head. When she placed her hand on his neck, he immediately calmed down. She looked at the stable attendant. "Any idea what happened?"

"None whatsoever."

"I'm going back to the front. I don't want to take Bucky until the way is clear."

"You might not want to move him forward anyway."

She frowned. "Why not?"

"Well," he ran a large hand through his salt and pepper gray hair, "the nearest station is behind us."

"Good to know. If you don't mind, I'll relay information of these people and horses to the people up front."

"Thank you. Let them know Jay is still alive, would you?"

She held out her hand. "And you would be Jay?"

He took her hand and gave her a firm handshake. "Yes ma'am."

"I'll relay the information. I would imagine I'll be back."

He nodded. Lucy patted Bucky one last time, then headed back the way she came.

⊱⊰⊱⊰⊱⊰

Now that she had seen how the passengers at the end of the train were doing, it seemed even more chaotic on the other side of the fallen car. There wasn't much room between the train and the wall on the right side; there was more room on the left, but no one was on that side of the tracks. She wondered why but then realized those in charge might not know if the other train was going to come down the tracks. Lucy filed that away for the moment as she moved through the crowds, looking for those in charge. She spotted Roger first, nodded to him, but continued looking around. Finally, she saw a group of people in Rail uniforms and moved to them. They looked just as shocked and scared as the rest of the people.

"Hi. Jay wanted you to know he's still alive."

"Oh, thank goodness!" a woman who looked about as old as Jay answered. She was plump and had white hair tied in a bun. "You saw him?"

Lucy smiled at the question. "Yes, I talked to him. I had to see about my horse. The last two cars didn't leave the track."

"Is it easy to go over the fallen car?"

"It's probably safe if not too many people do that, but I usually err on the side of caution."

The woman nodded and looked to the others. "We need to get that car out of the way."

Lucy cleared her throat. "Who's in charge?"

"The conductors died. We're not really sure who is."

"One of you needs to take that role. These people need someone to be in charge. Do you know what caused this?" Lucy tried to keep her voice calm to help the others in the group.

The woman with the white hair looked at the others in the group. "Fred, you're the next senior member. You should take charge."

"I've never been in charge." Fred rubbed a nervous hand over his short, thick, curly hair. His lips quivered.

"But do you remember the training?" the woman asked.

Lucy watched Fred as he took a deep breath. She heard more than saw him release it and stand taller. "Yes, I do." He looked at Lucy. "I need helpers."

"I can help, and I'm with people who can help as well," Lucy volunteered.

"Thank you. First order of business, separate the very hurt from those who aren't."

Lucy nodded. "Yes, sir. Can we use the entire tunnel or is there a chance the other train will come down that track?"

"We passed it before we crashed. Use the entire tunnel. This is the same train they would use in the morning."

"So nothing else will be on this track?"

"No ma'am."

"Good." Lucy sighed and looked at all those gathered. "Any idea what caused this?"

They all shook their heads, but Fred answered. "None."

"Maybe that's best?" Lucy made it a point to emphasize she was asking a question.

The others looked at each other, then at Fred. The man sighed. "Probably."

All were silent for a moment, then Lucy nodded to Fred. "I'll get people who can help."

"And we'll get things going with the rest of the crowd," Fred stated with confidence.

They nodded at each other, and Lucy left as Fred spoke to the people at large.

"Can I have your attention please? If anyone is able, we need to get people organized! If you can help, please step forward! Thank you!"

Lucy walked to Roger and nodded to the small group. Ms. Bauer, Dietrich, and Mortimer all looked in good shape. "I volunteered us to help, unless anyone has a problem with that?"

The group seemed to think about it for a moment, then all nodded. Ms. Bauer spoke up. "We can help. I've spoken to a few other people. I know who wants to help."

"Good. Go get them." Lucy looked forward and saw no one had come forward to help yet. "People are sometimes reluctant to help others when they're scared. No one else is volunteering yet."

"Well, then let's do it." Mortimer moved forward, raised his hand, and spoke loudly. "I'll help. Tell me how!"

That seemed to trigger others. Soon, a good group of people had moved toward the Rail employees to help them out.

TWENTY-SEVEN

Organizing the survivors took some time, but eventually, the injured were patched up and sitting against the far wall of the tunnel. Those who could, helped move the injured. Those who were willing moved the dead. Not too many lost their lives, but enough had that they were now in the car that had housed the horses. Fred and Jay felt it best to keep the bodies out of sight. Fred had asked for and received help from most of the strong people in the tunnel to move the fallen cars. It was a lot of work and was done very slowly, but the way was now clear. There weren't that many cars in the way, but it would help with cleanup when that could be done officially.

Fred also asked one of the horse owners to ride down to the nearest station to alert the officials of the incident. A telegram wire ran through the tunnel, and there were telegraph keys at regular intervals. A volunteer was sent by horse down both sides of the tunnel to find the nearest ones, but unfortunately, the two closest didn't work. He told this quietly to Lucy and a few other helpers but asked them to keep it quiet as he didn't want to scare people worse.

Once the rider was on her way to the closest station, and the injured cared for, Fred stood around with his helpers for the next step. "I don't like that the wire isn't working. It could mean there was some kind of disaster."

"You think we got Bombarded?" one of the helpers asked.

"This area does get earthquakes. It could have been that. That'll knock out communications too. It could be a bad storm, coupled with something derailing us down here."

The others murmured to themselves. No one had really thought of all the possible reasons for derailment.

Lucy raised her hand and spoke when Fred called her name. The group found it easier to raise their hand and wait for acknowledgement when working together.

"What are our options then?"

"We can wait here until the horse returns or go toward the station now."

"How long will it take for the horse to come back?"

"The station is less than ten miles away. If they're running, it shouldn't take more than an hour to get there and back."

"That's if the tunnel is clear." This was from Jay, who'd had a tendency throughout the night to temper what Fred said with some amount of pessimism.

Roger raised his hand and was called on. "Well, if we don't know if the way is clear, maybe we should wait. There's enough food in the dining car."

Fred cleared his throat and spoke in a near whisper. "There are some injured who might not make it."

"If we start walking in the wrong direction, they might not make it anyway." This was from another volunteer, who was the main caretaker for the injured.

As the man spoke, and the others ruminated on his words, Lucy tried to remember if he was a doctor or nurse and then gave up. He had been a great help with the injured people. She and Roger had lent a hand as well, but he had taken care of the most injured. He knew what he was doing.

The group thought for a few moments before Fred spoke up again. "Well, what should we do?"

"We sent the rider more than half an hour ago." This was Jay, who spoke as he looked at his pocket watch. "Let's wait another half hour, then put it to a vote with more of the people here."

"Votes don't usually work in situations like this," Fred stated. "But let's wait and hope the rider comes back."

The group nodded and dispersed throughout the crowd to take care of those who needed it.

࠶ࡃ࠶ࡃ࠶ࡃ

When the rider, a young woman on her racehorse, came back, she immediately went to Fred. Lucy and others watched her return and slowly made their way to him. To Lucy, she looked upset.

As Lucy approached them, Roger whispered in her ear. "Doesn't look good."

"No, it doesn't."

Once the volunteers were gathered, Fred took them farther down the tunnel. The rider, who had already dismounted, stayed close. Her horse didn't look winded. It impressed Lucy. Not many people had racehorses. It was shorter than Bucky but looked sleek and wiry. Despite all that was going on, Lucy really wanted to ride that horse. She was pretty sure it would be fun to run at full gallop on a racehorse.

Fred started to speak, and Lucy brought her attention to him.

"Got some bad news. The town is fine, but there was a Bombardment farther south."

The others murmured as Lucy raised her hand. When Fred acknowledged her, she asked, "Do you know what town?"

Fred shook his head. "It was closer to Obispo."

Lucy shook her head. "I just realized I have no idea where we are."

Fred nodded. "We're north of Jose. Obispo is less than two hundred miles away."

The group was silent as they pondered the situation.

Ms. Bauer was the first to speak. "Aren't we too far away to be affected by the Bombardment?"

Fred cleared his throat. "It's been a while since I heard of a Bombardment, but my grandparents talked of the first one. When it comes, it's designed to take out the entire targeted area, and it wipes it out completely. They don't use large meteors, but they use enough to do the job. It causes a shockwave that can be felt for a long way off."

The others were quiet for a long time. The group allowed it as it was needed. Finally, a voice spoke up. "Do we go to the town then?"

"It's clear all the way, according to Dawn. She told the station what happened. The person there said the town is fine and are sending help."

"So we can go to the town now if we want." Jay sounded optimistic for the first time in a while.

"Sure, but we still have the injured to worry about. And do we let people take their things?" another employee asked.

Fred shook his head. "We should tell people how far it is and to only take what they think they can carry for that distance. We should also ask for volunteers to stay with the injured. If I remember correctly, the station will send a handcar or two for the injured and for those who can't walk far."

Lucy raised her hand but spoke before Fred saw her. "Is there a possibility of Bandits coming down here?"

"There are enough stops along this railway that the only entrances are at stations. They can't get down here without notice."

"Even in an emergency?"

Fred shook his head. "The Rail has guards for such occasions."

Lucy nodded, satisfied.

Fred clapped his hands. "All right. Let's get people organized. Those who want to walk and those who need to stay. For those who want to wait, but can walk, let's find out why they don't want to leave. I don't want to leave too many people behind. Though the dining car has food, it's not enough to sustain too many people if it takes too long to get those handcars here."

The volunteers nodded and got moving.

&8003&8003&8003

Lucy rolled her head from left to right and stretched her arms over her head. It was hours later, and they were in the Jose station. She had walked the entire way, in order to allow an elderly woman to ride Bucky. She was tired and ached. It had been a long walk in a nearly dark tunnel. There were lanterns, but the light didn't stretch that far. She wanted a bed, some food, and a hot bath. It didn't matter what order she got them in.

Fred was on the station platform, helping people up. He had already let the train survivors know that most would have to stay underground, in the station. The water pumps were down; the town couldn't risk an increase in people. Some had already started the trip to Jose Under. The elevator down was in the station but could only take so many people. The injured were being taken down, as there was a bigger hospital below.

The woman on Bucky was waiting her turn to dismount. There were stretchers and helpers. She was nice enough, but Lucy was too exhausted to converse with anyone. Ms. Bauer, Dietrich, and even Mortimer were in poor spirits. Roger seemed fine, but Lucy knew he was hiding how he felt. That was his way when he was tired.

Finally, the woman, whose name Lucy forgot completely, was taken off Bucky. That allowed her to go to the makeshift refugee area set up in the tunnel. There were rolls laid out in the dirt and some cots. The cots were reserved for older people. Lucy didn't care. She took Bucky to a post that had been erected, unfurled her own bedroll away from the others, and lay down. In moments, she was fast asleep.

ഓരോ ഓരോ ഓരോ

The smell of coffee woke her in the morning. She had her hands wrapped around the mug before her eyes were open. Roger's laugh got her to open her eyes. She glared at him.

"What?"

"I knew that would wake you."

She made a noise and took a nice slow sip of coffee.

"They have doctors, nurses, and other medics looking over the survivors. We're all checked out. They're asking those of us who can leave to let them know our plans."

She pulled the mug away from her lips. "So they need to check me out and then we can leave?"

"Well, the five of us have to have a plan, but yes."

"I need to get Dietrich back to Meridune. Did you start talking about what you all what to do?"

Roger shook his head. "Ms. Bauer would like to know what our options are. We don't really know the state of the train. She has some things in storage in Sacramento."

Lucy frowned. "How much did she take?"

"Since she rented the train car when she came out here, she was offered the option of furnishing it with her own things. The price of the car included storage at her destination until her return trip."

Lucy opened her mouth to speak, realized she had no idea how she felt about all that, and took another sip of coffee instead.

Roger had the audacity to laugh.

She glared at him, then pulled the mug away. "So she wants to know when she can retrieve her things?"

He nodded as he spoke. "Retrieve her things and return with all of it to the East Coast."

"What about Mortimer and Dietrich?"

"Mortimer wants to stay with you. Dietrich is being unbelievably silent."

Lucy nodded, finished her cup of coffee, and handed the mug to Roger. When he took it, she moved the thin blanket off her body and stood carefully. She stretched her limbs, noted the ones that hurt, and stretched some more. Done, she turned to the mat and blanket on the ground.

"Blanket isn't mine . . .?"

"They handed some out. I saw you didn't have one and threw it over you."

"Thank you." She reached down and grabbed the blanket. "I'm going to fold this up, roll up my mat, and check on Bucky. I'll be with y'all in a moment."

"Don't forget to let the docs check you out."

"Yep," Lucy stated as she started folding the blanket. She looked at Roger. "Where's the group, anyway?"

"We're closer to the platform. You'll see us."

Lucy nodded and turned back to the task at hand.

ஐ⍥ஐ⍥ஐ⍥

The medic who checked her out looked and sounded tired. "How familiar are you with your own aches and pains?"

"I'm a Hired Hand. I have training."

He looked at her right lapel and nodded. "Unfortunately, I've known some Hired Hands who weren't that familiar with their own bodies. They were fairly new to the trade, though."

"I've been at this for," she thought about it for a moment, "thirty years. I know my body. Nothing is broken. I haven't checked for bruises, but I imagine I have some from the way I feel."

He wrote something down on his clipboard. "Ever break any bones?"

"One of the times I was shot, it broke my radius. I remember well what that feels like."

He looked at her. "If you're certain nothing is broken, I can give you the 'all clear.'"

"I'm sure," she said in a confident voice.

He nodded, wrote something on the clipboard, then tore off the paper. He handed it to her and gave her a tired smile. "You're good. Just

253

see a doctor if any of your aches and pains last too long, all right?"

She saluted him with the paper in hand. "Yes, sir."

He nodded and turned to the person waiting behind Lucy. "Next!"

Lucy moved toward Roger and the rest of the group and tamped down the desire to wave the paper in triumph. She instead nodded and said good morning.

"Do we have any information on the train situation?"

"There was a cave-in just this side of Bend. The train to and from Sacramento has been delayed; they're not sure how long."

Lucy nodded and sighed. "I can ride back to Meridune. I don't want to wait for the train. Grace may be dead by then." She looked at Dietrich. "I'll get you there safe."

Ms. Bauer stood taller. "My cousin and I are going back to Sacramento to wait for the train."

Lucy gave the woman a steady, deadly look. "My Assignment is to get Dietrich to Grace so she can talk to him. She is dying because of him. You will not stop me from completing my Assignment."

TWENTY-EIGHT

n appalled look came to Ms. Bauer's face as she opened her mouth to speak.

"I'm going with Lucy!" The words cut through the din of the other people in the tunnel. In the silence, Dietrich stood taller and started talking to his cousin in Deutsche. They argued for a few minutes until Dietrich spoke loudly again, and in English.

"*Nein*! Do you trust Lucy?"

Ms. Bauer grew quiet, lowered her head for a moment, then looked at Lucy. "Yes. I do."

"So do I. I go with her in good faith. I go with her, I talk to Grace, and I listen to her. When we are done talking, I will think about the situation more. It is the best lesson you taught me."

Even in the dim light, Lucy could see the blush rising to Ms. Bauer's cheeks. The woman cleared her throat, then rubbed her arms, as if cold. "Fine. We'll join you in Meridune once we are able."

Lucy noticed the look on Dietrich's face when Ms. Bauer agreed with him. The man looked surprised. He then smiled and nodded. "Good." He looked at Lucy. "How soon should we go?"

"A soon as possible." She looked at Roger. He would be following Ms. Bauer. "I think this is where we part ways again."

He held out his hand. "Until we meet again."

Lucy shook his hand. "Keep safe."

They nodded to each other, then Roger looked at Ms. Bauer. "Let's go find out how we can get to Sacramento."

She nodded, and both headed off to find the right officials.

Lucy looked at Mortimer. "Where are you going, old timer?"

"With you, if that's all right?"

"Fine by me. Can you handle a gun?"

"I'm a bit shaky," he said with reluctant confidence.

Lucy nodded and looked at Dietrich. "Do you know how to use a gun?"

He shook his head. "*Nein*, but I want to learn."

"We'll have to hire someone for the trip. I can't defend two people at once. Let's go find out where we're supposed to go from here. Once we do, I'll figure out where the Hired Hands are."

The men nodded, gathered their meager belongings, and headed to the group of officials who were helping people out.

℠ℂ℠ℂ℠ℂ

Lucy was directed to the hotel, where there was a room of Hired Hands. They were on the first floor, in what looked like a meeting room. At the entrance sat two people at a small table. They had small stacks of papers in front of them. One looked at Lucy as she approached.

"Have you hired a . . ." His eyes caught on her lapel pin. "Oh. We're only asking for local Hired Hands."

She smiled. "I'm looking to hire someone. I'm with two men, neither of whom can shoot. We need to get to Meridune, which means long days on horses through some rough wilderness."

The man nodded. "We can either appoint someone to you, or you can look around and see if you want someone in particular."

Lucy nodded, moved away from the table, and started to scan the faces of the people seated. Some looked at her, some didn't. There were a few faces she almost recognized but wasn't sure if it was due to knowing them or having seen their faces on "Hire Me" or "Wanted" posters. Some Hired Hands advertised; some made big mistakes. Lucy immediately ruled out anyone who didn't make eye contact. Lucy moved a bit to see everyone, and at the back was a familiar face.

"Jing?"

The woman smirked, stood, and removed her hat in greeting. She was dressed similarly to Lucy with a cowboy hat, blue denim shirt, jeans, and tall leather boots. "Lucy my dear! How are you?"

"What are you doing out here?"

"I got stuck." Her eyes narrowed. "For the past five years."

Lucy laughed. "Well, do you want to get closer to home?"

"Maybe." The petite Asian woman moved closer to Lucy. "What's the job?"

"I'm traveling with two people to Meridune. They don't shoot."

"Guarding. All right. I'll take it."

"That was easy."

Jing gave an exaggerated wink that included a click of her tongue. "You know me well."

Lucy snickered. "Let's go."

The women moved to the front of the room, where they gave their names and quick information about the job. The man filled out the paperwork, which included the cost of the job, had them sign it, and placed the paper to the side.

"You're all set. We'll get it filed for you with the others at the end of the day."

The ladies nodded and left the room to join Mortimer and Dietrich, who waited at the bar. Introductions were made, then the group took a seat at a table to discuss what supplies were needed. Jing pulled out a well-used map and laid it out on the table, which helped the group to understand how far they really had to travel. Once plans were set, Jing took them to the ranch she had called home for the past year. It was a working farm and had a couple small barracks. The group would be welcome to spend the night, for a price.

They set their belongings in the footlockers at the end of their beds and went about shopping for their supplies. Lucy only hoped that, with the influx of people from the train wreck, the stores wouldn't be low on supplies. She was most worried about transportation. Though Jing had her own horse, they needed two more. If they couldn't find two horses, they would have to get a wagon. Lucy knew horses were a better idea for the long voyage, especially if they had to get out of a situation quickly.

‘’

The next morning, after a hardy breakfast, the quartet set out. They were able to get two horses, a pack mule, some clothing, and enough rations to get them through the first week of travel. Mortimer had purchased a shotgun and ammo. They all decided to have Dietrich learn how to shoot before buying him a gun.

"How long do we think this journey will take?"

"It's two thousand miles to Meridune, and the horses can walk about twenty to thirty miles per day. If we only used horses, it would take over three months to get there," Lucy said lazily.

"That's . . ." Dietrich's voice sounded disheartened.

"It's a long time. So we're heading to Bend, which is about three hundred miles away. From here, that's about two weeks on horseback. I'm hoping they still have trains working on that line heading east. If they do, we take the train. If they don't have a train, they may have other means by the time we get there, like carriages."

"That's a lot of speculation, Luce." Jing didn't sound too happy about the prospect either, but Lucy knew the woman would have worked out the length of the journey when she accepted the job. Lucy felt Jing was continuing the conversation to air out all grievances. It was something Jing liked doing, Lucy knew, as it later led to her looking like she had changed her mind. She would then try and get others in her group to change their minds as well. It sometimes worked and sometimes didn't. As Lucy knew Jing's methods, she knew she could use it to her advantage if needed.

"I've talked to enough Rail employees in my time. Most of them either speculate or confirm that there are contingency plans in case a Bombardment hits the rails." Lucy's voice was calm and reassuring. "The trains are still the best bet for long distance, fast travel. They should have something."

Dietrich cleared his throat. "And if they do not?"

She glanced at him out of the corner of her eye. He looked worried. "Then we ride."

The look on his face went from worried, to thoughtful, to acceptance faster than she would have thought possible. When he nodded, straightened his back, and looked forward, Lucy knew he would do whatever she told him to, which would be helpful if they ended up in a bad situation.

"All right. I trust you."

Lucy smiled and looked at Mortimer. He shrugged. "I have no plans."

That earned a laugh from Jing. "Well, that's the spirit!"

Lucy smiled and turned her attention to the road ahead. Since it was morning, and the sun was out, she didn't anticipate too many issues. In the coming days, though, there could be Bandits or wild animals. It was best to be on her guard now, to make sure it didn't slip when it was needed.

"Well, at least we're all on the same page," Lucy stated. "Dietrich, at night, I'll teach you how to hold and point a gun. If we do have to be on horseback the entire time, it's best if we all have guns."

"Just don't put me behind anyone if we have to shoot at anything, and we'll be all right." This was from Mortimer.

Jing made a concerned noise in the back of her throat. "Eyes or hands?"

"Hands. My eyes are probably going bad too, but my hands shake when I try to hold 'em steady."

"My dad had that. It was a shame, too. He set a couple records when he was my age."

"Oh, yeah? What was his name?" Mortimer sounded genuinely curious. Lucy, to Mortimer's left, wondered if Jing's dad was as well-known as the man used to proclaim. Jing grew up in Nawlyns. Her dad taught her everything she knew.

"His name was Gang Chen."

"Huh! I know that name. He came around on a tour once with those Orators. Did a few tricks, if I remember right."

Jing laughed. "Yeah, that was Dad. He liked going on those tours. He tried to take me once, but I was too busy with my new Teacher, learning this trade."

"Wasn't Mr. Chen also a Hired Hand?"

"Yeah, but he liked going on tour and trying to beat records more than getting hired to do odd jobs." She took a deep breath, and everyone in the group could hear the sadness in the heavy sigh she let out. "When his hands started to shake, and he knew he was too old to tour any more, he paid a Hired Hand to kill him. He left a note for us that said he didn't want to be condemned to a life he didn't want because his hands were betraying him."

"I'm sorry to hear that." Mortimer's voice reflected grief.

"Thanks, but don't be too sad about it. His note also said he thought about hiring me to take his life, as he knew his eldest would understand his decision. And he's right. Had he hired me, I would have done it. I knew what he loved about life. I wouldn't want him to be miserable."

"But that doesn't mean you aren't sad about his passing." Dietrich's voice sounded contemplative.

"True."

Dietrich cleared his throat. "I would have killed my father. Not because he was dying. He was a bastard and did not treat myself or my cousin fairly."

"Seemed like the two of you get along well, though, you and Ms. Bauer." Lucy was half guessing. They did argue a lot, but there still seemed to be love between the family members.

"*Ja*, yes, but we saw the unfairness. Adelia saw it more than I, as she was raised by her parents first, then us."

"I have a question about the two of you, if you don't mind?" Mortimer asked gently.

"*Ja.* Go ahead."

"Why do you have an accent when she does not?"

Mortimer rode to Lucy's right, then Jing, then Dietrich, which meant that Lucy saw the awful look Dietrich sent Mortimer. She didn't like the look. It was full of hate. When Dietrich spoke, it explained the expression.

"Adelia came here when she was ten. She knew English but had thicker accent than I. Father believed women were more attractive if they had no accent. Men were more attractive if they had accent. When she came here, he beat her until she pronounced the words correctly."

The group was stunned into silence, but only for a moment.

Jing broke the awkward silence. "Well, now I can see why you wanted him dead."

"One of many reasons." Dietrich's voice was almost too soft to hear.

"So that's my dad, and Dietrich's dad. Lucy doesn't talk about her past. What about you, Mortimer? What type of dad did you have?"

"An absent one. My mom raised me with my grandparents' help, on their farm. Dad was a Scavenger. He'd stop by every year, but never for very long. He always had a present for me and Ma. Then, the year I turned sixteen, he didn't show up. It took us some time to find out he died by Bandits."

"I'm sorry to hear that."

"Thank you."

"All right, enough depressing stories. Let's keep an eye on the road for a while and play a game." Lucy's voice held authority.

"What game?" Jing sounded intrigued.

"I spy."

"There are a few different rules to that one. Or at least, I've heard a few different versions."

"The rules I learned are: find a thing in the distance that you think only you can see and describe it. The rest of us will try and find it too." Cecil had taught Lucy this game before she took any bodyguard jobs. Though it had the appearance of a game, what it did was keep people's eyes on their surroundings. It also helped people find wild animals or Bandits before it was too late. It had saved her on a few different jobs.

"Sounds like fun!"

"Let me go first," Mortimer requested as he turned his head to look at his surroundings. "My eyes aren't that good."

Lucy gave a small laugh. "I'll bet Mortimer sees something that's too far for the rest of us to see."

"That's not really funny, young lady."

Lucy smiled at him. "Wasn't poking fun. I've known plenty of farmers who can see much farther than non-farmers. It's part of their job to scan the horizon for trouble."

Mortimer looked like he didn't believe her and made a noncommittal sound in the back of his throat.

Lucy looked him up and down. "Go ahead. Choose something."

He gave her another perturbed look before looking forward to scan the horizon.

TWENTY-NINE

That night, the quartet had to set up camp. They had left a town a few hours earlier and figured they could reach the next town by nightfall. Unfortunately, a flood had washed out a bridge over a small river. They thought to cross it on horseback, but it ended up being deeper than it looked. It took some time to find a way to cross, which left them no choice but to camp. Lucy didn't mind; she liked the outdoors. Mortimer didn't really complain, and Jing had been a Hired Hand as long as Lucy had. She knew what to expect. As they removed bedrolls and supplies from the horses, Lucy looked over at Dietrich and wondered how he would fare.

It became obvious rather quickly that Dietrich, though he was trying to help, didn't know what to do. Lucy saw him looking at her and the others as they took down their bedrolls. He watched as they set theirs up, then he placed his down as well. It was the same for his blanket and for his food. Meanwhile Mortimer, Lucy, and Jing moved around each other as if they had choreographed their movements. It surprised Lucy that Mortimer was at ease, but when he offered to go hunting for their dinner she started to understand.

"How often did you hunt when you were on your farm?"

"Lots when my wife and kids were still alive and around. When it was just me, it was a lot cheaper and safer to buy meat in town. Then, as I got older, and the town kept growing, I found I liked hunting better."

"Did you find a group to hunt with?"

"Some of the people who helped me work the farm liked to hunt, so I went with them."

She nodded and understood why he knew what to do. "Jing, want to go hunting with Mortimer?"

"Sure." She looked around, grabbed one last thing off her horse, then turned to Mortimer. "I saw some rabbits not too far away. Might be other game near them."

Mortimer nodded, and the two headed off. Lucy turned to Dietrich. "How much water do you have?"

He held the canteen in his hand up to his ear and shook it. "Some?"

"We'll need more. I can hear a river nearby. Do you mind filling everyone's canteens, or do you want me to do it?"

"Do I hold the open canteen under the water to fill it?"

"Sure, but you also have to know how to tell if the water is safe enough to drink."

He gave her a blank look, then shook his head.

Lucy nodded, as she wasn't surprised. "Do you know how to build a fire?"

"With matches?"

She had hoped he had learned how to build a fire in a fireplace at least. "You've never started a fire from nothing? Build up the wood, that sort of thing?"

"Father believed that was servant work."

"Of course he did." She gave a quiet sigh. "Do you know how to cook?"

He shook his head.

"Do you know how to hobble a horse?" She felt sure his answer would be no, but at this point, she didn't know what else to ask.

Dietrich shook his head.

"All right. I'm going to teach you all of that."

An odd look crossed Dietrich's face, but in the end he nodded and Lucy could only be grateful he wasn't fighting her.

ഇൽജ്ഇൽജ്ഇൽജ്

"Does anyone smell fire?" Mortimer asked, his face contorted as he tried to sniff the almost non-existent wind.

The group had been travelling for a couple days now and found that though Mortimer's eyesight was no better than the others, his sense of smell was top-notch. When he asked about the smell, the others stopped their horses. Bucky stopped but pranced a step or two, even with Lucy still mounted. She calmed him and wondered about his behavior. This wasn't like him. Distracted, she was not the first to answer Mortimer.

"No, but I can't always tell if there's an odd scent in the air." Jing took another deep breath. "Nah. Nothing."

Dietrich made a grand show of sniffing the air, then shook his head. "*Nein*. Nothing for me."

After calming Bucky down, Lucy sniffed the air. "I think I smell food. I don't know about fire. But if there is food, there should be fire."

Mortimer shook his head. "Smells like a forest fire."

"It's possible the Bombardment caused some fires. That has

happened before."

"How far away was the Bombardment, anyway? Not sure I caught that."

Lucy thought back and shook her head. "I don't recall. Might just be a normal forest fire?"

Mortimer shook his head. "I know it's been dry the past week, but before that, we had a lot of rain. More rain than usual in fall and winter. It's been too wet for a forest fire."

Lucy shrugged and got Bucky moving again. "Well, we won't find out anything just standing around here. Let's find a town. I think the marker said there was a town south and to the east a mile or two."

The others nodded and started moving again.

ℴℴℴ

The town looked like most other towns in the Broken States: wooden buildings grouped together to form a center, and a few outlying buildings that were residential homes. There were a few more people than usual, though, including two at the town entrance who were stopping anyone coming or going. There was a small line, which Lucy and the others joined. Lucy placed herself in front, and no one seemed to mind. The man at the front of the line looked in her eyes. His pencil hovered over the clipboard in his hand.

"Number of people in your party?"

"Four."

"Where you headed?"

"Final destination is Meridune, Arkansas, but we're trying to get to Bend to see if the trains are running west to east."

The man shook his head. "The fireball set too much on fire. You're not getting through for a while."

"Fireball?" four voices echoed.

The man looked at the four. "You hadn't heard?"

They all shook their heads, but Lucy spoke. "We've been traveling for two days now. We were on a train when the Bombardment happened."

The man folded his arms and moved the clipboard to his side. "The meteorites exploded over the ground, not sure how high up. It caused fireballs, which destroyed who knows how many buildings and houses and burnt a huge area down. The fire's still spreading, and we don't have the means to stop it. It'll stop when it hits the desert, but we're not encouraging anyone to travel south right now."

Lucy heard Dietrich and Jing talking but ignored them. "Where was the epicenter?"

"At first we heard it hit Obispo. Then other towns were mentioned. Either there were several fireballs or no one's sure which was hit. The names of the towns mentioned though, run from south of Parson to north of Los Angeles."

"That's a large area." Jing's eyes were wide.

"Though the telegraph lines weren't affected, it seems like many towns were, as most aren't answering our messages. We're hearing information from survivors as they stagger in, but," he shook his head, "most of the people are still in shock. And most seem to be from the areas affected by the fire, not the Bombardment."

Lucy nodded in understanding and sighed. "So what are our options?"

"Well, unfortunately, not much. We're getting a lot of visitors, so we're asking people to go into the tunnels under the town. Decide what you're going to do, then leave. You can stay in the tunnels for a few days at most."

"We don't even know our options." Jing's voice carried from behind Lucy.

The man looked past Lucy to Jing. "We can't advise that you go south, but in the end, it's up to you." He looked at Lucy again. "Did you want to talk to your group some more? There are more people coming in. We're going to have to start turning people away."

"Is there food down in the tunnels?"

"Yes. It ain't fancy, but it's edible."

Lucy nodded and looked at the other three. "What do we want to do?"

"Shit, I don't know what to do from here."

"We can regroup in the tunnels." Lucy looked at the man. "Can we take our horses?"

He nodded. "Yep. And all your things too."

Lucy turned back to the others, who shrugged and nodded. She turned back to the man. "All right. We'll go to the tunnels."

"Great." He unfolded his arms, and his pencil hovered over his clipboard again. "Let me get your names, then one of our helpers will take you to the tunnel entrance. They'll even give you a history lesson on why those tunnels exist, if you want."

Lucy smiled and gave her and her companions' names.

ഇരുഇരുഇരു

Half an hour later, the four were settled in the tunnels. There were a lot of people, but it wasn't crowded. The tunnels were built some years ago, as part of the rail system, but were abandoned when an underground lake was found. As the train couldn't go through the cavern, it had to go around. The tunnels were left, and the town found another way into the cavern. It was almost a tourist attraction now.

The tunnels were prettied up. Some sections were made into barracks, and one was made into a kitchen and dining area, but it was still obvious it was tunnels. The walls were bare dirt, as was the floor. Lucy hated it but tried not to mind. They had to figure out what to do. The four were seated at a table in the dining area, waiting on food. It was a small menu, a couple cold and hot sandwiches, soup, and some dessert. It smelled good, though, and looked tasty. No one around them was complaining about the food at least.

"So, what do we do?" Jing spoke as soon as the server took their orders.

"What can we do?" Dietrich looked perplexed.

Mortimer, beside Dietrich and across from Lucy, shrugged. "We can always go over the mountain, but that adds, what? Another week on our journey, easy? There's probably already snow on the mountain tops. Or we can go back to Sacramento, or we can try going south, but that doesn't seem like a good idea."

Lucy suddenly sat up taller in her chair. "Shoot. I haven't checked my messages in a while."

Jing gave a small frown. "Is that really necessary?"

"If there are no messages, I can send one and let my employer know the situation. Maybe get some direction."

"You just ordered; you want to wait?" Mortimer asked.

Lucy looked at him as she realized his voice sounded different. Lighter, perhaps. She pushed the thought to the side and shook her head. "I'm supposed to take Dietrich to Meridune, preferably before my employer dies. I need her input."

Mortimer nodded. Without another word, Lucy left the table and went to the tunnel entrance. There were a few townsfolk with clipboards by the tunnel entrance. She went to the one not occupied.

The woman looked at her with mild disinterest. "Yes?"

"I need to send a telegram and check my messages."

"Oh um . . ." She looked around and called out a name. "Victor! She wants to go to the post office to send a message. We don't have protocol for that."

The man, a lanky fellow with gray hair and beard, nodded and came over. He aimed his words at the woman, but his soft voice was loud enough for Lucy to hear. "Put it under visit the town for supplies." He turned to Lucy. "What with the Bombardment that just happened, we're bein' real careful with how many people are in town."

"What's your usual population?"

"Two hundred, so we gotta be careful."

Lucy nodded. "I understand. So can I go send a message?"

"Ayeah, just make sure to check in when you're done." He nodded to Lucy and the woman with the clipboard and left to help another.

The woman and Lucy looked at each other.

"Ok, so name?"

Lucy gave her information quickly, asked for directions to the post office, and left.

❧❦❧❦❧❦

There were three people in the post office, two behind the desk and one in front of it, bent over a bit, a pen in their hand. One of the people at the counter called a hello, but Lucy wasn't sure which one. A man stood at the counter, obscured by the one writing. The other was farther back. Lucy grabbed a paper and pencil off the table by the door and filled out her information. Once done, she looked up and caught the clerk's eyes.

The short man, who had brown hair and eyes, saw her and talked to the person in front of them. "Chris, move to the side, would you? I have an actual customer."

The person grumbled but moved out of the way. The clerk looked at Lucy again. "Help you?"

She stepped forward and laid the paper face up on the counter. It had her name and Hired Hand designation number. "I'd like to check my messages and then send one, please."

He grabbed the paper she had lain on the counter. "Do you know what you want to say?"

"I won't until I know if there are any messages."

"Sure." He started to tap his finger against the transmitter key. It didn't take long to get the message sent to the Hired Hands office. Receiving an answer, though, might take some time. But so far this trip, it hadn't.

Once he was done transmitting, the man looked at Lucy. "Shouldn't take too long. Few minutes at most."

She frowned. "Yeah, why is that? It's taken much longer on other trips."

"There's more than one office now, I think. If you filled out your paperwork like you were supposed to, the messages get sent to the office that's closest to where you're going."

Lucy grinned. "You mean I don't have to wait hours anymore?"

"Shouldn't, but don't be too excited. We're not sure what this firestorm is doing."

"Yeah, but the HH offices are Under."

He gave her a look she couldn't identify. "Sure, but if the fires block or even destroy the vents, the Under is going to have a lot of problems."

Lucy's eyes went wide. "I hadn't thought of that."

"Yeah, it's wild." The telegraph started to chatter, and his eyes immediately cast downwards. He wrote furiously as the machine clacked out its message. It was over quickly, and as the machine fell silent, Lucy heard the man inhale sharply. He handed Lucy the paper he'd been writing on. "Uh, it's for you. We're not supposed to say anything, but," he looked away then back, "I'm sorry."

The look on Lucy's face was a mixture of worry and curiosity. She took the paper with no hesitation though, as this was part of her job. Take the messages, proceed as needed. The paper had pre-written fields, with spaces after each field that were to be filled out by the clerk. It didn't say much.

To: Lucy Marsh 25-2.09-03-2072A
From: Irene, Meridune, Arkansas
Subject: Grace miscarried

THIRTY

Lucy stared at the paper as a small part of her willed it to change. Grace didn't deserve that. No woman did, but Lucy worried greatly as Grace was too far along.

"Ma'am, I'm sorry. Can you move to the side? I need to help Chris."

She nodded and moved toward the table by the door and placed her hands on the top. She laid the paper down and stared at it some more. Grace had to be close to term now, and all Lucy wanted to do was ask what happened. But she knew what happened. Grace was prone to illnesses. Since she had the Red Death, it was probably even easier for her to get sick.

Lucy shook her head and picked up more paper. She filled it out with her name and number, addressed it to Irene in Meridune, Arkansas and wrote out a two-sentence message. She then turned around and waited for Chris to be done with the clerk. He was done quickly and left without a word. Lucy took her paper to the clerk and laid it down on the counter with a couple coins for payment. He picked it up, read it, and looked at Lucy.

"This is going to take longer to get a response."

"I know. I can come back."

"You waiting at the hotel or the tunnels?"

"Tunnels."

He nodded and placed the paper on the counter in front of him. "I can send someone when you get a response, if you need me to."

"I would appreciate that."

The man nodded and continued tapping the transmission key.

ಹಂಡಹಂಡಹಂಡ

It took a couple hours for a messenger to bring her the response. Until the young girl arrived, Lucy didn't say much. She refused to plan and only stated, "I don't have all the information I need. Let's wait."

The others tried to get more out of her, but she shut them down each time. After lunch was done, she went off to Bucky's stall and sat against the wall, which placed her behind her horse. It effectively blocked most people from seeing her. Jing brought the messenger to her.

"I figured you would be hiding back here. This girl has your message and won't give it to anyone else."

Lucy stood and moved Bucky out of the way. The young girl was in jeans and a black T-shirt. She looked Lucy in the eye. "Name and number?"

Lucy gave the girl her information, and a coin, then took the message. The girl nodded and ran off. Lucy sighed and looked at the message. She had sent, "I found Deter. Does Grace want to talk to him?"

The answer was, "No."

Lucy looked up into Jing's eyes. "Where are the men?"

"Playing cards in the common area."

"I was supposed to bring Dietrich to Grace. He got her pregnant and gave her the Red Death. She wanted to let him know she's pregnant."

"All right?" Jing seemed confused as to why Lucy was giving her this information.

Lucy took a breath and released it slowly. "Grace miscarried and now doesn't want to talk to him."

Jing's eyes went wide, and she covered her mouth with her hand. "Oh!" Her hand dropped. "Well, ain't that some shit."

"You're telling me."

They were silent for a moment, then Jing shrugged. "Well, at least now you don't have to figure out how to get to Meridune."

Lucy nodded.

"This is affecting you bad. I'm trying to be lighthearted and you're missing it completely." Jing's voice held confusion.

Lucy ducked her head a bit as if embarrassed. "I had a romantic notion that somehow, he would meet Grace, Grace would have the baby, and he would take the baby and Grace's oldest, and all would live as a happy family."

Jing looked shocked, then realization dawned on her face. "Grace is a friend of yours, isn't she?"

Lucy rolled her eyes. "Yeah."

"Woman, you have got to learn not to take Assignments from friends. You always do this to yourself."

"Yeah, well." There was resignation in Lucy's voice, as if to say she wasn't going to change.

Jing shook her head. "Let's go talk to the men. But get that happy ending out of your brain. Life doesn't have many of those."

"I know. I know," she said in a huff.

Jing swung her arm around Lucy's waist, and the women walked slowly toward the common area to join the men.

❧❧❧

Dietrich sat staring at his hands, which were palm down on the table in front of him. He wouldn't look Lucy in the eye.

"The baby died?"

To make sure he understood, Lucy emphasized, "She miscarried, yes."

"She doesn't want to see me?"

"No."

Lucy watched as he turned his hands over, flexed his fingers as if making fists, then relaxed his hands. He finally looked at her. "What am I supposed to do now?"

Mortimer cleared his throat. He sat to Dietrich's left, shuffling the cards absentmindedly. "Your cousin's in Sacramento. You can go back to her."

Dietrich looked back at the table. "I have questions . . ."

"Unfortunately, we don't always get answers to the questions we have." Lucy stated this matter-of-factly. That earned her a sharp look from Dietrich. She met his gaze and didn't look away until he did.

Mortimer cleared his throat again. "So what now? How do things work with having hired Jing?"

"We'll end her contract early, unless one of you need her." Lucy stared at Dietrich for a moment or two, then finally sat down at the table. Jing came to the table a moment after that. She had been waiting, at Lucy's request, out of earshot. Her cue to return was Lucy sitting.

Once the woman was at the table, Lucy looked her way. "We're trying to decide what to do. We may have to end your contract early."

277

"Well, I already figured that one out when we were told we couldn't continue south." Jing smiled. "What are the options for this group, anyway?"

"I still want to get to Meridune, if possible, before Grace dies. That means trying to head south regardless of the fires. Traveling closer to the mountains might work."

"What about you, Mortimer?" Jing asked.

Lucy watched as Mortimer looked around the room, smiled a bit, then looked back at Jing. She wondered about it, but didn't point it out and let him speak.

"I want to settle someplace new, so I'll keep riding until I find it. I know I don't want to stay on the coast. If Lucy'll have me, I'll travel with her for a bit."

"Company's always nice." Lucy's voice was inviting.

Seemingly taking control again, Jing nodded and turned to Dietrich. "Do you know what you want to do?"

Dietrich shrugged. "I suppose I go to Sacramento and find Adelia. Then, when we can, I go home with her." He looked from Jing to Lucy. "But I need guard."

"You can hire me," Jing answered quickly.

Dietrich looked at Lucy, who shook her head.

"I'm still under employment. My job is to get back to Grace." As she said the words, she realized she didn't know if Grace needed her to get back home as soon as possible, but the contract was still intact. The messages hadn't indicated Grace was breaking the contract, and Lucy wasn't either.

Dietrich looked at Jing again. "How much?"

"We'll work it out. Let me get my current contract ended. Lucy?"

"Let's get that squared away later. I want to make sure we all know what we're doing first."

Mortimer piped up. "Do you think we can even get farther south?"

"I'm going to find out. Someone has to have more information."

The group nodded, and Lucy went looking for the information she needed.

❧❦❧❦❧❦

It took a while, but eventually, the sheriff's office was able to supply information about the current state of things. Most of the area south of Parson was on fire. It looked to be heading east due to the winds, but if the winds shifted, it could head in any direction. Travel south was heavily discouraged. As Thompson, the town Lucy was in, was slowly filling well beyond capacity, people were being encouraged to move north. Lucy didn't like it. She wanted to get back to Meridune.

Offput by the situation, Lucy went back to the post office to send another telegram to Grace via Irene. She asked point blank if Grace needed anything more from her or if Grace considered the job done. Instead of going back to the tunnels, Lucy looked around the town, and found a barbershop/salon. When she realized they weren't busy, she went in and asked to have her hair done. She had let it go too long. It had been more than a month since she last took care of it. The man shampooed her hair, oiled and conditioned it and braided it.

It took a while and the entire time, Lucy had her eyes closed, and listened to the conversation in the shop. A lot of town gossip was being thrown around. As Lucy didn't live here, she didn't know who they were talking about, but enjoyed the sound of the people's voices as the barber took care of her hair. As she was paying, a messenger showed up and handed Lucy a slip of paper. It was the same messenger as before. This time, she simply handed the paper over rather than asking for Lucy's information. Lucy left the shop, leaned against a post and read the message.

No, Grace didn't need anything from her; she considered the job done and would put payment aside for Lucy.

Officially released from her duties, Lucy headed back to the tunnels, albeit reluctantly, and was surprised to find that most people were already going to sleep. She thought this was odd, but upon inquiring, found it was eight o'clock at night. The day had gotten away from her. Instead of trying to wake anyone, Lucy grabbed an apple from the restaurant, ate it in an out of the way corner, and then went to sleep. She could tend to things in the morning.

⁕⁖⁕⁖⁕⁖

The next morning, Lucy let the others get ready before letting them know she had more news. They went to the common area and found a table easily enough. Dietrich started to talk with people at another table, and to Lucy's surprise, he spoke to them in Deutsche. Their conversation ended quickly enough, and he turned back to look at Lucy. Mortimer and Jing were looking at her as well.

"So, what's the word?" Jing asked as she flagged down a server.

"I am released from my job. I can take as long as I like to get home, I guess."

"You don't sound too happy about that," Mortimer said quietly.

Lucy frowned. "Something feels off, and I don't know what. I feel like I'm needed."

Dietrich nodded. "*Ja*, you're needed with us. I can hire you, yes?"

She looked at Dietrich and realized she had no desire to help him get back to Sacramento. Her spine seemed to tingle, and she knew she was forgetting something. There was something else she needed to do, and it wasn't in Sacramento.

"You folks know what you want for breakfast?" the server asked as she looked at the quartet.

Lucy let her thoughts go as she looked at the server. The young woman stood near the table, notepad in hand. She was tall, with brown hair and eyes. She wore a black skirt and a blouse with roses all over it.

"Rose," Lucy said as her eyes went wide.

"You feelin' all right, Luce?" Jing asked.

Lucy realized she had spoken loudly enough for everyone to hear and shook her head. "I made a promise to a woman in Bend name Rose that I would stop by on my way back home."

"You forgot?"

"Lots going on, and as that's a stop on the train, I would have seen her anyway. I didn't feel it was necessary to keep it in my forethoughts."

Mortimer spoke to the waitress, and Lucy heard a kindness there she hadn't heard in his voice before. "Miss, I'm sorry, I know Jing flagged you down, but we probably need a few more minutes. Mind coming back?"

"Sure thing! But before you decide, we're starting to run out of hot sandwiches. So if that's what you want, get it now. And we have fresh pastries, but I can tell you about those when I come back."

"Much obliged." Mortimer smiled as the woman walked away.

Lucy leaned back in her chair and frowned at Mortimer in concentration. He saw the look and shook his head. It made Lucy even more curious about his attitude, but she let it drop and turned to Dietrich.

"I'm not going back to Sacramento until I find out if there is any way to get to Bend." She turned to Jing. "Rose wants to be my Apprentice."

Jing looked surprised. "As far as I know, you've never taken on an Apprentice."

"Never felt right until Rose asked me."

Jing nodded. "I understand. I don't take on an Apprentice unless I have a good feeling about them either."

"Lucy?" All eyes went to Dietrich. "This means we are splitting up?"

Lucy nodded. "It does. If Mortimer and I head east and a bit north, we may be able to avoid the fires. Though a lot of towns have done a good job of irrigating and getting trees to grow again, there still aren't a lot of forests the farther east you go, from what I've heard. There's a good break between the mountains and most of the coastline. We should be able to get south closer to the mountain."

"And if you can't?" Jing looked skeptical.

Lucy shrugged. "We'll head back to Sacramento or hole up in another city until the fires burn out. How long can they really burn for?" She turned to Mortimer. "You still with me?"

"I'm looking for a new place to live. This sounds like it'll give me lots of new places to see."

"All right." Lucy smiled at Mortimer, then looked at Jing and Dietrich. "Will the two of you be all right?"

"Yeah." Jing waved off any worry. "I've been talking to people. A lot of others from here are heading up to Sacramento. We'll go as a group. We'll be safe."

Lucy looked at Dietrich. "How do you feel about all this?"

"It doesn't sound like I have choice?"

Lucy thought about it for a moment before answering. "Well, you could hire someone completely different."

"*Nein*. I know you. You know Jing. I trust her because you trust her."

"This has been a rather odd job," Lucy stated as she shook her head. "Let's get some food and then talk to the others heading to Sacramento. It's probably safer to be in a bigger group."

The others nodded as Lucy flagged down their server. She hadn't expected her job to end this way, but she knew that's how things worked sometimes. She would be paid when she returned to Meridune, and until then, she could take an odd job or two if she needed it. She hadn't blown through the money earned from Ms. Bauer yet, and didn't expect to.

As the server came over and everyone placed their order, Lucy looked at Mortimer. He was looking at the young lady with a slight smile again. She wondered if he would tell her what that was about when they were by themselves. A small thought crept into her mind that, perhaps, this woman was the one he was seeking out. Lucy pushed the thought away. Like many things in life, that would have to wait. She just hoped she wouldn't have to wait too long.

Once the server was gone, the group fell into travel plans. It didn't take much to find the others who were travelling to Sacramento. As the people gathered and started to plan, Lucy looked over at Mortimer. They were both done with their food and they were no longer needed. None of the plans involved them. With a nod to each other, they stood from the table.

"Well, since we're not headed to Sacramento, there's no reason for us to stick around. Jing, it was nice to see you again. Drop in when you're in my area next, ok?"

"Sure thing!"

The women shook hands, and Lucy turned to Dietrich. "Life doesn't work the way we want it to, but I hope you and your cousin do well at whatever it is you plan on doing when you get home."

Dietrich stood and offered Lucy his hand. "*Danke*. Thank you."

She shook his hand. "Tell Roger I said hello."

"I will."

They nodded to each other, then Lucy turned to Mortimer and waited until he said his goodbyes. Then with a smile, the two left the tables and went to gather their things for the journey ahead.

ABOUT THE AUTHOR

Cat Stark writes novels with assertive protagonists who form strong bounds. Until this book, she wrote romance novels with many adult themes. When this book didn't have any romance in it, no one was more surprised than she.

Cat earned a B.A. in English from Rockford University in 1999. This is her seventh self-published novel. She also has short stories published in *Contagion: War Stories* and *Revolution: a RAW Anthology*.

Find her here:

catstark.com
@catstarkwriter
facebook.com/catstarkwriter/

* 9 7 8 1 7 3 3 3 9 8 5 7 2 *